RED WINTER

*One Woman's Struggle to Survive
the Russian Revolution...*

KYRA KAPTZAN ROBINOV

Second Edition

Copyright ©2016 by Kyra Robinov

ISBN-13: 978-1533393470
ISBN-10: 1533393478

For information about booking a speaking event, please contact:
AuthorKyraRobinov@gmail.com

Cover Designed by Judy Bullard (http://www.customebookcovers.com)

Map Designed by Estelle Kim (www.estellekim.com)

Formatted by Therin Knite (http://www.knitedaydesign.com/)

DANCING IN THE DARK PRESS
New York, NY

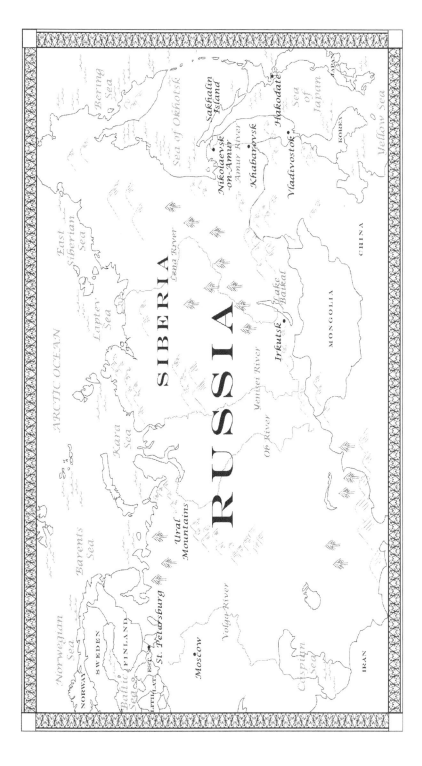

Index of Characters

The Kaptzan Family

Simon ~ deceased patriarch; fishery owner; originally from the Ukraine.

Riva ~ Simon's widow; bossy matriarch; originally from Poland.

Raissa ~ eldest daughter.

Ilya ~ eldest son; lawyer, newspaper editor and businessman; married to Luba Lury; father of Katya, Misha, Veronika and Viktor.

Pavel ~ wayward 2nd son.

Esther ~ feisty 4th child; married to Nikolai Lury; mother of Tolya and Sophie.

Nessia ~ youngest daughter; epileptic.

Yumiko-san ~ Japanese *amah* of Ilya and Luba's children.

Cook-san ~ Chinese cook and manservant.

Ivan ~ Family coachman; Russian.

The Lury Family

Moses ~ deceased patriarch; originally from Lithuania.

Anya ~ Moses' widow; originally from Moscow.

Matvei ~ eldest son; thriving entrepreneur; married to Raya.

Nikolai ~ personable middle child; White soldier; married to Esther Kaptzan; affectionately referred to as Kolya.

Luba ~ youngest child; married to Ilya Kaptzan; mother of Katya, Misha, Veronika and Viktor.

Vasya ~ Family cook and manservant; Russian.

Locals of Nikolaevsk-on-Amur

Syoma Maremant ~ brother of Anya Lury; husband of Tuula.

Tuula Maremant ~ wife of Syoma; originally from Finland.

Lyonya Minkov ~ town doctor; neighbor of Kaptzans.

Ludmilla Minkov ~ wife of Lyonya.

Judi and Abram Avshalumov ~ prominent citizens;
neighbors/friends of Kaptzans/Lurys.

Andrei and Iulia Sharpov ~ friends; neighbors.

Efraim and Mira Gorbatov ~ friends; neighbors.

Sammy and Eda Shimkin ~ friends; neighbors.

Piotr Nikolaevich Shimada ~ local merchant; friend.

Major Ishikawa ~ leader of Japanese forces stationed in
Nikolaevsk.

Colonel Vits ~ leader of White Russian forces stationed at
nearby Fort DeKastri.

Colonel Medvedev ~ retired leader of White Russian forces
residing in Nikolaevsk.

Iosef and Oksana Dimchin ~ local peasants.

Bolsheviks

Yakov Triapitsin ~ charismatic leader of the Red takeover.

Nina Lebedeva ~ consort and co-conspirator of Triapitsin.

Zhelezin ~ former school teacher turned Commissar.

Nelibuov ~ former peasant turned Red leader.

Glossary of Terms

Amah ~ Japanese nurse

Baba, Babushka ~ Grandmother

Babka ~ Coffee cake

Blini ~ Russian pancakes

Borscht ~ Beet soup

Burzhui ~ Bourgeoisie

-chan; -san ~ Japanese way of addressing children; adults

Da ~ Yes

Dacha ~ Summer house

Dobre Dyen ~ Good Morning

Gospodeen; Gospozha ~ Mister; Missus

Gymnazia ~ High school

Gyoza ~ Chinese dumplings

Hai ~ Yes (Japanese)

Hoopah ~ Bridal canopy

Kimono ~ Japanese robe/dress

Kopek ~ Russian penny

Krassavitsa ~ Beauty

Kto Eto? ~ Who's this?

Kulibiaka ~ Russian fish pie

Lubachka, Nessyinka, Milla ~ Affectionate derivatives of Luba, Nessia, Ludmilla

Moy Lyubimov, Moya Lyubimova ~ My love (masc.; fem.)

Nogoodnik ~ Troublemaker

Nu ~ So

Nyet ~ No

Partisan ~ Supporter of the Bolshevik cause

Pelmeni ~ Meat-filled dumplings

Pervaya Ulitsa ~ First Street

Pirogue ~ Meat or fish pie

Piroshki ~ Savory meat-filled pastry

Pozhalsta ~ Please

Red ~ Bolshevik; revolutionary

Samovar ~ Highly decorated tea urn

Sembeh ~ Japanese rice crackers

Sinich ~ Son

Spacibo ~ Thank you

Tsaritsa ~ Little Empress

Tyotia ~ Aunt

Varenya ~ Jam

Varenyaki ~ Large, meat-filled dumplings, usually fried

Versts ~ Russian measure of length; 1 verst is slightly more than 1 kilometer

White ~ Counter-revolutionary

Yarmulke ~ Skullcap worn by Orthodox Jewish men

Zakuski ~ Assortment of hors d'oeuvres

Zoris ~ Japanese footwear

Author's Note

In 1917, the workers of Russia united to overthrow the Tsar and his government, a system of rule that favored wealthy landowners and nobles—the 1% of the day, so to speak. Most Russians had lost faith in their leader's ability to guide the country. Corruption was rampant. Having recently come out of a disastrous involvement in the first world war, the economy had been crippled by the costly war effort. Emerging radicals—Reds—called for a new beginning.

At the time, my family was living in the far eastern corner of Siberia, in the city of Nikolaevsk-on-Amur. Closer to Japan than to Moscow and St. Petersburg, Nikolaevsk was an anomaly: a prosperous town settled by adventurers as well as foreigners, unrestricted by the harsh rules that governed the rest of the vast country. Cut off from the world for seven months a year because of snow and ice, Nikolaevsk offered its inhabitants freedom of speech and religion as well as abundant business opportunities for those hardy enough to weather the climate. Side by side, Christians, Jews and Muslims abided peacefully as they created idealized lives. Nobody suspected that the events uprooting the western part of Russia would ever reach—or have any effect—on their remote outpost.

Yet, in the winter of 1919-1920, the city was taken over by a band of Reds who considered entrepreneurs like my family to be capitalist enemies of "the People." Their aim: to bring down the bourgeoisie in the name of freedom. My father's family was among those targeted for annihilation.

I grew up hearing my father and grandmother tell stories

of that winter. Though their accounts contained villains and executions, peril and pain, they always seemed more like escapades than reality. Listeners were always mesmerized by these tales and, from an early age, I felt compelled to capture them in writing. However, once I began to do research, I found a large disparity between the romanticized details that had been related to me and the actual facts and written testimonies I uncovered of those who'd survived the events in Nikolaevsk. Had my father misremembered? Had my grandmother blotted out the horrors of her past? How could I ever weave together the conflicting information?

Based on true events, **Red Winter** is a fictionalized account of one of the more harrowing episodes in my family's history. It is told from my grandmother Luba's point of view, as I imagined she might have told it herself.

For my father and grandmother Luba

"You live as long as you are remembered."
— **Russian proverb**

Part One

1

Nikolaevsk-on-Amur, Siberia ~ February 29, 1920

O pen up! Open up in the name of the People," came the impatient demand.

It felt like an earthquake was reverberating in my head. I wrestled with my comforter, realizing I'd been having a nightmare. But the pounding continued, growing more insistent. Across the room, Ilya was pulling on his robe and reaching for the door, looking as if he was trying to slip out before I awoke. I could barely make out his retreating figure but for the dim glow of the lamp he carried.

"What's going on?" I called, my voice an octave higher than usual. The noise hadn't stopped and I realized it was coming from our front door. Rough male voices were thundering from outside. It sounded like an angry mob. "Ilya, stay here," I called. "Please."

He glanced back over his shoulder, then ducked into the hall. I reached for my housecoat and hurried to be close to my husband. Shivering, not so much from the Siberian winter as from panic, I hugged myself to keep warm.

"Alright. Alright! I'm coming," Ilya shouted toward the door. I rushed down the narrow corridor after him and the wooden planks creaked under my feet. Ilya appeared outwardly unflustered, his posture erect and his face serious, but fearless.

"Wait…" I pleaded as he reached to unlatch the bolt.

"If you don't open the door immediately, we'll open it for you," the voice snarled from the other side. I clutched Ilya's arm and felt my alarm shoot through him like an electric shock. "Shh, *Lubachka*." He squeezed my shoulder with one arm, then threw open the door.

An enormous figure filled the frame. I recognized him as the man who had spoken at the rally in the town square the day before. Zhelezin. How could anyone forget such a creature? A coarse, black beard encircled his red face like the dirty wiry tendrils of a beet just pulled from the earth. The frigid air turned his breath into puffs of smoke. Small icicles clung to his whiskers and his eyes shone from the cold, but the tears in them weren't sympathetic in the least. In his long fur coat, he resembled the bear whose skin he was wrapped in. A long rifle was slung over one shoulder and the butt of a revolver poked from the belt that encircled his thick waist.

Behind him lurked more than a dozen men, some on horses, others on skis. The scene looked hazy because with each breath the men exhaled, they disappeared behind a frosty screen. It reminded me of the shadow puppet shows I sometimes took the children to. Dark shapes loomed against the white drifts of snow which reflected the faint glow of the moon. The animals snorted restlessly—the horses and the men. The rest of the street remained quietly in slumber.

Zhelezin stepped across the threshold and entered our house. "Ilya Semyonovich Kaptzan?" He didn't bother to stomp the snow off his hefty boots and swept several mounds into the hallway with him. It melted slowly into a puddle at our feet. "I have here a warrant for your arrest." He shoved a crumpled paper forward and in the brief instant that Ilya considered what to do, the beast lost his temper and threw the document on the floor, forcing him to bend down to retrieve it. "Get your coat and come with me," he growled.

I tightened my grasp on my husband's arm. "No! Please, you mustn't! You can't..." I turned toward the interloper. "Please…" I begged him. "There must be a mistake." I knew I sounded desperate, but I didn't care. My pulse was pounding in my ears.

"What's going on? What have I done?" Ilya addressed Zhelezin.

"You will learn. Later."

"Can't this wait until morning?" Ilya appealed. "I'm not going to disappear and I can't leave my wife alone in the middle of the night in the state she's in."

"Your wife won't be alone...." Ugly, frightening thoughts scrambled through my brain. I shrunk into my robe, pulling it tighter and wishing it wasn't so pretty.

"I thought everything was to be peaceful—" Ilya tried to break in, but the bully pushed ahead like an ox breaking up the soil in its path.

"If you don't come of your free will, I will gladly assist you." Zhelezin brandished his pistol.

"Have you no compassion? My wife is not a well woman." I tried to look weaker than I felt which wasn't so difficult considering the circumstances.

"She looks extremely well to me," he sniggered. Ilya and I grimaced at his leering tone. He plowed on. "Do you have any firearms in the house—any ammunition...?"

"Of course not. We handed everything over at the rally yesterday morning. We were promised that the changeover was to be without incident..." Ilya was getting worked up. I knew that he hadn't turned in any arms, having claimed not to own any, and I wondered if this monster was going to find his pistol when he searched our house. A chill ran through me.

"If we find any weapons—even a single rifle or one bullet..." The monster's eyes narrowed into slits. "...you will be executed on the spot. Let's go." He pointed his gun directly at Ilya's chest.

My legs buckled. "Don't worry," Ilya whispered to me. "Everything will be straightened out in the morning." He didn't sound convincing. "Please get a hold of yourself and be strong." To the brute he said, "I need to put on some clothes."

"Be quick," he barked. I watched as Ilya headed to the bedroom, not wanting to let go of him. Unconsciously, my body leaned in his direction. But Zhelezin blocked my way. "You—" He pointed at me. "Get his coat." Ilya indicated, with a nod over his shoulder, that I should comply.

Surprised that the boor was letting us out of his sight, I hurried to the small room off the kitchen where our outerwear hung on hooks. The reassuring odor of pine emanated from the rough hewn walls. Ilya's boots were where he always neatly placed them, under the bench on which he sat to pull them on. I reached for his black woolen overcoat with the sable collar in which he looked so distinguished. His plaid scarf was tucked into one sleeve and its softness reminded me of his skin, the scent of his cologne as much a part of the weave as the white accent threads. I burrowed my nose in this cloud of Ilya as I felt a flood of tears building behind my lids. I pressed my face against the icy wall. Grabbing his warmest hat, I hastened into the hall, drawn by the need to be next to him.

Zhelezin was stepping out of our living room. He was pocketing something and, from the look of relish on his face, it was something of value. He caught me staring at him but before he could say anything, Ilya returned from the bedroom. He'd put on a suit and tie, proper and elegant as always, but he couldn't mask the nervous twitching of his mouth and cheek. He fingered his moustache, trying to veil the tic. I scanned his body, wondering if he'd taken the gun and if he planned to use it. Where might he have concealed it? And what would they do if they found it on him?

"You won't be needing that," Zhelezin snapped, snatching the pipe from Ilya's hand. I wanted to smack the barbarian for treating my husband so indignantly. He shoved Ilya toward the door as he slipped the pipe into his pocket.

I lunged forward offering Ilya his coat and hat. As he wriggled into it, I wrapped the woolen muffler around his neck, wanting to bind myself to him forever. I pulled down the flaps of his hat and stared into his eyes. They were rimmed with red from all the worry and lack of sleep during the last weeks. I was about to hug him when the beast pried us apart. Like a big cat pawing its quarry, the large man mocked the smaller.

"Ilya!" I cried and dashed out into the snow after him, despite my slippered feet. He turned and stared at me for one brief moment before he was shoved onto a waiting wagon.

I watched him disappear, feeling the freezing snow envelop my toes. Standing there in the moonlight, the gazes of the churlish soldiers burning into me, I wanted to rush after him, but my feet and body were numb. All I could do was stare at the fading figure of my husband and wonder if I would ever see him again.

2

*L*et's go! It's cold out here!" I was brought back into the moment when one of the men filling our yard prodded me back toward the house.

As I watched the wagon transporting my husband creak out of sight, my breath left my body. It felt like I was losing one of my limbs. The soldier was red-faced and smug under a shearling cap that was pulled down over most of his face. His teeth were like jagged amber rocks, yellow and uneven. His eyes were shifty. He looked familiar, though I couldn't place him. "Let's go!" he said again. I moved forward as if in a trance. He seized my arm and I snapped out of my stupor.

"I can manage." I pulled free of his grip and entered the house. I started to slam the door behind me, but he interrupted with a sweep of his arm, pushing the door back open.

"Is that so?" he asked as he followed me inside. I

wanted to stand my ground, but every ounce of courage bled out of me when I glimpsed the cold glare on his face. "I have papers here that state we are to occupy your house, 'in the name of the People.'" His voice sounded far away, as if I were dreaming. If only I could wake up. "That's right," he continued, unfurling some more documents. "It says so right here."

"But—"

"The same goes for all your property." He glanced around. "Since I'm in a generous mood tonight," he laughed coarsely, "I'll let you gather a few things…"

"What do you mean...?"

"Who lives here besides yourself?"

"My mother-in-law, my sister-in-law. My children and their *amah*…" The man looked so familiar. There was a shimmer in his eyes that vacillated between sincerity and scorn. I'd definitely seen that face before.

"Why do you keep a Japanese *amah* in the house? Let her go and take a Russian woman." His voice was a blend of sugar and vinegar. I didn't know how to respond. "Well...! Get everyone up. I have many tired men here who need to rest. We need your rooms. Your beds."

"Our beds? But my mother-in-law is old. Her daughter is sick..." I thought of Ilya as I said that.

"What's wrong with her?" His eyes bore into me as if I were making this up.

"She's epileptic." There was a glint in his eye and I wondered if he had a wife and family and where they might be. How would he feel if they were being treated like this?

We were interrupted as Riva came down the hall from the back of the house. With the assurance of a peacock, she strode toward us, tying the belt to her dressing gown and trying to cover herself up as she noticed our interloper.

"Luba? What's going on?" Though I rarely lit up at her presence, for once I was thrilled that this fearless woman shared our home and was there just then. Riva could handle anything.

"Oh, Mama!" I flung myself into the older woman's arms and all my strength seeped away. I melted into her strong embrace. Meanwhile, two other men appeared in the doorway.

Riva looked in their direction. "What's going on? Who are—?"

"I am a Commissar of the People's Army," the leader announced. "We've come to set up our new headquarters in your house." He offered her the official papers. Even his bombastic demeanor was slightly tamped in Riva's presence.

"What? Now? In the middle of the night?" Riva wasn't going to take any orders from him.

"That's correct, *Babushka*. As you can see right here…"

"What kind of men are you?" She took the papers he offered her and scanned them.

"Patriotic Bolsheviks. Under the command of Yakov Triapitsin."

"They took Ilya away! They just took him…" I whispered.

Riva's effort to remain stoic was countered by the sound of her son's name. Her voice wavered as she spoke. "What do you want with us anyway? We're just innocent women and children here."

"There are no innocent Whites!" retorted one of the men behind us and his superior shot him a threatening glare, but the man just guffawed. I noticed his left ear looked as if it had been gnawed off.

"*Babushka...*" the officer softened a little. "We don't want to make trouble. We just need rooms. And beds. I'm sure you understand how tired and hungry my men must be. How many bedrooms do you have?"

"The children sleep in two rooms. I share a third with my daughter," Riva informed him.

"And of course there's the master," he interceded. He folded his arms across his chest and assumed a Herculean stance.

"My son and daughter—"

"Your daughter is welcome to remain in her room," he said. "You and your other daughter can stay with the children. Since you are an old lady, I'll allow you to take two pillows with you from your room. Go and get them and your other daughter now."

Riva was not unaccustomed to humble living. She'd grown up in a remote village near the Polish border in Lithuania. She was familiar with the sort of bullying that propelled these partisan upstarts. "I'm sure there has been some terrible misunderstanding," she said. "Can't this wait until morning?"

"No. Now!" The man was losing his patience. He almost pointed his revolver at her, but controlled himself.

Riva disentangled herself from my grip. I was clutching her with all my might. "I'm going to get Nessia. And my pillows…" she added sarcastically. "You go to the children. But don't let them see you like this."

I reluctantly let go of her arm and headed toward the back of the house in a haze of disbelief, thankful for her leadership. I felt the man's eyes boring into my back and I moved quickly so that he wouldn't make me return. The lamplight cast sinister shadows and the portraits on the walls stared down at me. Everything felt so familiar, yet so foreign.

I opened the door to the nursery and peered in at my sleeping children. Moonlight streamed through the window. It fell across Misha, sprawled in the tangle of his comforter. I could see Ilya's face in the composure of his expression and I felt a stab of grief. Above him, on a shelf with his model boats and toy soldiers, was his Grandfather Simon's violin, the one Ilya had proudly passed on to him but which Misha loathed playing. Reverberating in my head was the endless screeching that his weekly lessons produced. When his hour was up and the maestro released him from the living room, Misha always bounded into the kitchen, eager for a glass of fresh milk and a treat for his efforts. If only I could let go of my throbbing dread and do the same.

On the other side of the room, flanking the window, stood the twin beds of Katya and Veronika. Watching over them from a nearby bureau was their assortment of dolls, festooned in fancy hats and regional costumes. Katya loved to arrange tea parties and balls for them, but Veronika preferred Oleg, her stuffed bear with the crooked scar on his belly. Practically buried inside her down cocoon, I knew Veronika had Oleg nestled in her arms.

Katya slept serenely, her beautiful face composed as it usually was when she was awake. She was almost eleven. No longer a child. Her long hair fanned across her pillow. It seemed barely a moment ago that I was her age. In the next room, Yumiko-san slept with Baby Viktor. As I looked at my sleeping children, I wondered how I would ever explain the circumstances to them.

Noises from outside made me peer through the window. In

the yard, men were wresting open the door to the barn. Others beat the ground with their boots and clapped their gloved hands together to keep warm. There were about ten of them. In their shearling coats and bushy beards they looked like a herd of caribou. Where was Ivan, I wondered. Our coachman lived in a small room in the back of the structure.

I stared past the men, trying to make out Mama's house at the far end of the courtyard. Were she and Esther sleeping through this? Or were they also being roused from their beds and roughly ordered about? I didn't want to imagine what they might be going through. But I was glad Mama had Esther with her.

3

A baseline of gruff male voices gained momentum in the front of the house. I peeked into the hallway from the children's room. The front door had been hurled open again, by a gale of wind, and the commander filled the portal, signaling his men to enter. He stepped back outside and soldiers sauntered in as if it were a dirty railway station.

Curious, I inched forward, hugging the wall so as not to be noticed, staying close to the alcove where the firewood for our furnace was stacked. I tried to categorize each of the intruders, wondering if a compassionate soul might exist among the band of rough, repulsive men. Ranging from gruff looking grandpas to stealthy young men, their faces were masked by thick beards and moustaches and their countenances resembled neglected gardens. They were heavily cloaked against the cold. Some were uniformed, but most wore a haphazard collection of buttoned cloth overcoats and boots. Their head coverings were an array of close-fitting homespun felt caps propped on their heads like tea cozies and helmets crafted from animal skins with furry ear flaps that revealed only the slimmest gash of a face. These men lacked the panache of real military men and their coarse conduct furthered the incongruity of their newly official status. From the way they acted, I doubted any one of them had ever been in a home like ours.

The men piled into the living room where they threw off their coats and hats and instantly made themselves comfortable on the velvet divan and brocade chairs. They looked absurdly out of place sprawling beneath the crystal chandelier and on the ornate Mongolian rug. Several men made a bee-line for the liquor cart. After filling some glasses for his comrades, the scraggly bartender lifted the remains to his lips and drained the glass container crooning "*Na zdarovya!* To our health!" and clinked glasses all around. A short fellow, almost as wide as he was tall, picked up the brandy decanter and admired the geometric design scored into the crystal. He seemed to recognize the craftsmanship and picture the look that would appear on his wife's face when he presented it to her.

Other soldiers plundered the ornaments on the mantel. Drawers were thrown open and being explored. The intricate ivory figurines which my brother Matvei always brought me as gifts from his travels to China and Japan were disappearing into pockets. A silver ashtray evoked a nod of approval before being stowed under a shifty-eyed partisan's coat. Each theft felt like a jab to my heart. But it was nothing compared to my worry about Ilya. What was going to become of him? Of all of us? As I watched from the hallway, I swallowed hard and tried to remain calm and rational.

The lights flickered on and off as a young soldier discovered the switch on the wall and flipped it up and down with glee. Noticing the Victrola, a string bean of a man with a cobweb beard began thumbing through our stack of records. He selected a disc and lay it on the phonograph bed. As he prepared to wind it up, one of his comrades sat down at the piano and began to bang out a loud tune. Several of his comrades sang along. I thought of Ivan's calm deep voice and how different it was from the cacophony of this tribe. It was clear the men were heavily inebriated. Their condition, more than the icy weather outside, accounted for their rosy complexions.

The commissar returned. He didn't seem as boorish and overwhelming as Zhelezin, who'd taken Ilya away. But he was sweaty and nervous. A few stray wiry curls protruded from his hat and, when he removed it, his orange hair was flattened and damp with perspiration. His small ears stuck out like dried apricots. He looked up and our eyes met. In an instant, I realized who he was. I tried to untangle my gaze, but it was as if I was locked in a spell. He grinned sheepishly at me.

Finally, I managed to turn away. I hurried to the room Riva and Nessia shared.

"Sounds like a brothel out there," Riva was muttering as she tugged on the brass pulls and picked through the drawers of her wooden bureau. "Who do they think they are? Who do they think we are?"

"Mama, what's all the noise?" Nessia said. "What—"

"Hurry, Nessyinka..." She interrupted her daughter. "Put on your robe and take our pillows. They've arrested Ilya and—"

Nessia wrapped her lissome body in the dressing gown that was draped over the spindly iron frame of the bed as Riva gathered a few personal belongings. "Arrested...? What do you mean?" her face blanched. A web of blue veins quivered under her alabaster skin.

Riva pulled the satin collar of her daughter's robe tighter so as to better conceal her daughter's inviting figure. She looked up and saw me standing in the doorway.

"Do you know who that man is?" I blurted out, unable to remain silent any longer. They both stared at me. "Dmitri Nelibuov!" I spat out his name. That put an end to their chatter.

"What?"

"You mean—?"

"Yes," I cut them off.

"I thought he looked familiar." Riva shook her head. "How dare he—?" She huffed as she emptied the contents of a simple wooden jewelry box onto her bed. "Well, maybe we can use that to our advantage," she said.

I watched, dumbfounded, as she used an amethyst brooch to make a slight tear along the seam of one of the pillows, then carefully enlarged the gash just enough to wedge some of her jewelry in among the feathers. She slipped the rings off her fingers and hid them in her underwear.

I was outraged. "What are you trying to do? Don't you realize what they'll do to us if they find that?"

"Shh. We're going to need something of worth. I don't think we'll have access to our safe—not that our money has value these days anyway. We're going to have to pay dearly for our status as wealthy *burzhui*."

"Will it be worth it if this barbarian finds the jewelry first?

He'll have us all arrested—" I didn't want to think what else he might do.

"We'll have to make sure he doesn't find them."

Riva left a few inconsequential items in the box, then replaced it on her dresser. "Alright, come." She indicated it was time for us to go. But at the last moment she caught sight of a sepia photo in a silver frame and snatched it. Just as she was pondering where to hide it, Nelibuov surged into the room.

"Ah. What a lovely memento, *Babushka*!" He eased the frame from her grasp and turned it over, inspecting the photograph.

She glared at him. "Thank you. It's my husband."

"Very handsome man. And an officer, I see." He set the frame back on the bureau, pretending to admire it.

"Yes," Riva couldn't conceal her pride. "He was."

"A White officer?"

"What else would you expect him to be?" I sucked in my breath at her audacity.

"You weren't intending to take this with you?" he inquired menacingly.

"Why not? It's mine." Riva reached for it.

"There is no longer such a thing as *personal property*. Everything belongs to the People."

"Well, I'm sure 'the People' won't mind if I keep a picture of my dead husband." She grabbed the frame and slid the photo from its casing. I was awed by Riva's arrogance, but also glad for her confidence. She would be able to manage the situation. "You can have the frame, if that's what you're worried about. It's silver." She proffered it to him. "But the photo's not worth—"

"Thank you. I will," he replied, accepting it. "But I still

don't think I can allow you to carry such a slanderous memento," he said, indicating the picture. Simon was clearly in the Tsar's *White* Army in his youth. Twin tracks of brass buttons adorned his chest and a visored hat with the double headed eagle insignia crowned his head. I hadn't seen this photo in a while and was struck by the resemblance of Ilya to his father.

Riva was disgusted. "Of what use is this photograph to you?"

"I'm only trying to protect you. If it were to be found on your person…" The insincerity of his tone revolted me.

"If you were that concerned with my well being, you wouldn't be here at all." The Bolshevik paused for a moment, as if mulling over whether to snatch the photo back or not. "You of all people…." As her last words landed, Riva dropped the photo into her pocket and turned to leave.

"Perhaps I can make an exception just this once." I could tell he was trying to save face. As much as he reveled in his new authority, he had to have a conscience, feel some remorse about unseating the man who had saved his life.

"Come, girls," she said, picking up her pillows and ushering Nessia and me toward the part of the house in which the Reds were allowing us to remain. Our captor watched us go. He seemed almost relieved that he hadn't had to push the matter further. Before reaching the end of the hall, we could hear him sorting through the drawers and shelves.

While we were together, Riva suggested we duck into the master bedroom and gather some belongings as we might not have another opportunity. I pulled open the wardrobe and pulled out two of my favorite blouses and skirts and then some undergarments from my bureau.

"Where do you keep your jewelry?" Riva demanded. I

nodded toward a lacquer box with ivory inlay on my dressing table. She picked it up and started to go through it, selecting more pieces to take with us, but again left enough behind so it didn't look as if we'd looted it. I scanned the familiar room for anything else and stuffed my silver handled brush into my pocket as Riva nudged me toward the door.

On our way to the nursery, we had to pass through the kitchen. Another contingent of men had made themselves comfortable around the table by the window. They'd already raided the larder and were lounging about, enjoying its contents. A kettle boiled on the iron stove and one of the men was pumping the handle by the sink, trying to elicit a stream of water. When we appeared, the men ogled us. "I'm so lonely, my beauty, won't you come sit with me a while?" one voice sang out at Nessia.

"Come here. And see what I have to offer!" a second one taunted. I forced my eyes down and hoped that made me invisible.

The square lid that covered the entrance to our cellar popped up and two scoundrels climbed out hauling all sorts of food. "Look what we have here," the first announced, throwing a gleaming side of salmon on the table before them.

"And a sack of rice," said his mate.

"And caviar," a third chimed in.

"How about cooking us a meal, Grandma?" said another.

Riva pushed Nessia ahead of her through the unruly throng. A partisan reached out and I felt him paw my robe. I picked up my pace and gritted my teeth, clutching the bundle in my arms and hoping to disappear behind it.

"What's that in your arms?" I heard someone asking.

"It's just a change of clothing," Riva addressed the man, nudging us forward. We continued through the dining room where more scavengers were attacking food, their filthy boots on the burnished table, eating with their hands and spitting chicken bones right out onto the floor.

I winced, about to say something.

"Don't tempt them," Riva pre-empted me.

All the commotion had woken Viktor. His cries pierced the silence. I hurried into the room where Yumiko-san was tending to him. I could tell she was startled to see me at that time of night. Rarely did I rouse myself from the warmth of my bed to rush back there to comfort the children. Usually, our *amah* handled everything. But when I walked in, she brought the bundled boy to me.

Though he was too old for nightly feedings, being a year already, I felt a sudden urge to unbutton my nightgown and offer him my breast. I only continued feeding him because it was a good precaution against getting pregnant again. Stunned at the unexpected surprise, Viktor delightedly latched on and sucked fiercely. Oddly, I was as reassured by his neediness and my ability to soothe him as he was.

The loud banging of the piano started again in the background. It brought back memories of the German horror movie shown the year before in the cinema downtown. The story of a macabre carnival hypnotist, the film had been filled with disturbing images and distorted sounds. Esther had laughed when I made Ilya leave the theatre early with me; she and Nikolai stayed to the end.

In the adjoining room, the older children were waking up,

though they still had one foot mired in their dreams. We turned our attention to them.

"Savages!" Riva huffed, referring to the intruders, as she rushed to take a frightened Katya and sleepy Veronika into her arms.

I looked at my mother-in-law who was addressing the girls, her voice serious, but calm. The family was pressed around her. Normally, I would resent her taking over, but just then I was grateful for her courage. Looking from one to the next as if calculating how much she should say, Riva told the children they were going to have to be very brave. "The next few days are not going to be easy. A group of Bolshevik soldiers has come to stay in part of our house." This information jolted them from their grogginess. I realized I was shivering uncontrollably. I hugged Viktor closer, wishing I were as oblivious as he.

Riva continued before the children could jump in with questions. "I want you to keep as far away from these men as you can. Try not to talk to them. If you have to, say as little as possible. But be polite. Even though they're a bunch of beasts, our lives depend on their kindness. We must not antagonize them." Seeing their non-comprehending faces, she modified her instructions. "We mustn't make them angry. I know you're a little young to understand what's going on and I don't want you to be scared. But we are in a dangerous situation. Everything is going to be alright…somehow…but we are going to have to act very cautiously. So, don't any of you wander away from your mother, Yumiko-san, Nessia or me. And don't ask any questions in front of those men. Understand?"

Katya and Veronika nodded as they took this in. Viktor started to bawl again. I jiggled him.

Misha tugged on my sleeve and cried out, "Where's Papa?"

"Yes, where's Father? What's all that noise? What's going on?" Like a container that's just crashed to the floor, its contents escaping in every direction, the questions poured out of the children.

Before I could think of what to say to them, Riva stepped in again. "Veronachka, I want you to stay very close to Katya and do whatever she tells you. We don't have time for arguments. Alright?" Veronika assented reluctantly. Free-spirited and decisive already at the age of seven, she didn't like to be restrained by anyone, least of all her responsible older sister. Katya, her eyes wide with consternation, was thrilled with the authority her assignment granted her. She blinked back her fear and raised her head a little higher as she put her arm around her younger sister who squirmed away. "Misha, you are going to have to be the man of the family until your father comes home." I saw Katya grimace as the competition over who held the trump position between my two eldest children arose. Surely she would later allude to the unfairness of her younger brother's elite status just because he was a male.

"But where is he?" my little boy demanded.

"Misha..." The tone of his granny's voice made it clear that Ilya's whereabouts were not a subject she wanted to discuss.

"Alright, Granny," he said.

Riva motioned for us to gather closer. We put our arms around one another and remained in a huddle. "Let's all say a quiet prayer for your father." I closed my eyes and tried not to picture what might be happening to Ilya at that moment. I willed my tears from triggering another deluge. Riva, sensing a downpour, glowered at me and held out the lace kerchief that was tucked into the sleeve of her gown. It exuded her favorite Caswell-Massey fragrance. I silently sopped up the moisture on my face, knowing my tears were upsetting the children. My mind was racing, trying to figure out how we were going to get ourselves out of this situation.

4

Eleven Months Earlier ~ March 1919

*I*t was the morning of Ilya's big trial. Though I may have preferred to eke out a few extra hours of sleep rather than put myself under the scrutiny of my mother-in-law as she served her son breakfast with Cook-san's help, I wanted to show Ilya my full support. Sometimes I wished I had a job, like him, to run off to everyday instead of remaining home to oversee the running of our household. But this was one of my wifely duties. I didn't want to abdicate my position to Riva who would be more than happy to subsume it at my slightest delinquency.

Riva was in the kitchen, overseeing the morning baking. Garbed in her customary black skirt and white blouse, stock-inged feet in sensible thick-soled shoes, she was sturdy as an oak, imposing and formidable. Legs astride for balance, she stood before the wooden table. Her fine hair was parted and rolled into a bun, tucked under a crocheted snood. White wisps framed her flushed face. The faint crinkles at the sides of her gray eyes were like rays emitted from them. Her skin might be aging, but her gaze was alert. Riva missed nothing. Sleeves were rolled up over her ample arms and an apron shielded her clothing. Both were splotched with flour. Fiercely kneading the dough in front of her as if trying to tame a wrestling opponent, my mother-in-law seemed content. She'd already been awake for hours and even at her age it was clear she had more energy than me. At least in the morning hours. She sprinkled more flour on the wooden board and flipped the yeasty blob around, finishing it off with her fists. Despite knuckles both swollen and red, Riva was the victor of the battle.

As I reached the doorway, our eyes met. I detected a flicker of amusement from her that I was awake at this early hour. Not seeing Ilya, I immediately withdrew, to avoid conversation. I peeked into the dining room. The table was set for breakfast, but remained untouched. Ilya must be in his study, gathering his papers.

Loud squawking outside caught my attention. I pulled the brocade curtain back and peered through the frosted panes. Like a graceful skater, his feet in slim black envelopes, Cook-san was chasing a chicken around the yard, lunging after the cackling creature as it nervously evaded his grasp. Each failed attempt was followed by the flustered flutter of wings beating relief as the poor hen escaped her death—at least temporarily. Then, a great deal of screeching from both Cook-san and his victim. Another dive, another thump. Some more nervous titter. Cook-san stopped to catch his breath, then decided to try a different tack. The thin, wiry man put his hands in the pockets

of his quilted blue jacket. His ears were bright red, uncovered
as they were. A black satin cap didn't seem to offer much
warmth. It reminded me more of a *yarmulke* than a buffer from
the cold. Nonchalantly, Cook-san strolled away, keeping track
of the errant bird out of the corner of his eye. Suddenly, he
pounced. Success! He caught his prey and dragged it over to
a tree stump in which a hatchet was poised. Deftly grabbing
the handle, Cook-san eased the weapon from its mooring in
gloveless hands and lifted it over his head, all the while bat-
tling to restrain the frantic hen. He lay the bird's neck on the
stump. With one triumphant blow, he decapitated it. Blood
seeped into the wood and speckled the carpet of snow as the
body of the chicken continued to race around the yard even
though its head had been removed. I could tell Cook-san was
pleased by the glint of his silver front tooth as it flashed from
the window of his smile.

I closed the curtain to shut out the scene, relieved that this
chore was his responsibility and not mine. I'd seen women
in their yards performing this identical dance with their creatures, trying to coax them into a tango that would lead to one
partner's demise and the other one's dinner. Fortunately, we
had servants. I didn't know how we'd survive without them.
My mama couldn't catch a hen to save her life. Her eyesight
was so poor she could barely read a book or do embroidery.
Sometimes I wondered if she was as blind as she claimed or if
she just relished being read to and doted upon. But I assumed
she wouldn't wear those unattractive tinted spectacles if she
didn't need them. Mama had a vain streak.

Ilya's mother didn't approve of either one of us. She
claimed I took after Mama and needed constant pampering.
Well, I had a successful husband willing to shower me with

candies and servants. Why should I sit all day in the kitchen with my mother-in-law, baking bread and making soup? I wanted rings on my fingers...not flour and grease. I wanted to dine in restaurants, not at home every evening. I'd be old and fat like her before I knew it. Four children—six, if you counted the two we'd buried—had already taken their toll on me. At twenty-nine, I was too old for any more little ones. For as long as I could remember—most of the twelve years Ilya and I had been married—I'd been with child. My last pregnancy had been the worst. I'd thought being enormous in the heat of the sweltering summer was uncomfortable. Trying to keep my balance on the ice with all that extra baggage protruding from my mid-section proved to be even more of a challenge. Viktor was my only winter baby. Six weeks after his birth I was still plump as a pillow.

I missed looking and feeling alluring, though my misshapen form didn't seem to deter my husband. I relished his attention, but detested the restrictions of another pregnancy. How I longed to go dancing or skating and not worry about exerting myself or falling. I couldn't remember the last time I'd been admired by anyone other than him. Like Mama, I basked in being singled out. An only daughter with two older brothers, I'd always been pampered and praised.

"Misha! Up so early?" Riva's throaty alto addressed my seven year old son who had tromped into her arena. I returned to the periphery of the kitchen to watch their interaction, knowing I'd be ignored now that her favorite grandchild was occupying her attention. I felt a twinge of jealousy that he was so drawn to her. I knew he reminded his granny of Ilya as a child; and nobody could compare with her son, except perhaps Misha. Why were she and I always competing for the attention of our men? Riva opened the metal door to the brick oven and stoked the embers, sweeping them aside so she could slide in her tins of dough. Tottering on tiptoes, Misha followed every movement. When finished with her task, she enveloped the boy in her softness.

All knees and elbows, he climbed onto a stool. "I couldn't sleep," he told her, wiping the drowsiness from his eyes. "The chickens were making too much noise." Disheveled by slumber, his thick, dark hair stood askew. I remained in the doorway while I waited for Ilya to join us.

"Let me get your yogurt. The bread will be a while yet." Riva turned to the black stove where a row of glass jars were lined up like soldiers. She handed him one with a spoon and Misha dug into the creamy contents. His *babushka* watched with pleasure as he emptied the glass. "This will keep you healthy and strong!" When he finished, she took the nearly empty receptacle and poured fresh milk into it from a copper pitcher. By morning, the heat from the oven would turn it and the remaining culture into more yogurt.

Riva resumed her baking as Cook-san came in from outside. Though Chinese, Cook-san had adopted the Japanese form of address, adding the "san" to his name. In his grip, his prey dangled by its scrawny claws. A stream of freezing air swept in with him. Small and spindly, the man was not much larger than my son. Depositing the chicken in a corner, he greeted the boy. His smile revealed not only his shiny capped tooth but also a gap at the side where other teeth were missing.

As to the plucking of the bird, he would get to that after the morning meal was served. At that moment, a glistening slab of fish lay on a wooden cutting board, beckoning. Rubbing his chapped fingers together, Cook-san approached it and, with a sharp knife, began slicing it into thin filaments which he draped onto a china platter garlanded with rosebuds.

"Are we going to have smoked salmon for breakfast?" Misha asked hopefully as Cook-san carried the plate into the next room.

"Your father is," *Babushka* Riva informed him. "He's got a big trial today, so when he comes in, you be a good boy and don't bother him with a lot of talk, understand? He should be here any minute." Misha nodded.

I thought of the impending court case and wished I was allowed to attend. But, as with so much else, women weren't welcome. I wanted to see Ilya in action, presenting his evidence to the judge. I wanted to see the defendant about whom I'd heard so much but never seen. I wasn't sure I wanted the man to be freed; yet, I was rooting for my husband to win.

Cook-san returned and focused his attention on the gleaming silver samovar. He retrieved a woven basket filled with twigs and pine cones and stuffed the kindling into the chimney of the urn. Using a sliver of wood lit from the stove, he ignited it and carried the samovar into the other room

"When will the bread be ready?" Misha fidgeted as irresistible scents wafted from the oven. It smelled so good I, too, was looking forward to it.

"Patience, *moi lyubimov…*" said Riva. She always had endless amounts for him, unlike her threshold for me.

"*Dobre Dyen!*" Ilya entered the room with a flourish and Misha ran to hug him. "How is everyone this fine morning?" he asked as he led us into the dining room. The large table was laid for the whole family, but the breakfast offerings were confined to one end. After holding my chair for me, Ilya draped his suit coat over the back of his own and took his place at the head. He unfurled his napkin and tucked a corner of the square into his neck. Everything he did was so methodical. Never the slightest deviation from his daily routine. "Don't want to have to change my clothes," he said, winking at Misha. The boy chuckled. "Come here, son," he motioned to the boy who was hanging back at Riva's side. "Sit with me while I eat." The boy looked at his granny for confirmation that it was alright. When she nodded, he happily seated himself.

The nutty aroma from the oven floated in from the kitchen. Father and son looked at each other in anticipation. "Nobody bakes bread like your *babushka*," Ilya noted. Riva returned with her efforts and, alongside the brown mounds of pumpernickel, studded with seeds, was a small dark pretzel baked just for her grandson.

"*Vot!* Here you go." She placed it before him, after first serving her son.

Ilya took several slices of salmon and put some on Misha's plate. The boy looked up, thrilled. This was his favorite food. Ilya cut into the loaf and a geyser of steam spewed forth. He handed Misha and me slices and then built a fortress of fish upon the warm brown base. Misha watched as his father decorated the orange strips with a mosaic of diced raw onion and chopped hard boiled egg and imitated every movement. I loved watching my two men together, even if I felt like an outsider, an intruder in their private tête-à-tête. It was obvious they adored one another. Misha was a little miniature of his father, not only his facial features—the cheekbones, the eyes—but his mannerisms mirrored his idol's, too.

As the samovar percolated, Cook-san served us cups of tea. I spread butter on my bread and watched as it was absorbed like ice melting into the Amur River during the Spring thaw. I glanced out the window and surmised that it would be doing that any day now that it was almost April. I placed a chunk of sugar in my mouth and sipped the liquid through it, sucking in the sweetness as it dissolved into slush on my tongue. Maybe if I drank enough, it would wake me up. Or maybe I'd go back to bed after Ilya left and lose myself in the dunes of my comforter.

Misha reached for the sugar bowl but Ilya put a hand over his eager little one. "If you're going to eat smoked salmon like a man, you must learn to drink your tea without sugar. It doesn't mix with the fish." Misha withdrew and nodded gravely that he would do as his father bid. "That's a boy," Ilya reassured him. "And soon you can go off to court and try my cases for me, eh?"

Misha nodded. "Are you going to win, Father?"

"I hope so. Today is the conclusion of a very important case." Ilya took a large bite of his breakfast and washed it down with the steaming liquid. He wiped both corners of his moustache and continued. "A man is being tried for a murder he didn't commit. He's being used as a scapegoat, to set an example. Do you know what that is—a scapegoat?" Misha shrugged uncertainly, but Ilya, absorbed with his story, continued. "Well, I believe this man is innocent and I've been doing my best to convince everyone else of it. After all, that is one of the major reasons we here in Siberia are so proud of our government. Because it's fair. Not like in the rest of Russia where you can be persecuted because you're poor…or Jewish…."

Misha's eyes were glued to his father's, even as he gobbled up his own portion. "I hope you win," he said, his mouth full of food. The pride and affection I saw in the boy's eyes reminded me of myself when I first fell in love with Ilya. Everything he did and said was mesmerizing. I wanted to linger at his side endlessly. I wished I still felt so blindly enamored.

In the small room between the kitchen and the back door, Ilya tugged on his tall wool-lined boots. He put on his fur-collared coat and hat, hugged Misha and then planted a kiss on my lips. The familiar tickle of his moustache made me smile. He pulled gloves from his pocket and thrust his fingers into the pliant leather. Another whoosh of icy air hit us as he opened the door. I pulled my dressing gown tighter around me, wishing it were wool instead of satin. I hadn't combed my hair properly in my rush to join Ilya at breakfast and the wind blew a few loose strands from my braid. I tucked them behind my ear.

Ivan, our coachman, waited in the snowy drive, having hitched the horses to the sleigh. He bowed to me, his black hair and eyes like smudges of coal against his ruddy complexion. Once Ilya was comfortably seated, Ivan climbed onto his own bench, in front. Ilya burrowed beneath a thick bear rug, keeping his head under the slight overhang. With a reassuring cluck and an experienced nudge with the reins, there was no need for Ivan to employ his whip. Cook-san held open the gate and then closed it as the sleigh drove off.

"I wish I could go with him," Misha said. He hurried to the kitchen window to wave, but Ilya had already disappeared.

I shook my head and wondered what the outcome of the trial would be, unhappy that I had to content myself with hearsay.

Only a month earlier, our Sunday lunch had been interrupted by the arrival of a local woman beseeching Ilya to speak with her. Kerchiefed in red, her cheeks a similar hue, be it from worry or perspiration, I could tell she was desperate for his help. Ilya had invited her into his study and when they'd emerged after a short consultation, her brow, which had been waffled with concern, was smooth with relief. Ilya had seen to it that Cook-san gave her a warm meal before asking Ivan to drive her back to her village. The reverence in her eyes made it clear that Ilya had once again worked his magic.

After she left, Ilya explained that the woman's husband, the peasant Dmitri Nelibuov, had been accused of murder. Ilya had agreed to represent him. Gratis. The shock stamped on my face prompted Ilya to explain that if he could exonerate this fellow, that would be payment enough. "The man deserves a fair trial just as any of us. Perhaps he steals. Cheats on his wife even. That doesn't make him a murderer. He has a family who needs his support. Who knows how many little ones...?" It occurred to me that this woman might be better rid of her husband, but I kept my mouth shut. "This case may not bring in any income," Ilya had said, "but think of the respect I would garner if we win." Previously, the only law suits that had fallen to him involved neighbors squabbling over stolen livestock or spouses accusing one another of infidelity. This case presented a challenge. A break from his work at the fisheries and as editor of *The Amursky Liman*. When he saw I wasn't appeased, Ilya had continued. "How can you of all people pass judgement so quickly? Your own father was exiled to Sakhalin Island for a crime he swore he didn't commit. Just because he was a Jew. If he'd had a fair trial—or even a trial at all—" That was true, but....

"I just think you're making a mistake," I'd said. The rest of the town echoed my sentiments, claiming Nelibuov to be a loiterer, a *nogoodnik*. Since the Tsar and his family had been ruthlessly murdered by bloodthirsty Bolsheviks a year before, the entire country had been in the throes of a civil war. We, in our remote corner of Siberia, on the shoulder of Japan, were immune to the political prattle. But this trial had polarized our city.

Ilya persevered despite the naysayers. He lived by a personal code of honour and always gave others the benefit of the doubt. Sometimes, I even joked that he had Bolshevik tendencies. If Nelibuov was found guilty and sentenced to death, my husband would take it personally that he hadn't been able to save the man's life.

5

My sister-in-law, Esther and I were headed into town to do some shopping. Esther was voluptuous and though her girth made her appear older than her thirty-two years, she was full of exuberance. I envied her tobacco hair which was flecked with auburn tints and shined in both sun and candle-light. Mine was longer and thicker, but was merely brown. I felt like I was the plow horse to Esther's stallion. Whereas Ilya was a reflection of his father, I imagined Esther looked like Riva had in her youth. Jolly, but with a sharp wit, she was frank and funny and she and I got along famously. It was odd, because everything about her mother made me cringe these days. I admired Esther's daring and wished I could be more like her. She was the older sister I'd always wanted.

Esther was married to my brother, Nikolai, and we joked that we were especially compatible because we were doubly related. We teased one another about having to live—and put up—with our respective mothers-in-law, which, since they were our own mothers, we could definitely relate to. We were both close to our older brothers and it was Esther who'd played a vital role in bringing Ilya and me together. I always felt svelte beside her as she was positively rotund, but I also felt young and naive. Her expansiveness didn't seem to bother her—or my brother. Esther bragged that he loved to bury himself in the thick dough of her flesh. In fact, she was constantly whispering the most outlandish details of how she and my brother kept themselves entertained in the bedroom. Though Ilya and I had what I considered to be a passionate marriage, Esther definitely made me blush at her descriptions. I knew she was trying to shock me and I wished I could ask her for details, but I was too bashful. I didn't want to be considered prudish, so I played along with her, insinuating that Ilya and I were not as puritan as I suspected we might be.

We drove through the wide streets of Nikolaevsk in our sleigh with Ivan at the helm. The ground was still upholstered in white, so we hadn't reverted to tires on the carriage yet. But a few weeks of April sunshine had sufficiently melted the accumulation along the route into town. Wooden planks were strewn along the sides of the roadways to prevent pedestrians from sinking too deeply into the muck of mud and melting snow. The sun was warm, but a lingering bite in the air made me snuggle against Esther's soft, warm body under the bearskin.

On my lap, I held a copy of the French fashion magazine—*Vogue*—that my eldest brother, Matvei, had brought back from his last trip. It came from Paris by way of St. Petersburg and was full of glossy illustrations of beautiful women outfitted in everything from ball gowns to everyday wear. If only we could travel to Paris and see some of those creations in person!

"I like this one," Esther indicated a cinnamon colored dress with chiffon sleeves and a revealing neckline on a tall slender model. "What do you think?"

"Mm...That shade would be nice for you." I wasn't sure how to tactfully steer her in a more flattering direction. Since the Great War had begun in 1914, Esther and I had been organizing bi-annual balls to raise funds to feed and clothe the soldiers at the front. In addition, we held monthly afternoon gatherings to help the war effort. Over tea and conversation, we and our lady friends would cut up old tablecloths and roll them into bandages. We'd solicit donations of clothing; and money to pay for medication. Once everything was accumulated, we'd pack the care boxes to be sent to the West. I relished the diversity these activities added to my days and felt good about doing something other than planning meals and making sure the children's schoolwork got done. There wasn't much a woman in my position could do outside the home that made a mark on society. Though the war had ended, we'd kept up our charity efforts knowing that there was still plenty of need, both near and far. And it gave us a good excuse to get dressed up and go out.

I thumbed through the pages in search of something more appropriate for Esther to wear. I thought of how hard it had been to clasp my skirt that morning and hoped I wouldn't end up looking like my sister-in-law. Even if I did, I would never have the chutzpah to appear in the frocks she put herself into. Esther loved attention of any kind. I only liked approval.

As we neared the center of town, we passed the main

square located at one end of the city. Three sides of the quadrangle were represented by the differing faiths of our community. The stone synagogue, with its imposing columns and stained glass windows, had been built and funded by both our fathers to replace the small wooden structure that had originally graced the area. The building now held its own against the ornate mosque facing it. But the Russian Orthodox cathedral, whose golden onion domes shimmered in the morning light, overruled the prevalence of its neighbors, dominating the patch of land where, in summer months, townspeople gathered for concerts, dances or strolls.

Two priests stood deep in conversation on the steps of the cathedral. The men looked so serious in their long black robes and mitres. Heavy silver crosses hung from their necks. I wondered what they were discussing. "Probably the sermon for Easter Sunday," Esther offered. The archpriest was known to be outspoken in his views, especially on the subject of the Tsar. Though the horrific execution of the royals had occurred over a year before, the priest couldn't seem to reconcile their fate and was constantly issuing warnings to his congregation to beware of the growing revolutionary threat. At least that's what we'd heard from our Gentile friends. Nobody seemed to pay it much mind, but scary thoughts were constantly bombarding my thoughts and dreams. I wanted to bring the subject up with Esther, but knew she'd pooh-pooh them just like Ilya always did.

Off the square, radiating like strands in a spider web, streets branched off toward the various quarters of the city. At the far end of one boulevard loomed the Town Hall, the Bank and the foreign business offices; and at the other end, like anchors, stood the police station and the prison. We veered left toward the center of town, passing the Amur Hotel, with its uniformed doorman who lifted his cap at Ivan in greeting. Finally, we reached our destination: Kunst and Albers, one of the largest establishments in town. Modeled on European emporiums, K&A was two stories high, made of yellow stone, with white trim and large arched windows that overlooked the street. The stately building always reminded me of a tiered wedding cake. Vying for trade on the other side of the avenue was Svenson's Department Store, and a little further on the right, Shimada's Dry Goods. Ivan steered the panting horses out of the main thoroughfare and helped us down from the sleigh. We disappeared inside, anxious to peruse the latest imports.

An hour or so later, our ears sated with gossip, Esther and I re-emerged onto the street. Our arms were overflowing with purchases wrapped up like presents in cardboard boxes secured with ribbons. Ivan relieved us of our bundles, but we told him we wanted to stroll a bit before returning home.

"Isn't that a pretty brooch?" I pointed at a pale pink cameo nestled on a cushion of red satin in the window display at the jeweler's.

"Mm-hm," Esther nodded, but she linked her arm through mine and pulled me along.

"Shall we stop at Marfa's for a new hat?" I slowed down for a glance as we passed the milliner's.

"Maybe afterwards. I've got a hankering for something sweet and buttery right now." She nudged me past the bookstore and telegraph office, but at the printer's, I stopped to peer through the glass to see if I might catch a glimpse of Ilya conferring with Gennadi Richter. Ilya's law office was situated directly above the printer's, which was particularly convenient since Ilya was also the editor of *The Amursky Liman*, the city's most read gazette. As it was mid-afternoon, the shop wasn't its usually bustling hive. A few aproned men bent over steel presses. Richter, his shiny pate ringed with graying florets, sat hunched at a raised desk, his shirt restrained by sleeve garters.

"Ilya must be upstairs," Esther commented.

"Busy at work, as usual." I shook my head. As it turned out, he'd won his murder trial and the peasant Nelibuov had been freed. The verdict had bolstered Ilya's faith that good indeed could win out over evil. It had also increased his work load. Though I'd been opposed to his taking on the case, his victory filled me with pride. My husband was a principled man and he stood up for his beliefs. If only I could be as blind to the public's opinion and as forgiving and honorable in my outlook as he was.

We walked by Shimada's, then crossed the wide boulevard, skirting a small marsh of mud in the middle. I lifted my skirt and tiptoed carefully so as not to soil my favorite red boots, but Esther forged ahead, unconcerned. Billboards advertising the latest movie framed the ticket booth at the cinema. "'*Das Kabinett Des Doktor Caligari*'" Esther moved in closer to read the caption. "'The story of a macabre somnambulist and his deadly predictions.' Ooh! We'll have to get Kolya and Ilya to take us to see that after the holidays."

I shuddered at the stark poster. A man, clad in black, stared out from beneath a hooded cape. His long crooked fingers clasped the shoulder of a female corpse, wrapped in a milky shroud. The whites of his eyes stared sinisterly at us. I pulled my woolen cape tighter and nuzzled the fur trim at my neck. "Looks rather spooky, doesn't it?"

"You're such a coward," Esther chided, poking me in jest. "It'll be fun!" She steered us into Konditorei Keller, the German café next door to the cinema.

The atmosphere in Keller's was cosmopolitan. Chandeliers hung from the ceiling and a long marble counter offered a display of tempting confections. Small geometric *petits fours* draped with pastel marzipan vied for attention alongside dark chocolate cakes and colorful glazed tartlets. People sat at small round tables on wire-backed chairs and read the newspaper or gossiped with friends. The smell of burnt sugar filled the air. Aproned waiters balanced trays as they zigzagged from table to table. The elegantly suited proprietor manned the elaborate cash register whose ping rang out every so often.

Herr Keller greeted us with a satisfied smile and led us to a table in the midst of his bustling establishment. Esther and I sipped our tea, served in glasses with cherry *varenya*, and nibbled on an assortment of shortbread and cakes. I picked out a chocolate-bathed crescent and dunked it into my tea. "I hear there are cafés on every corner in Paris," I confided wistfully. "And the women are all so chic!" I longed to see the exotic city, but knew I'd probably stick out like a bruised pear among the sleeker, more exotic fruit in France's orchard. No need to worry, though. My chances of ever making the trip were remote.

"So says Matvei, I presume?"

I nodded. "Do you think we'll ever have a chance to visit there?" How I wished Ilya's work would take him abroad like Matvei's did. But ever since he returned from university in St. Petersburg, he seemed content to remain in Nikolaevsk.

"Perhaps someday. But Kolya's not a world traveler like his brother." Esther garbled through a mouthful of éclair.

Her lips were shiny from the cream. "Don't look now," she said, swallowing, but I immediately turned my attention to the doorway as two women entered. "I told you not to look," Esther admonished.

Mira Gorbatova was a petite woman with a plain face and tiny dark eyes. She wore an evergreen coat with fox trim and carried a matching muff. It was almost as if she'd costumed herself to resemble the animal. Beside her towered Iulia Sharpova, in a Persian lamb cape that hung stylishly on her slender frame, all height and no width. Her blond hair was pulled into a twist and she looked very elegant. Almost like one of the models Esther and I had admired in the *Vogue Magazine* earlier. I wished I could enter a room like her, drawing all gazes without even acknowledging their existence.

"What a pair!" Esther whispered. Both Iulia and Mira had set their sights on marrying Ilya back when they'd been in school together. I could understand his being disenchanted by Mira's constant chatter and opinions, but Iulia's cool beauty was hard to resist. The only reason I could find for his rejecting her was that she was taller than him which no doubt deflated his self-esteem. The fact that I had won him in the end had not endeared me to either of the women.

Having made eye contact, they approached. "Hello, Luba...Esther," they chimed.

"Iulia! Mira! What a lovely surprise," Esther transformed her sarcasm into charm, as if by magic.

"How is Andrei?" I asked after Iulia's husband, then turned to Mira. "And Efraim?"

Unable to quell her eagerness to gossip, Mira leapt to juicier topics. "Have you heard?" she asked.

"Heard?" Esther said.

"About the schoolteacher," Mira rolled on.

"The one who was due here in January..." Iulia filled in.

"...who never arrived...." The two women tripped over one another in their zeal to convey the news.

"No. What about him?" I asked.

"Remember how everyone wondered what had become of him? Well," Mira sputtered, "his body was found frozen in the forest."

Iulia gasped, as if she hadn't already heard. I looked at Esther and listened more closely.

"Just this morning Igor Blogodovich came into town, his sled piled high with pelts. And on top of them all was the frozen corpse of the teacher!"

"And he hadn't just died from the cold," Iulia informed us. "No, there was a bullet wound in his chest."

"What do you think happened?" I asked. By this time, half the restaurant's ears were tuned to our conversation. I realized I was gripping the silver holder of my tea glass a little too tightly.

"People are saying that Bolshevik soldiers are working their way north from Vladivostok..."

"And from St. Petersburg. Taking over villages..."

"Trying to establish a foothold up here." The women worked in perfect synchronicity, like dance partners.

"In Nikolaevsk?" My eyes bulged like the macaroon I'd been eying. Could the rumors actually be true?

Because of our harsh winters when the river froze for seven months and the only means of transport was by dogsled, travelers were often delayed. The unlucky often met their demise due to the frigid temperature. Not from attacks by roving bands of marauders. In Nikolaevsk, as Ilya always pointed out, we were worlds away from Moscow and St. Petersburg where trouble had been brewing for years. It was as if we lived in a different country. People like our fathers had settled here because of the region's acceptance of different religions, not to mention all the business opportunities. In our remote corner, we minded our own affairs and nobody bothered us. Until recently.

In the past two years, even our local government seemed to be on a roller coaster. One minute, the Reds were in power; the next, the Whites seized it back. We had two sets of arm bands and, during periods of upheaval, we switched from one to the other, displaying our loyalty to the party in command on the sleeves of our coats. There had been a frightening period just the year before, in 1918, when it looked like the Reds might remain in control. There had been many arrests and a great deal of threatening. Despite Ilya's constant reassuring, I found the circumstances unsettling.

Fortunately, the Whites had prevailed and the tide once again turned in our favor. Lately, the political situation had simmered down. But that hadn't reassured me. Whenever talk turned to suspicions that partisan soldiers were hiding in the woods or villages along our Amur River or that the Reds were gaining strength and heading our way, Ilya would brush such notions aside, insisting that we were perfectly safe in Nikolaevsk. Yet I couldn't quell a growing uneasiness as I found myself listening to our neighbors voicing their fears about approaching danger.

When he returned home that evening, I ran straight to him with the news. "We are not the enemy, Luba. Haven't you ever seen how dirty my hands get from the inky news-paper presses?" he dismissed me. "They are hardly 'white,'" he laughed. "You have much more important things to worry about, darling. Like what you're going to wear for the holiday celebration next week. Did you find some material in town today? I want my wife to be the most beautiful woman of all!"

Being beautiful was the least of my concerns. For once, I wanted to feel safe, not pretty. I wished my husband would understand that. Would understand me. He suggested I blow my worries away like the fluff of a dandelion. In my mind it was he who was being too frivolous these days.

———

My father had been among the earliest settlers in Nikolaevsk. Having been released from an unjust exile on Sakhalin Island in 1874, he was making his way back to Lithuania, where he'd been born. He'd been wary of returning to a life of restrictions not all that different from imprisonment but had wanted to see his family again. Passing through Nikolaevsk, which at the time was not much more than a bustling frontier town, he quickly became convinced that he could re-build his life there.

The far eastern region of Siberia was bursting with untapped resources. The Amur River teemed with life, salmon and sturgeon being dominant headliners. The city was encircled by vast forests providing homes for wildlife that included elk, bear, boar, sable and mink. Father's business mind calculated that the excellent fishing and hunting would not only provide food and sport, but the valuable skins could also be exported and sold. He'd eyed the trees and seen lumber. During his years of incarceration, Father had labored in copper and gold mines in Sakhalin. He had learned a great deal, acquiring technical skills and observing the ill treatment of workers as well as encountering such behaviour first hand. He once told me that the experience had left him resolute to never work for anyone again and to treat any employees he might have fairly. It was Father who stressed that it was our duty as wealthy citizens to look out for those less fortunate than ourselves. Simon had passed on similar sentiments to Ilya and his siblings.

It didn't take Father long to acquire enough funds to start his first mill, becoming an owner and leaving his menial past behind him. Following this venture, Father added mines to his holdings, excavating gold, copper and silver from the depths of the rich Siberian earth. A few years later, he began to lease land along the river and build fisheries. So far away from the central body of Russia, there were no religious restrictions in Nikolaevsk. Christians, Muslims, Jews lived and worked side by side. The international make-up was equally diverse. British, German and even American speculators, undaunted by the brutal elements and hungry to strike it rich, had offices in town. In this free atmosphere, Father thrived.

He purchased a large tract of land on *Pervaya Ulitsa*, the main residential street in town, and built himself a handsome, two-story dwelling that many considered palatial. At least by Nikolaevsk's modest standards. I grew up in that house. The city was increasing in population and size and Father was at the forefront of all the expansion. On a business trip to the West, he'd met my mother, Anna Maremant, the daughter of a wealthy intellectual. Father's charm and ambition were such that he was able to woo her away from the comforts of Moscow. Also inspired was Mama's brother, Syoma, who moved to Nikolaevsk a few years later. My brother Matvei was my parents' firstborn, followed by Nikolai and then me, in 1890.

Every Spring, tracts of land along the Amur were auctioned off to the highest bidders and that was how Papa met Ilya's father, Simon. Both men were vying for the same lots on which to establish fisheries. After their initial competition, there proved to be more than enough for each of them and their rivalry turned into a lasting friendship. As their camaraderie grew, Father sold off a parcel of his estate to Simon who built his own house on Second Street. Between the two homes lay a sprawling expanse which was eventually tamed into fruit groves, vegetable gardens, barns and chicken coops. I literally grew up back to back with Ilya's family and when we married, I simply moved across the yard. Esther did the same and she and Nikolai lived with Mama and Matvei's family in my childhood home.

Because Nikolaevsk was cut off from the world for seven long months every winter, not only our relatives but the entire community considered one another family, despite differing backgrounds. And because of the dark, cold months of isolation, any opportunity to celebrate was a good one.

Passover and Easter usually fell concurrently near the end of the deep freeze. It was a happy and festive time. Besides the formal religious observances, this was also a time of gratitude rather than ceremony, a welcoming of Spring. My eldest brother Matvei followed the tradition set by our father. Every year, he hosted the holiday dinner at his house.

———

When we convened for the annual party the following week, a lavish *zakuski* was laid out on a side table in the living room. Guests helped themselves to deviled eggs, smoked salmon, sturgeon and sausage, spooning dollops of eggplant caviar, pickled cucumbers and marinated mushrooms onto plates that bobbled under heaping cascades. Women in aprons buzzed about the room, toting platters. Food was such a prominent factor in our lives. We loved to eat it, prepare it, and it was the perfect backdrop for community gatherings.

I felt luminous in my new velvet gown, sapphire teardrops dancing from my ears. Though it hugged my still ample hips and mid-section, the dress also accentuated my eyes. I could tell from Ilya's glance that he approved of my choice. He looked crisp in his tuxedo and was holding court at the bar helping my brother Nikolai pour drinks for the guests. Esther was squeezed into a sheath that resembled the *Vogue Magazine* illustration she'd admired. She was laughing bawdily with Sammy Shimkin, our childhood playmate. Sammy was a timorous fellow and he was blushing from whatever Esther had just whispered in his ear. I could only imagine what she might have said. It seemed to have something to do with Mira Gorbatova and Iulia Sharpova who'd just arrived with their husbands. Mama and Riva were in the kitchen with Matvei's wife, Raya, overseeing preparations. They were like salt and pepper mills, Riva white haired and imposing, Mama stout and severe, her black hair pulled tight and her tiny spectacles veiling her periwinkle eyes.

The front door opened and closed, spewing more guests in with the regularity of a cuckoo clock. Two servants relieved the arrivals of their stoles, coats and top hats. The conversation in the house created a steady hum punctuated only by occasional squeals from the children running underfoot or laughing at one of Uncle Kolya's magic tricks. Matvei roamed the room, ensuring that his guests had everything they wanted.

A cannonball—stout, solid and powerful—Matvei dashed through life, full of energy and purpose, much like our father had. Sparkling eyes, deeply set, gazed over a bulbous nose never missing a detail. His hands slashed the air like an impresario as he emphasized whatever point he was trying to make. He was always outfitted in the finest fabrics and enjoyed looking debonair, even if his starched shirts stretched tautly across an increasing paunch marring the perfection of his portrait.

He reminded me so much of Papa, who'd vanished years ago during a hunting trip, the winter I was seven. The details surrounding his disappearance had always been murky. Had he simply vanished? Been eaten by a bear? Frozen to death? Or had he left Mama for another woman, as I once heard rumored. Matvei, who was seventeen at the time, had stepped up and assumed Father's role, caring for Mama and helping her raise Kolya and me. He refused to answer my questions and Mama never wanted to discuss the subject either, claiming it was too painful, which also gave me pause.

The dining table had been appended for our large number and jutted into the hallway. It gleamed with silver and goblets like a showgirl seeking a beau. Bottles of red and white wine from Crimea's renowned vineyards stood like sentinels, alternating along the vast stretch. The tinkling of a silver bell announced that dinner was about to be served. As everyone searched for markers inscribed with their names, the living room swell ebbed. I followed in the wake and as I passed the front door, I caught sight of Syoma and Tuula Maremant, my mother's brother and his wife, standing awkwardly in the foyer. I greeted them.

Aunt Tuula, an angular woman with a mass of black corkscrew curls on her head, pecked my cheek. Uncle Syoma wrapped me in an enthusiastic grip. I could feel the strength of his torso through his suit jacket. Although Syoma was Mama's brother, the Maremants rarely socialized with the rest of our family. I suspected it was the result of a fissure that existed between Tuula and Mama. Not only had Papa given my mother a life of grandeur and leisure, he'd also bestowed three children on her. Tuula came from a modest background. She and Uncle Syoma were childless and their lifestyle remained modest.

The women's coolness might have been the result of something else, but knowing how judgmental Mama was, I doubted it. Whatever the case, the holidays were the only time everyone congregated. It wouldn't do to exclude less affluent relations from well attended events.

"How lovely to see you both," I said as I ushered them to the two unoccupied seats they'd been assigned, at an extreme diagonal from Mama.

No gathering was immune to the topic of the day: the changing landscape of Russia's governmental and class structure. It was 1919 and the world had just come out of the Great War. At home, our country was embroiled in civil strife. The Tsar had been deposed and Russia's opposing forces were boldly etched in red or white. As I listened to the discussion, I absent-mindedly pushed my Beef Stroganoff in its creamy sauce on my plate. It made me angry that everyone ignored the danger I felt was so imminent, Ilya in particular.

"We're not nobles and our employees are not serfs," he said as he dug into his meal with relish.

I reached for my wineglass and took a large swallow, letting the liquid warm my throat and cheeks. "Meaning we're good Whites and they're bad ones?" I dared my husband across the table. I could feel everybody's eyes on me.

"We don't take advantage of our workers. We pay them fair wages, not like the peasants who toil on vast estates and are more like feudal serfs." Ilya said. He washed down another bite with a gulp of wine, then sighed, whether from satisfaction at the meal or frustration with me, it wasn't clear. Ever since Dmitri Nelibuov had been acquitted, Ilya's faith in mankind and in the citizens of Nikolaevsk had been renewed. The triumph had also cemented my husband's resolve that there was nothing for us to worry about and that all rumors of Bolshevik incursions were groundless. And, yes, his success had increased his clout and gone to his head. "Mamatchkas, this meal is delicious!" He raised his glass with a grandiose gesture and glanced at Riva and Mama at the other end of the table in an obvious attempt to change the subject.

"Regarding our army," my brother Nikolai jumped in, returning to the subject, "I can vouch for them." Kolya had been granted leave from his military post at Fort DeKastri, for the holiday. Ever the entertainer, he had a biting sense of humor, like Esther, and always kept company entertained. Kolya had joined the military as an escape from the entrapments of the family business. Though more of a jokester than a soldier, his uniform fed into his need to pontificate. "They're well equipped, well trained—isn't that right, Colonel Vits?"

"Absolutely," Nikolai's commanding officer boomed. "There's no need for concern." The big man whose ruddy cheeks contrasted with his thick white sideburns lifted his goblet, swallowing its contents as if it were only a thimbleful,

then stretched his arm toward Nikolai who was already holding a new bottle aloft. "Isn't that correct, Ishikawa-san?" Vits
addressed the Japanese major sitting opposite, who quickly
concurred.

Since Japan had won the Russo-Japanese War in 1905,
Japanese forces had been stationed in Nikolaevsk to oversee
their country's interests in Russia and maintain peace. The
Japanese command was situated at the edge of town. They
were eight hundred strong. The officers and soldiers resided in
nearby barracks and their families and the rest of the Japanese
population built their homes in the adjoining neighborhood
so as to be close to their compatriots. Major Ishikawa had
lived in Nikolaevsk for close to fifteen years and he and Ilya
had been friends for most of that time. Beyond the Japanese
district lay Chinatown, a less affluent area where the Chinese
locals resided. Whereas the Japanese who were not enlisted
worked mostly in the fisheries and lumber mills outside of
the city, the Chinese population were generally employed as
cooks and servants by the wealthier households like our own.
As far as I could remember, there had always been Chinese,
Japanese and Koreans in Nikolaevsk and there had never been
any animosity. The Chinese generally stuck to themselves and
the Koreans usually returned home after the fishing season
ended. The Japanese, on the other hand, were more integrated
into our local society.

Mr. Shimada, the owner of the dry goods store in town,
was so much a part of our community that, rather than being
addressed as Shimada-san, in the Japanese fashion, he was
known to everyone as Piotr Nikolaevich and had even given
Russian names to his sons, born in Nikolaevsk. We bought
many of our provisions at his store. There was also a Japanese

barber who doubled as a dentist. One always knew which profession he was practicing by the noises emanating from his window at a given time. I used to think one of the worst things in the world was being dragged to that office with a toothache, the only thing worse being the toothache itself. That was before I started worrying about bigger threats like the increasing uprisings and discontent of people far less fortunate than ourselves exploding in spurts across the country like fireworks on Chinese New Year's.

As the dinner conversation continued, our host, my brother Matvei, who frequently traveled throughout Russia as well as China, Mongolia and Japan, had the last word. "Between Colonel Vits, Major Ishikawa and their combined troops, we have plenty of manpower to defend ourselves, should there ever be a need."

6

My bare feet propelled me back and forth as I swayed in my rocker on the porch of our *dacha*. Viktor lay in my arms, having fallen asleep after nursing. At five months, he was just beginning to show a curiosity in his surroundings, but as yet he was an easy baby. I settled him in a large wicker basket by my side and he slept on, unperturbed. I knew I should help Riva and Nessia prepare lunch, but it was so peaceful, sitting there alone. I leaned back and sighed contentedly. I was wearing a comfortable skirt and blouse of light cotton, sleeves rolled up, and my long braid was coiled around my head and off my neck. The sky was a swath of blue with just a few cloud freckles and the July sun baked us as if we were pies in an oven, turning our skin brown as crust if we weren't careful.

Though I missed the active social life of Nikolaevsk and especially the attention I garnered when with Ilya, whether in public or in private, I loved the quiet of the country. No newspapers or rumors of threatening Reds. Only the monotonous hooting of an owl at night, the excited chatter of crickets at dusk, the subdued buzz of bees making their rounds. The chirp and crowing of nature soothed me.

I tuned out the voices that drifted from the house and watched as two dragonflies flitted in front of me, their gossamer wings and slender bodies darting among the rose bushes nearby. The first one circled back and landed on my knee. The other followed. It hovered, then softly lowered itself onto its mate's back. After a moment, they flew away together. How romantic. A breeze countered the humidity and the air was thick with perfume.

Every summer, the children and I traveled upriver to Mago to escape the oppressive heat and dust that settled on Nikolaevsk. Of course, Riva and her daughter, Nessia, who lived with us, came, too; as did Yumiko-san, the children's *amah*. My mama, Esther and her two children had their own place nearby. Ilya remained in Nikolaevsk with Ivan and Cook-san to wait on him. He visited from time to time, when work permitted, and would arrive the following day in time to celebrate Misha's eighth birthday.

Our *dacha* was tucked in a copse of birches and pines from which the house and most of its furnishings had been constructed. We had neither plumbing, a telephone nor electricity here, those being relatively new innovations even at home. But the proximity of the river, the green expanse of yard and the awning of forest that encompassed us made up for the lack of conveniences. In fact, the simplicity eased some of the pressure of city life. How nice not to have to always wear a corset or look one's best.

We filled our days tending to our garden or berry picking, carrying our bounty back to make preserves and pies. Twice a week, on Wednesdays and Saturdays, we went into the village to shop at the market. Local peasants cooked and cleaned for us; but, as usual, Riva led the brigade. She and Nessia were unfurling a bright embroidered cloth, covering a picnic table in the shade. They laid out plates, glasses and cutlery, then accented their tableau with a meal of hard boiled eggs, pickles, cucumbers, bread and cheese.

Slender as a fishing pole, with sad brown eyes, Nessia was such a quiet presence in our lives that half the time I didn't even realize she was in our midst. A year older than me, she remained unmarried. I knew she suffered from epilepsy and I felt badly for her. But I didn't understand how that affected the rest of her well being. In the years I'd known her, she'd had four or five seizures. The rest of the time she was like everyone else. Except that there was nothing youthful or engaging about her. She didn't have any close friends and rarely ventured from her mother's side. If I thought I was shy, Nessia made me look like a firecracker.

In the distance, I heard Yumiko-san's lilting voice mingling with the shouts and laughter of the children as they trooped forth through the bushes. Katya's long braids swung at her sides and her dimpled face looked radiant with health. She had been born with one blue eye and one green and this asymmetry gave her a unique presence. She ran over to give me a hug and peeked at her sleeping baby brother. Misha and Veronika, baskets in hand, broke from their older sister and headed straight for the table, scrambling onto the benches and reaching for the food. They must have been tumbling about because their clothes were smudged with dirt and there were bits of leaves and grass in their hair. Misha tucked his favorite wooden toy, a small cup on a handle with a ball attached that Ivan had made for him, into his pocket and Veronika pulled a wooden pistol out of hers and lay it on the table. Ever the tomboy, she worshipped her older brother and coveted his belongings. The children wriggled as Yumiko-san covered their fronts with napkins. Riva and Nessia bustled about serving everyone.

"Sounds like you had a wonderful time!" I said as I sauntered through the grass, carrying Viktor in his bassinet. I stepped over a wooden duck on a string and dodged a collection of toy soldiers and horses scattered in my path.

"Will you come play with us later, Mama?" the children wanted to know.

"We'll see. Probably." I enjoyed engaging in family activities, but my favorite pastime of all was reading. I liked to take advantage of Ilya's absence and Yumiko-san's presence to lose myself in books. I'd recently been given a collection of short stories by Anton Chekov which I was enjoying; but it didn't hold a candle to *Anna Karenina*, which I'd read the previous summer and hadn't been able to put down.

The children were perfectly happy in their *amah*'s company. Small boned and built like a child, Yumiko-san never lost her temper with them. I was astounded by her composure and gentle affection. I loved my children, but I often felt overwhelmed by their constant demands. I wanted to play with them, but found their games dull. And I didn't have the patience to follow their fleeting instincts and abrupt changes in direction.

Not Yumiko-san. Though she wore a traditional *kimono* with *zoris* on her feet, she didn't let the constricting outfit deter her from getting on her knees and playing with her wards in the grass. And though it was clear how much they adored her, she never flaunted their fondness or tried to make me feel jealous. I couldn't have been more thankful for her assistance.

"We brought berries, yes?" Yumiko-san prompted. The children looked up from their meal and pushed forth their baskets, nodding and smiling as they chewed. I reached my hand in and popped a handful of raspberries, still warm from the sun, into my mouth. Their tartness whet my taste buds.

"Can we make ice cream tonight?" Veronika asked.

"Yes! With the berries," Misha agreed. "I'll do the cranking!"

"Me, too!" Veronika echoed. It wasn't difficult to get them to join in as they were aware of the special treat that would result from their hard work.

"Alright. But then we'll have to pick more so that we can make Papa's favorite jam," I winked.

The crunch of twigs underfoot announced the arrival of Mama, Esther and Esther's children from their *dacha* nearby. Mama was a dumpling of a woman and wasn't so comfortable navigating the rough path with its protruding branches. Her once thick black hair was pulled back in a severe bun and in her black cotton dress, she was the antithesis of summer cheer. I sensed that her uneasiness stemmed both from her poor vision as well as her unsteady carriage. She was sturdy, but hardly agile. Esther, who was surprisingly fleet for someone of her dimensions, helped her along. Five-year-old Sophie bounded ahead, all skinny limbs and missing teeth, and squirmed in between Veronika and Misha at the table. Her brother Tolya, ten, loped dreamily along in a world of his own. He called to mind a poet, right out of Tolstoy.

When they reached us, Mama was panting and her dress was stained with perspiration. I lit up at Esther's presence, knowing that whether we joined the children later or stayed back on the porch, there would be lots of laughter as Esther found humor in everyone and everything. Even cleaning up would be less of a chore with her at my side.

Indeed, after the hike and the meal, Mama was too tired to return home. She could have sat on the veranda with Riva and Nessia, but they weren't her idea of good company. She decided she'd like to take a nap. "You can sleep in my bed," said Katya. The girl offered her *babushka* her arm and led her into the house. Mama beamed.

"Let's play croquet!" Misha suggested and Veronika and Sophie galloped to help him set up the hoops. A curtain of freshly washed sheets fluttered in the breeze and the children ducked through the billowing folds to get to an open swathe of lawn. Misha directed the girls who happily obeyed his orders. They looked like a litter of happy puppies turning circles in the grass. I could almost see tails wagging!

Convinced the older children were fine under Riva's watchful eye, Yumiko-san picked up Viktor's basket and took him inside. For someone so diminutive, Yumiko-san was very hardy.

After clearing the table and shaking the crumbs into the bushes for the squirrels and hares, Esther and I linked arms and headed toward the river. "We'll fold the sheets and clothes later," I called to Riva as we disappeared down the rocky path.

Perched on a rock, our skirts lifted to our knees, we

dangled our feet in the clear water, kicking softly at the little fish who nibbled our ankles. I could hear the clack of mallets meeting balls in our yard and could guess who was winning from the pitch of the children's voices.

"Do you think Kolya will come with Ilya tomorrow?" I asked. "It will make for a great celebration for Misha's birthday."

"I don't think he can take another leave so soon after his last one," Esther said, braiding a wreath of daisies. "If your brother had known how disciplined military life was, I doubt he'd have enlisted rather than continuing to work at the fisheries with Matvei."

"Kolya can't work with Matvei. He hates to work at all. And for his older brother...? Never!"

"You're right. Besides, he loves strutting around in his brass buttons and boots," Esther tittered.

"He always did enjoy playing army games when we were young." I remembered him constantly recruiting me for snowball fights in our yard. I'd join in with glee, but would quit after being pummeled by his enthusiastic assaults. I'd run inside to get warm and dry. Sitting by the fire with a good book and a cup of warm cocoa was much more satisfying. It occurred to me that when Katya played with Misha and Veronika for a short while, she would bow out similarly. Like mother, like daughter, I smiled to myself.

"I must say I find his riding crop enticing." Esther nudged me with her elbow, her eyes full of mischief. As she tucked the last stem into her creation, she lay the floral crown on her head.

"Esther!" I admonished her, feeling a twinge of jealousy mixed with curiosity, but too shy to pry.

"Maybe Ilya should get one of his own?"

"That's alright. We do fine without it." My face felt as red as the raspberries I'd just eaten.

"Perhaps that's because Ilya's such an older man. So distinguished." Esther was mocking him, but since he was her brother, I supposed it was alright. "I would have thought he'd be too stern to let loose, but maybe not. Maybe you could teach me a thing or two."

Grasping the folds of my skirt, I hopped into the shallow water and waded toward the inlet of sand just opposite in an effort to change the subject and put some distance between us. The river felt so cool.

"Come on," I said before she could push the subject further. "Let's put away the laundry before Riva does it herself and then complains we weren't there."

———

The cicadas were gossiping in full force, competing for our attention. We were gathered around the table, enjoying Misha's birthday dinner the next evening. Ilya had arrived that afternoon and spent several hours playing croquet with the children on the lawn. He looked so dashing, his sleeves rolled past his elbows and his cravat-less shirt unbuttoned at the neck, like a university student. I glanced at his strong forearms and his gentle, tapered fingers and looked forward to being alone with him after the children went to sleep.

"I wasn't able to bring your present with me this year," he told Misha as Riva put a homemade chocolate cake adorned with raspberries in front of our son. "It's waiting for you at home."

"Is it a pony, Father? Did you get me a pony?" Misha was

breathless with anticipation. He'd been pleading for a pony for a long time.

"You'll have to wait and see," his father said, but his smile gave the answer away. "Meanwhile, let's enjoy this scrumptious looking cake."

"Too bad there's no ice cream left from last night," I said, recalling how quickly that treat had been consumed.

The sun had set completely and we were almost too full to move. But when the air lit up with fireflies, Ilya followed the children across the lawn in pursuit of them. "Here! I've got one," he called, his hands cupped together. "Take a peek," he whispered to Veronika as he knelt before our little girl. She squealed with delight as he opened his hands and the lightening bug flew away. "Come on," he said, taking her hand in his, "let's go catch another. His ability to focus on each child warmed my heart.

The children were in their nightshirts, fresh from the line where they'd been hanging all day. They scrambled into bed as Ilya and I came to kiss them goodnight. The room was stark, reflecting the simplicity of our country life. Wooden walls, floors and bed frames stood out against the white linen sheets and shirts that retained the sun's freshness. At home, there would be an apple and a piece of chocolate on each pillow and Ilya would cut up the fruit for the children as he caught up on the events of their day. Being summertime, chocolate didn't transport well and after birthday cake, no one seemed to miss the bedtime ritual.

"I do have another surprise for you, Misha," Ilya said as he tucked the boy in. "I thought perhaps you'd like to accompany me to the fisheries tomorrow. Now that you're a young man, it's time you learned a little about the family business, eh?" Misha beamed.

"Can I come, too?" Katya sat up on the cot next to her brother's.

"And me? Me, too?" Veronika chimed in.

"Ilya Semyonovich," I chided when we were finally alone, "how you spoil that boy!"

"What am I to do?" he asked with a chuckle. "He's my eldest son." As if that were justification enough. I couldn't help noticing the jealous twinge that had swept over Katya's face. She was our oldest child but she resented her brother's male position. Having grown up with two brothers, I understood my daughter's feelings. That's why I'd insisted that she and I be allowed to accompany them to the fisheries.

———

The sky was striped with the pink of dawn when we awoke. The symphony of wildlife that announced daybreak was leveling off. Our carriage drove along the path that hemmed the river. The pulsing motion and the lull of the water flowing beside us was hypnotic. All was quiet except for the bells on the harnesses, the clopping of the horses' hooves and Ivan's deep baritone. As he crooned Russian folk tunes, I lost myself in the tranquility. The sun rose over the cliffs on the opposite bank and hawks began to shriek as they swooped in search of breakfast. We neared the fisheries and noticed that the Amur had become an undulating ribbon, shimmering like a sequin dress in the sunlight. Our mouths were agape.

"See the salmon running?" Ilya pointed out the incredible sight. It took the children a moment to realize that what we were looking at were the backs of hundreds of salmon swimming upstream to lay their eggs. There were so many fish we couldn't even see the water. "Three times a year, during the spring and summer, the salmon run like that. In droves," Ilya explained. "They make runs upstream to lay their eggs." Katya was awed by the beauty, Misha by the immensity.

Along the banks, shirtless men in high rubber boots were hurling huge screens of hemp into the middle of the river. The fishermen were a mixture of Japanese and Koreans. Their muscular backs and hairless chests gleamed with sweat, as shiny as the salmon skins. Bits of their conversation peppered the air—a tinkling of Korean and Japanese. As the fish fought to get to their spawning grounds, many were trapped in the holes. The heavy nets were hauled in and so were the fish. The sight reminded me of trips I'd taken with my own father whom my brothers and I sometimes accompanied on his rounds. Matvei and Nikolai would whoop with delight when Father invited them along. Like Katya, I'd always clamored to be included, then regretted my decision when I got there.

We got out of the carriage and followed Ilya to the dock where a sea of salmon was being slaughtered. Misha and Katya winced as they watched the men clobber their frightened prey. Under thick wooden clubs, their frantic movements slowed. Others plucked the slippery creatures from the nets and gutted them, sliding sharp steel blades into their bellies and slicing the fish in half. With agile hands, they reached in and disemboweled the fish, carefully depositing the valuable roe into barrels of salt for shipment as caviar and throwing the slimy entrails aside. The remainder of the catch were separated into other, larger barrels. Some would be salted, pickled and exported; others, taken to the huge smokehouses where they'd be hung and slowly cured. Katya crinkled her nose at the powerful fish odor. Rumbling like thunder, cartloads of barrels were rolled to and from the docks.

The workers looked up as we passed. They greeted Ilya warmly. He proudly introduced us and the men nodded respectfully. "How come there are no Russian workers?" Misha asked.

"There are a few. But I suppose it's tradition," Ilya said after a pause. "Every year boatloads of workers come north from Japan and Korea for the four month salmon season. The men don't have enough work at home and they can make enough here to last them the entire winter. Fishing is in their blood as their countries are surrounded by water. Unlike our own. As winter approaches, most return home. But some remain in town where their families have settled."

Inside, the smokehouse was cavernous. Dark and cool, it took a moment to adjust to the lack of sunlight. Slowly, the room came into focus. Small stoves burned beneath rows of salmon hanging from the rafters, their silver backs glistening as oil dripped off them, their pink bellies growing orange as they aged.

"Mm..." Misha remarked.

"That's from the oak fires," Ilya explained. "It's how we smoke the fish."

"I love the smell! It's like breakfast at home with you," Misha grinned.

We made our way to the back of the warehouse where the latest catch was being prepared for smoking. Workers were prying the lids off wooden barrels and driving large steel hooks through the gaping mouths of the salted fish. They hung them on wires which they hoisted to the ceiling. Katya buried her face in my shoulder.

"Shall we go outside?" I suggested.

"Why do they have to hurt them like that?" she wanted to know, not making a move to leave.

"If we don't smoke the fish, they'll spoil and we won't have anything to eat all winter," Father explained.

"I don't like to see them suffer," Katya said.

"Don't worry," Ilya went on. "The fish don't feel anything. They're dead."

"But there's so much blood," she said.

"I feel sorry for them," Misha agreed.

"Nonsense! You don't feel sorry when you eat them, do you?"

"No…but…"

I wondered if it had been such a good idea to insist that Katya and I come along. I'd forgotten what the fisheries were like, not having been in years. I hadn't wanted her to feel left out, but I also didn't want to upset her. I certainly would have preferred being home, reading by myself or laughing with Esther.

Continuing through the huge space, we arrived at the small office where Ilya's managers had their desks. "You know, children, there's a difference between killing for necessity and killing for no reason," Ilya told them. "Many people enjoy overpowering something smaller or weaker than themselves—just for the thrill of it. That's murder. But when one kills with a purpose, for food or clothing, for instance, then that's a different story."

A stir outside diverted Ilya's attention. We followed him, keeping our distance. Behind the wooden building in a clearing, Anatol, the foreman, was arguing with three men. The leader wore a felt cap which partly concealed a scar running from forehead to ear. Despite his disfigurement, or perhaps because of it, he was ruggedly attractive. His mate had abrasions along his arms which he kept scratching. I couldn't see much of the third man. He kept his head bowed and pawed the ground with the ragged toe of his boot. All three shuffled their feet nervously in contrast with their aggressive attitudes. Anatol was wearing an oilskin apron and his sleeves were held up above his elbows with braces. "I thought I told you hooligans never to show your faces around here again!" As he pointed at the men, I noticed one of his fingers was missing.

"What seems to be the matter?" Ilya asked calmly. Then I saw him tense his shoulders. I pulled the children back.

"These ruffians!" Anatol said. His face was splotched with perspiration. "They're the ones I threw out of here last month. Tried to sneak back in unnoticed. Well...! I overheard them goading the workers to join their damned Bolshevik forces..."

I was about to go back inside when I heard Ilya address one of the men. "Dmitri Nelibuov...." I stopped and immediately swung around.

"Gospodeen Kaptzan...." The third man had looked up. He was cool, but polite.

"Is this what I got you out of prison for? Why I saved your neck from the noose?" Having not been allowed in the courtroom during the trial because I was a woman, I'd never glimpsed Nelibuov. I'd only heard details from Ilya at meals. From them, I had fashioned a composite in my mind. It had never been a favorable picture, but as I observed his arrogance now, I liked this man even less in person. His hair was a mass of thin, orange curls from which several unruly tendrils had loosened and drooped about ears that stuck out. His gray eyes darted nervously and his sideburns crawled down unshaven cheeks until they disappeared into a scraggly beard.

"We want our wages," the scabby skinned man interceded. "We've worked all week."

Anatol was furious. "Hooligans! You don't deserve a *kopek*!"

"And you wonder why we're trying to talk sense into your men," the leader muttered under his breath.

My husband glared at him. I could tell he was nervous because he was pulling at his moustache. "They haven't been paid?" Ilya turned to Anatol who was sputtering for words. "Give the men their due." Ilya always insisted on being fair.

"But...!" The foreman was livid. I agreed with him and had trouble understanding my husband's forgiving nature.

"Pay them what they've earned." Ilya's voice was cold. "We're not trying to take advantage of our workers."

Anatol wasn't as successful at maintaining his composure. "They deserve nothing! Less than that even!" he scoffed. But despite his muttering, he did as Ilya directed. The men pocketed their wages and disappeared through the bushes, though Dmitri Nelibuov slithered away a bit sheepishly.

We drove back to our *dacha* in subdued silence, lulled by the rhythmic trot of the horses. I couldn't believe that this man who'd been imprisoned and accused of murder, whose life Ilya had defended—and saved—against the entire city's better judgement, had the audacity to return the favor in this manner.

The jovial mood of our morning had fizzled. I stared at Ivan's back, suspenders over his linen shirt. His arms barely budged, so good was he at maneuvering the reins. When Katya and Misha leaned against us and succumbed to sleep, I finally turned to Ilya. "You've got to take us back to Nikolaevsk with you. I don't want to stay out here alone with men like that lurking in the area."

"Don't be silly, *Lubachka*." He draped his arm around me. But one look at my face combined with the stiff resistance of my upper body and he must have realized that he was not going to convince me otherwise.

7

"We are not moving to Japan," Ilya abruptly sat up, shrugging me off as if I were a snowflake on his collar. The tender mood of our morning tryst had evaporated.

"But...once the Amur freezes, there'll be no getting out until May." It was September and, some mornings, the river already had a sheer layer of ice in sections. My brother and his family had decided that rather than spend the winter months in Vladivostok as they usually did, this year they were moving to Japan.

"What will I do in Hakodate? I have no business there. I barely speak the language." What Ilya said made sense—on one level. But what about our safety?

"Matvei's offered for us to live with him. He has plenty of room in the house he's rented. You and he can work together." With the rising political tension, there had been much talk of moving amongst our friends, but the consensus had been that there was no need.

"I don't want to be his lackey."

"What are you talking about? He's my brother." I tugged on Ilya's shoulder. "You're good friends." It bothered me that my husband always had to be in charge. When we'd first been married, I'd been content to defer to him on all matters. His ubiquity had impressed me, but over the years it had begun to irritate me that he didn't consider my opinions viable.

Ilya pulled away. "Yes. When we're here, on equal footing. But I don't want to be beholden to him." Confronted by his back, I grazed my fingertips lightly across it as I knew he liked. Unconsciously, he turned to me.

"I know you're used to being your own boss, *Ilya moy*." I raked my hand across his chest and played with the brown tufts that sprouted in different directions. "But it would only be for the winter months. Until the trouble blows over."

Even though it irked me, I played the accommodating wife in the hope that he'd be assuaged by my touch. Ilya leaned into me and I thought he was capitulating, but then he pulled away, resisting the urge to soften. "The winter months make up more than half the year. And nobody else is moving away."

"Nobody else has a place to go," I pointed out.

Ilya ignored me. "The trouble's not here. It's in the west. In St. Petersburg. Moscow."

"Not anymore. You yourself told us the revolution was moving east."

"A little. To Irkutsk…"

"You said Vladivostok. That's about as far east as you

can get." I pictured the layout of our country on the globe in Ilya's study.

"Vladivostok is 500 miles south of here. And Vladivostok is not Nikolaevsk."

"Why is Matvei moving if there's no cause for concern? Don't you read your own newspaper?"

"Matvei and I have spoken. With his boys of high school age, he thinks they'll get a better education abroad." I huffed in frustration. "Stop being silly."

How I hated when he said that. I faced him squarely. "What if they take over, the Bolsheviks?"

"What if, what if...!"

I felt my blood pulsing, a volcano in my core starting to erupt. I tried to remain calm and in control. "Stop treating me like a child. I'm—"

"You sound like a child. You worry too much." Not another lecture. Why did we always have to argue lately? Once Ilya started, there was no stopping him. The lawyer in him took over. "Haven't I told you that our way of life here in Nikolaevsk represents what the revolutionaries are seeking? Freedom, business opportunities. Why would they want to cause trouble?"

"Because we're Jews?"

"The Jews hate the Tsar as much as the revolutionaries. Nobody's going to come here." He threaded his fingers through my hair. I could tell he wished I were still the adoring girl he'd married.

"But how do you know?" I wanted him to convince me, to hush the whirring that rushed through my veins making me hum like a telegraph wire.

"We're nestled way up here in the north. Like bears in a cave." He pushed me onto the mattress and canopied the comforter over us. "Hibernating for the winter," he chuckled as his hand reached for my breast.

I pulled back. "What about the rumors? All the upheaval everywhere?" How could my husband be so blind?

"That's been going on for years now. Up and down, up and down. In recent months, things have calmed considerably. Remember last year? It looked like the Reds were going to take over...and then, poof! We expelled them like that!" He snapped his fingers in my face. I pushed them away. He grabbed my hand and wrestled me back into the pillows, kissing and caressing. Couldn't he tell that I saw what he was doing? Finally, he gave up. "If you're so worried," he said, "why don't you take the children and move to Hakodate yourself?"

That caught me off guard. "Without you?"

"If it makes you happy." Oh, was I tempted. I pictured us living in surroundings akin to our *dacha*, but far from the reach of encroaching partisans. Could I live without Ilya for seven months? What would people say? And to leave him behind with his mother who surely would not desert her son like me? I'd never hear the end of it.

Ilya got out of bed. "I have to get to work. You wouldn't have me arrive late, would you?"

"Of course not," I grumbled under my breath. I watched him dress and leave, then plunged into my feather pillow. I didn't really want to move to Japan where none of us spoke the language and the only people we knew were my brother and his family. I just didn't want to remain in Nikolaevsk. I shook myself. Was I being silly after all? Could Ilya be right that the threats would melt like snow in Spring? I vowed to bury my fears and persevere.

———

It wasn't easy to watch Matvei and his family sail away for the winter the following week. The billows of their three masted clipper ship flapped angrily in the brisk wind, mirroring the furious beating of my heart. Their vessel sailed gracefully downstream that chilly September day and Mama and I stood on the dock, watching as it grew tinier and tinier. Many boats still remained in the harbor: an American steamship with a black hull and red rimmed masts; Chinese gunboats and various smaller fishing vessels and junks. Sea gulls shrieked and dove around us for scraps of food floating in the harbor. Workers hustled to unload arriving cargo which they stored in the warehouse up the hill. They re-packed the boats with products for export. Matvei had promised to return one more time before the Amur froze, but first he wanted to settle his family in Hakodate and enroll his children in school there. Not wanting company, I sent Mama home in the carriage and dragged myself through town. My footsteps, heavy as my heart, I wondered if we hadn't made a mistake by not going with them.

Several weeks later, Matvei did return, but before he could say good-bye, winter hit us with bitter fury. It was only October, but practically overnight the river had become so solid that several Chinese gunboats, including the one that Matvei was going to board, found themselves frozen in the ice before they could head southward and home. The deep freeze was followed by a blizzard that raged for five long days. Snow in October was not uncommon, but storms of that magnitude didn't usually hit until late November or December. When the clouds had finally cried themselves out, our city had all but disappeared. It took days to tunnel our way to daylight and when we did, we could walk to town on the roofs of our neighbors. The only sign of life emerged from chimneys that dotted the landscape like the tombstones in our cemetery.

With the waterway now frozen solid for the winter, Matvei would have to take a sled downriver to Khabarovsk, whose port would remain open for another few weeks, and board a boat for Japan there. It was an arduous and lonely trip, but one my brother was used to. I remember hearing stories from Mama about her trip east from Moscow after she'd married my father. It had taken them months and they'd had to journey during the winter because it was easier to traverse the country on a sled with runners that could glide over the hard icy surface than to attempt the crossing by horse and carriage. Spring rains created mud in which tires would get mired. Even worse, landslides sometimes caused the beasts to lose their footing and carriages to overturn, resulting in fatalities.

Mama told me how Father's description of Nikolaevsk and his tales of adventure had made her affluent but predictable life in Moscow appear dull by comparison. However, once she'd left the comforts of home and family behind, she quickly became conscious of how large the gap between reality and Father's fantasy was. Not only was the trip long and cold, but being confined to a tiny sleigh day in and and day out for weeks on end with a man she barely knew was hardly how she'd envisioned her honeymoon and first days of married life. The couple would stop at ramshackle inns or primitive Mongolian tents at night. Having gotten pregnant and then miscarrying along the way only made Mama long for her own mother more. But it was too late to turn back and Papa refused to humor his bride. By the time she arrived in her new city, which was hardly more than a burgeoning outpost at the time, she'd been ready to shoot herself with one of Father's collection of shotguns and rifles. She immediately sent a letter home, pleading for her older brother, Syoma, to come and fetch her.

He did arrive the following winter, just before Easter and Passover; but the timing was such that brother and sister would not be able to make the return trip for another six months when the river froze again. In the meantime, Mama became pregnant and Syoma fell in love. Mama couldn't imagine traveling in her condition and her brother was happy to remain and settle down.

These thoughts were running through my mind as I walked out of the house I'd grown up in and saw a sled moored by a team of huskies barking in anticipation out front. The dogs' silver tipped fur reflected the bright sun on that sub-zero day. They were beautiful and their clear blue eyes were like glacial pools. Matvei was loading the last of his valises onto the sled and securing them with cords. He was bundled from head to toe in fur and I was sure Mama had made him put pepper flakes in his socks to keep his feet warm. He carried several flasks of vodka for the ride, and his pockets were filled with dried elk and salmon jerky to munch on during his trip. Cook-san and Mama's servant, Vasya, had tied half a dozen burlap packages to the runners. Each one contained portions of frozen soup, *borscht* or chicken broth with *pelmeni*. There was little habitation along the route to Khabarovsk, but when the sled came upon a remote village where it might stop for the night, to rest and feed the animals, Matvei would bring in one of the soup servings. His host would heat it for him and Matvei could enjoy a delicious home-cooked meal.

I could barely get my arms around my brother as I hugged him through all his layers. Mama was wiping away tears with a crumpled hanky. She laced her arm through mine as we watched Matvei climb aboard and bury himself under furry pelts. I know she wished she could've gone with him, and she would have had it not been for her loathing of traveling by sled. The driver cracked his whip and the dogs sprang forward. As the sled glided away, I eased myself from Mama's grip and ran after it, waving wildly and slowing only when it turned onto the vast white page of the frozen river. I prayed that Matvei wouldn't encounter any trouble on his journey south. The jingling of the harness bells gradually diminished, but the sled disappeared from sight less rapidly. I watched until it was a tiny dot, sending my strongest wishes his way.

A hollow fear filled my chest. This was it. We'd missed our last chance to leave Nikolaevsk. I was slightly reassured by all the snow because how could agitators who lacked food, clothing and shelter venture into such a frigid wasteland and cause trouble? Surely, they'd withdrawn by now. If they'd even survived.

I trudged home through the pristine landscape as if in a bubble. I breathed in the fresh air and my lungs tingled with the cold. My fingers lingered in the pockets of my sable jacket, searching for reassurance in the soft lining which reminded me of the tummy of a warm kitten. The silence was all encompassing and the vista as clean as a fresh blotter.

8

*D*mitri Nelibuov threw open the door and burst into the nursery, his breath infused with anger and vodka. "What did you do with your jewelry, *Babushka*?" he demanded.

I held my breath and glanced sideways at Riva. "Jewelry?" she said cooly. I could see Nessia quivering with trepidation.

"Don't be coy with me," the Red snarled as he hurled her now empty jewelry box onto the bed with such force that it bounced to the floor and the lid broke off. Veronika whimpered. Misha grabbed my arm and buried his head on my chest.

"Where did you find that?" Riva asked innocently.

"Where do you think?" He leaned in as if he was about to grab her by the collar of her flannel robe.

"In my bedroom, I assume. Where I left it when you

hurried me out of there without even the framed photograph of my husband. Why don't you question your men who are rooting through our belongings like boars in a forest?"

For a moment, Nelibuov seemed almost convinced by this clever woman. Before he could dispute her, he was summoned and relief flooded back into the room.

"Nessia, take out the jewelry from the pillow," Riva instructed. "Yumiko-san, can you please find me a needle and thread? Or a small pouch."

Before Nessia had a chance, Riva had grabbed the pillow and followed Yumiko-san into the next room.

"Where are you going?" I asked.

"Nowhere. I'll be back in a moment." When she returned, Riva sat next to Misha and took Simon's photo out of her pocket. "You're lucky you're not alive to see what's happening here," she whispered to his likeness. She was about to slide the photograph back into her robe when she realized she had a small pocket in her nightgown. I watched her stow the photo in there and then place her hand over her heart, as if to derive strength from the nearness of her husband. How I longed for Ilya. And for courage.

The sight of several figures trudging through the drifts in the courtyard outside suddenly caught my eye. They were moving toward our back door. "Look!" I called out. "Here comes Mama! And the children."

Everyone turned their attention outwards. "Where's Esther?" Riva asked, her voice shaking slightly.

"Do you think they'll be allowed in?" I asked. This gave Riva the idea to open the window. She motioned for them to come alongside the house, by our room. The children ran ahead, but Tolya quickly turned back to help his granny, who was having a difficult time of it. Sophie reached us first. "They've taken Mama!" she cried. I looked at Riva, then leaned out and helped pull the little girl through the window. Riva held her questions until Mama reached us, not wanting to have this conversation in front of the children. She whispered to Nessia to occupy the youngsters. Mama wasn't so sure she wanted to tackle the window. She leaned against the house, panting from the exertion of walking through the snow.

"They came with their guns and their stinking vodka breath. Just broke down the door and demanded to see Matvei and Nikolai," she spat in an angry whisper. "We told them we were alone but they wouldn't believe us. They searched the house, took all the guns in Matvei's study, then told us we needed to move out. Esther told them we needed the study in order to conduct business and because that's where the telephone is." Just like her mother, I thought—confident, even arrogant. "They just laughed and told us the telephone wires have been cut so there'd be no use for the telephone. They instructed us to move into the yardman's cottage and stay there because they were taking over. 'Everything is now the property of the state!' Can you imagine?"

"Are you to live in the yard with Grisha?" Riva scoffed.

"No. He was sent away to work for 'the People,'" Mama huffed. Riva nodded resignedly. "They demanded Esther give them her rings but she couldn't get them off her fingers." I pictured the jewelry embedded in her doughy digits. "The leader threatened to chop off her fingers. I winced. "'Esther,' I kept telling her, 'Just do what he says.' But you know what a temper she's got, your daughter. She was not going to be pushed around." Mama paused a moment. "So they took her." Riva inhaled deeply at the thought that a second of her children was in "their" hands and I kept trying to get the thought of those crude, disgusting men harassing my beloved Esther out of my head.

Mama explained that the children's *amah*, Shoko-san, had also been taken. I gasped and glanced at Yumiko-san. From the way she shrank against the wall I could tell she'd heard what my mother had said. "Told me I could take care of the children," Mama continued. "Gave us one pillow and blanket and told us to get out of the house. They wouldn't even let us wait until morning." She shivered as she related the details.

"Have you wood for the stove?" I asked.

"A little. But they said that after we use up what we have, we'll have to chop more ourselves."

"We'll help you," I assured her. "Or...stay here with us, Mama," I attempted to pull her in, but she was skeptical about climbing through the window.

"I'm certain that, as soon as he gets news of this, Nikolai and his men will come to our rescue." Mama had total confidence in her son.

Riva nodded, but I could tell she wasn't so sure. "Certainly. If he's able..."

"Who's there?" a harsh voice slashed the darkness. A figure rounded the corner of our house. When it neared the window, the glow from inside revealed a burly soldier with a substantial mustache.

"I've just come to see my daughter," Mama started to explain. "I thought we could stay together..."

"There is no room for you here. Go back home," he commanded.

"But—"

"I'm sure you're needed there. To cook for your guests!" He laughed at his joke and then prodded Mama away from the window. "But my grandchildren..." Sophie and Tolya were listening to the exchange from the other side of the room.

"Children," Riva motioned to them. "Go with your granny." We helped them out of the window and watched as the threesome straggled back across the snow, disappearing into the darkness. "Take care of one another..." Riva said under her breath. "Putting them in that tiny cottage..." She shook her head, her lips pursed. "What are these Bolsheviks thinking?"

We stared until we could no longer see them. In my mind, I pictured them entering the timbered structure which my father had built for his overseer. Grisha lived there alone, a wisp of a man with a stubbled chin. He had a pronounced limp from an accident years earlier, but that hadn't prevented him from making sure the grounds were always well tended. A small chimney emitted puffs of smoke when the stove was lit. Without Grisha, there would be more room, but less help. I imagined Tolya carrying logs for Mama and helping kindle a flame. I envisioned the small, dark space: a simple cot against the wall, a cupboard in a corner and the pot-bellied stove in the midst of it all. No running water or toilet like they had in the big house. No electricity or telephone, either.

"What's going to happen to Father?" Katya shook me from my thoughts.

"Everything will be fine," Misha reassured her calmly, sounding exactly like his father.

"I didn't ask you!" she retorted in her snidest "big sister" tone.

"Misha is right," Riva told her.

"What does he know?" Katya huffed.

"Misha knows lots of things!" Veronika, too, came to her brother's defense. She resented Katya's bossiness and looked up to him.

"Children!" Riva admonished, reminding them of the gravity of the situation. She reiterated how important it was that we all stick together and support one another. Then she separated them, putting the girls into their beds and Misha in his own. Nessia lay down next to him.

"Where are you going to sleep?" he asked me.

"I'm not sleepy."

I didn't really want to talk. Yumiko-san paced the floor, trying to soothe Viktor. I took him from her and settled in the rocking chair, giving him my breast again. It was the only thing that calmed us both. Every time I closed my eyes, I envisioned Ilya being taken away by those men. I imagined those same derelicts shoving Esther about, as she certainly wouldn't have complied without a fight. Were the two of them together? Who else was with them? And where had they been taken? What was going to happen? To them? To us? Like a blizzard, questions swirled around in my hazy, sleep-deprived mind. I was too scared to think or talk about it. Something told me I didn't want to know the answers. But the images and fears continued to stab at my brain.

9

As morning rays spilled into the room, I handed Viktor to Riva. "I'm going to find out where they are." My voice was surprisingly defiant. "I want to know what they plan to do with Ilya. And Esther. There must be some way we can help. Some price they'll accept."

"I'm going with you!" Misha chimed in bravely.

"Misha!" Riva exclaimed.

"No," I told him. "You stay here and help your granny. She needs you."

"So do you!" he blurted out. "What if they arrest you, too?"

"What would they arrest me for?" I swaggered, but wondered the same thing. What choice did I have? "Mama, give me some of the jewelry. The time you spoke of has come."

Riva stared at me appraisingly, then took me into the next

room. She slid her hand under an orderly stack of diapers and pulled out a few items—an amethyst brooch, ruby and pearl earrings—while I slipped into my clothes. "Not my pearl earrings," I said. "They were one of Ilya's first gifts—"

She weighed my request, then slipped the earrings back into the pile and pulled out an amber ring. I was attached to that one as well, perhaps my last links to Ilya; but I knew I couldn't quibble. "Don't let anyone know you have these," she said, handing them to me. "Especially not that Nelibuov."

"Don't worry," I cut her off as I buried the jewelry inside my underwear.

"Offer them only as a last resort. And let those Red officers know the advantage of releasing Ilya and Esther—Ilya's connections....Esther's..." She paused a moment, trying to come up with a selling point for her outspoken daughter, "...our family's reputation throughout the entire region..."

I turned toward the other room. "Let me go—before I lose my courage." I kissed the children and walked out. I could hear Misha burst into tears as the door shut. I pictured Riva gathering him in her ample embrace. "She'll be back. Don't worry." But I doubted that he'd be soothed. Neither was I.

In the kitchen, soldiers were ferreting about in the cabinets for food. "At last!" one of them declared. "Our chef has arrived!"

"I need to go into town to see about my husband," I said.

"Never mind him," Nelibuov said. He was leaning back in a wooden chair, his stockinged feet on the plank table. "We're hungry. Bake us some bread."

"The servants will be here any moment," I informed him.

"Servants?" Nelibuov scoffed. "YOU are the servant now! Come, krassavitsa, make us some breakfast." He sat forward.

"My mother-in-law is an excellent baker. If you let me go into town, I'll return with more goodies to fill your bellies."

Nelibuov mulled this over a moment. "How far can she go?" one of his comrades voiced a thought. "And we will be needing a great deal of food."

Nelibuov stared at me a moment, sizing me up. "I suppose," he relented. "But don't be long. And, before you leave, get the rest of your family in here so they can begin to serve us." As I turned, he added, "Know this: If any of the food or water is poisoned, your entire family will be killed."

I walked back to the nursery, his last words ringing in my ears. Everybody looked stunned to see me again so soon. Before they could decide whether my prompt return was a good sign or a bad one, the sound of a familiar voice outside made us all turn. Simultaneously Riva and I exclaimed, "Cook-san!" as our faces registered optimism. Our faithful servant had arrived for work, as usual. But outside the kitchen, he was stopped and reprimanded.

"Your services are no longer necessary here. Make yourself useful by going into town and joining one of the new cooperatives that are in need of your labor," one of the partisans commanded.

"This is where I—"

"Not any longer..."

"But Mastuh Kaptzan..."

"...is no longer in residence here. He has been taken to prison..." snapped the soldier.

"...Where he belongs!" seconded his comrade.

Prison? Until now, Ilya's whereabouts had all been

conjecture. I don't know where I'd assumed he'd been taken, but picturing him in a dark jail cell wasn't where I'd allowed my mind to wander. I'd never been to the prison, but I recalled Ilya's description of the cell in which Nelibuov had been held. The bucket in the corner that served as a toilet. The straw scattered on the floor that Ilya was certain was teeming with lice. I hadn't felt very sorry for his client at the time; but picturing Ilya now in his place, I shivered with disgust and apprehension. Stories of Marie Antoinette and the French Revolution filled my mind. How long until these brutes took me and my family in as well? The reality hit me with the force of Cook-san's axe on the neck of his helpless chickens. Only now it was me who was running around frantically without a head.

"But Mistress Luba-san and Baba Riva-san..." Cook-san was trying to make some sense of the situation.

"They will be all the servants we need for now."

"Ivan-san....? The coachman?"

"He's gone. As you better be. You must work for the People now. Otherwise, you will also be considered an enemy..."

From the window, we watched our beloved servant turned away from our front door. Riva stood beside me, aghast. I continued to stare, transfixed by the transformation of our courtyard. Several men were wheeling a cannon into the yard; others were pulling an ammunition-laden wagon. They positioned both at the foot of our drive, facing out toward the street. The wooden pickets of our fence had always reminded me of soldiers, protecting us from the outside world. Now, they'd become bars imprisoning us.

Heavy footsteps announced the arrival of Nelibuov who stomped into the room. "*Babushka*, come! My men are hungry.

We need to eat." As he caught sight of Nessia, he perked up. "Good morning, *Tsaritsa*! Did you have a nice sleep?"

"I'm ready. Let's go!" I could sense that Riva was trying to shift Nelibuov's focus away from her drowsy daughter.

"We're not going to leave without Sleeping Beauty. Come, come! Your courtiers await you!" Nessia pulled back the cover under which she huddled. Her long hair fell haphazardly over her shoulders, but it didn't detract from her attractive, if forlorn, face.

"We'll be there in a moment. Let us just get dressed." Riva tried to keep Nelibuov from staring.

"Bring the children along with you. They can collect eggs."

I slipped into the room off the kitchen where our coats and boots resided. I thrust myself into them, took hold of a large basket and disappeared out the back door as quickly as I could, afraid Nelibuov would change his mind or offer to send a soldier to escort me. I was rather amazed that he'd allowed me to go into town—and alone, at that. Then, the futility of my escaping or being able to gather forces sank in.

My first thought was where to go. The Minkovs next door? Shimada's...for food? The prison? Maybe the Japanese Consul for help and advice? I realized that the Japanese had been no help to us in averting the dire situation we were in. Just two days before, on his return from the meeting at Fort Chinnarakh, Ilya had ranted to me in disbelief that Major Ishikawa, who had all the Japanese troops in town under his control, would not step up and come to the aid of us, his Russian friends. If only Esther were here. She would know what to do and with her by my side, I'd feel much less frightened. I trudged through the snowy streets as if I were hauling a sack of bricks behind me.

I passed the Shimkin house, but seeing Red militants outside, I decided to bypass it. I wondered if Sammy and his family were home, or if he, too, had been arrested in the night. I thought of my friend Eda who had ended up marrying Sammy once Ilya and I became engaged. She was more timid even than Sammy and I couldn't picture her standing up to the rough partisans. Sammy's father lived with the family but Papa Shimkin was sickly and frail and wouldn't be as helpful as Riva. Riva! Imagine me being thankful for her presence.

Years ago, when I used to walk to school, I'd pass this way in the hopes that Sammy would see me and rush out to escort me. These days, Ivan drove me everywhere in our shiny coach or sleigh. I forced myself not to think about anything but putting one foot in front of the other so that I could get into town and determine what was going on. The vast Siberian sky had turned steely as clouds swept in, like the troops surrounding our city. The streets were quiet at this early hour. I spied two kerchiefed women on a side lane and a young boy pulling a sled laden with baskets passed in the opposite direction. Some partisans on horseback gained on me from behind but, thankfully, they were on a mission and didn't bother with me. My head bent, I picked up my pace, emitting a sigh of relief when I reached town without being harassed.

Shimada's General Store was like the roll top desk in Ilya's law office where everything was stowed in drawers and slots, every cranny full and spilling over. Even at this early hour, the store was alive with activity. Goods were stacked along walls and in the aisles. Hanging from the rafters were ropes and chains, shovels, rakes, lanterns. Shelves burst with anything and everything. Women congregated between pickle barrels and sacks of rice. I recognized many of them from synagogue or around town.

I searched for a friendly face. Iulia Sharpova, Mira Gorbatova and their mothers were gathered in a group at the back, next to the flour barrel. But no one was scooping or shopping. Never overly friendly, today all social pretenses had fallen away and I was welcomed into their midst. Leah, the rabbi's wife, usually jolly, had no smile on her face. Madame Keller, whose husband ran the cafe, was wringing her hands nervously. Ludmilla Minkova, the doctor's wife, who lived across the street from us, stood on the perimeter, looking uncomfortable. Her husband seemed to be the only one not arrested. Judi Avshalumova, who was older than both Riva and my mother, had also made her way into town that morning.

As I suspected, Ilya and Esther had not been the only casualties. Everyone in our midst, except for Ludmilla, had been visited by the Bolshevik Army and any husbands and sons old enough to fight had been dragged off to jail.

"Yes...they came to us, too...in the middle of the night... those cretins...with guns...so drunk and slovenly...took over our rooms...stole our clothes...our jewels...emptied our safe... ate our food...what to do?"

The cacophony of fearsome murmurings resembled the sounds of the saw at my brother Matvei's lumber mill, whirring as it gained speed and screeching as its teeth met the complacent wood being steered to its fate. Sometimes, the blade would slide smoothly through the wood as it was cleanly split in two. Other times, the teeth ground and gnashed as a knot in the lumber balked in argument.

"I need to buy some things," I said. "Then I'm going to the prison."

"You can't get near there," Mira informed me. "The place is surrounded by a screaming mob."

"They're yelling 'Death to the *burzhui*! Kill those White skunks!'" Her mother shook her head vehemently. Her gray hair, coiffed like a helmet, didn't budge.

"That's right," Leah confirmed. "'Beat them! Kick them!' they're shouting."

"Who *are* these people? Where have they come from?" I was still in shock.

"Plenty of them you'll recognize," Mira's mother informed me.

"Yes," Iulia's mother nodded, "People we've worked with...who've worked for us..."

"Drunk with power, they are!" Madame Keller voiced.

"...So happy for the opportunity to denounce us....God save you if you've had a run in with somebody—no matter how small the matter. It's their word against ours now...and with their working class background, it's not us the leaders will be listening to." There were so many melody lines, I couldn't follow who was saying what.

"No...they're only too happy to have an excuse to arrest and get rid of another *burzhui*!" Judi summed up.

I refused to cave in based on hearsay. "Maybe if we go together..."

"Don't even try," said Iulia's mother.

"Are you just going to give up? Give in?" I challenged them. "It's our husbands and families in there!" Their stony glares were my answer.

"Be careful," Judi whispered to me as I turned my back

on them. I filled my basket with sausages, caviar, chocolate. I needed to get out of that hive of pessimism before I lost my nerve.

Despite their warnings, I ventured down the street until I could discern the stone structure of the prison at the far end of town. As I got close, I heard the angry shouts. A crowd was making a ruckus near the gate. Armed soldiers surrounded the edifice and hindered my approach. They were pacing the perimeter like wolves guarding their kill before moving in to devour it. I glanced in their direction and considered trying to befriend one. But there were so many.

I turned down one of the side streets and wove through back alleys to the rear of the prison. There were no hordes demonstrating there. Two soldiers were sharing a cigarette near the fence. I tried to glean what they were whispering about, but the wind whistled piercingly in that open part of town. Even if I pulled up the flaps of my hat, I wouldn't be able to make out their words.

Finally, one of them flicked his butt into the snow and climbed the incline toward the jail. The other continued to smoke for a moment, sucking every last puff from his stub. He then proceeded to stalk back and forth, though there was nobody even trying to get close.

I watched the man intently from the safety of the last building on the street. His rifle was slung against his shoulder and his cheeks were chapped. He looked young, perhaps a teenager still. That boosted my confidence. I thought of the jewelry hidden in my clothing. It wouldn't be easy to get to, so I rummaged through my basket for something to offer him. The next time he passed, I stepped forward.

The guard was more startled than I was. He immediately

drew his gun, pointing the steel bayonet blade menacingly at me.

"*Pozhalsta*...please.... I thought you might be hungry," I held out a sausage in his direction. He gazed steadily at it, then planted the stem of his gun firmly in the snow.

"*Spacibo*. Thank you." After a moment, he snatched the meat and shoved it into his mouth. Realizing I wasn't feeding him out of mere generosity, the boy asked, "What do you want?"

"My husband." I could feel my emotions surging. Taking a deep breath, I began again. "Please...if you would be so kind... my husband...I think he's..." I nodded toward the concrete and stone structure, "...in there. Can I find out—"

"Nobody is allowed. No information. No visitors," he recited.

"I can get you more," I indicated the sausage. "If you would only take a message to him...or give me some information."

He considered the offer. "What's your husband's name?"

"Ilya Kaptzan. He was arrested last night." I wondered if the name meant anything to him. When the boy didn't respond, I continued. "Do you think you can find him?"

"There are many prisoners. More all the time."

"Are they being—do you know what the conditions are like?"

"*Kto eto?* Who's this?" The boy and I both jumped as two soldiers assaulted us. "Giorgi, what's going on?"

"I was just telling her she has to leave, Piotr Sergeyevich," the youngster uttered nervously. I nodded. To my surprise, I recognized the second man: Iosef Dimchin, the tinker from Mago whom I knew from our summer visits to the village and also the weekly market. Iosef's wife Oksana made Ilya's favorite cakes. We exchanged an awkward glance.

"Then, get out of here," the leader snarled. "Now."

I scrambled away, afraid the men would relieve me of all my purchases, if not my freedom. I looked back, wondering if there was any way I could speak with Iosef. He was a good man. Perhaps he could arrange for me to speak with my husband, to touch him. Even for just a moment. Ilya would tell me what to do. He always had answers. At the very least I could let him know....Know what? What could I tell him? But Iosef had disappeared into the prison with the others.

I blindly made my way through the maze of streets, my mind racing.

It was mid-afternoon when I reached home, exhausted and weary. I was greeted by two partisans who immediately relieved me of my basket. "Is this all?" they asked as they scrounged through my purchases, throwing them all over the place.

I was put to work alongside Riva and Nessia, who were busy cooking and serving. The soldiers were assembled around our family's dining table, as if at a banquet. When out of earshot of our captors, I conveyed the meager details of my trek into town. I didn't want to upset them, but neither did I have the strength to pull off a ruse. And to what purpose? We were in this together. My frank account quickly pierced any bubble of hope they had that I might return with optimistic news or a plan of action.

As I entered the dining room, struggling not to drop the heavy tureen of soup Riva had just put in my hands, I lowered the serving dish onto the center of the table, then located a ladle in the sideboard drawer. The sight of the men sprawled around the perimeter of our table gnawed at me. "Aren't you going to serve us?" Nelibuov asked. He was wearing Ilya's smoking jacket and one of my husband's pipes lay next to his plate. I lifted the tureen and carried it from man to man, trying to tune out their rude comments. When I got to Nelibuov, usurping Ilya's place, all I could think of was my husband who, every morning, sat at the head, looking like a prince in his ironed shirt and cravat, his linen napkin tucked into his vest so as not to stain his tailored clothes. Instead, here was this uncivilized criminal. How I wished I had the nerve to pour the hot soup into his lap.

"More!" His words brought me back to the present. I suddenly realized that I was holding an empty receptacle.

I rushed to the kitchen, promising to return in a minute.

10

It was morning and Ilya was at his office. In the garden, Katya was perched in our small sleigh. Her hands were burrowed inside a rabbit muff that matched the trim of the hood on her coat. Misha's pony was harnessed to the sled and the boy, wearing Ivan's cap, which practically covered his face, was holding the reins and steering. His features were further obscured by a long woolen scarf spooled around his neck and lower face. The children flew by my window, Ivan running alongside, making sure brother and sister were safe. Their laughter and shouts came through the closed window. Large icicles dangled from the eaves like walrus tusks and gleamed as the sunlight struck them.

At my dressing table, I guided the boar bristles of my brush through my hair. Smiling at my face in the mirror, I twirled a handful of tresses into a chignon and secured them with a tortoise shell comb in an attempt to recreate a style I'd seen on the actress who'd played the lead in a play Ilya had taken me to a few nights before: *A Doll's House*, by Henrik Ibsen. It had been his Valentine's Day treat. The whole evening had stayed with me: the actress; the subject matter, the scenery. To think that a man could write such an insightful work about women. Ilya was clearly like that husband, Torvald. He didn't understand me and preferred to keep me as his plaything, his little doll. I supposed it wasn't entirely his fault. Not only were most men like that, but Ilya was eight years older than me and, when I'd first fallen in love with him, I'd wanted nothing more than to be taken care of.

I'd known Ilya my entire life. Besides growing up on the same square plot of land, our families spent most holidays together. Even our mothers, though of different backgrounds and personalities, had been thrown together in the tiny, close knit circle of our city. Our lives were like the vines that covered Sleeping Beauty's castle in Katya's favorite fairy tale, intertwining at every turn. From a distance, they were beautiful, like the enchanting greenery; but, up close, they sometimes threatened to choke when the stems got too tangled.

Ilya had been a schoolmate of Nikolai's, although he was much more studious than my brother. After finishing *gymnazia*, everybody expected that he would join his father in business, especially since he was the eldest son. But Ilya wasn't so sure that was what he wanted. Having finished at the top of his class, he confided in Simon that he longed to attend university. Still very virile, Simon recalled his own youth and what it had been like to be in the captivity of military service. He didn't want to pin his son down, so he relented. I was still a child at the time, absorbed with schoolmates and young girl crushes.

Because of his splendid academic record, Ilya was one of a small quota of Jews allowed to attend university in St. Petersburg. Ilya continued to excel in his studies, so much so that, after receiving his diploma, his professors recommended he attain a law degree. He convinced his father that this would only help the business in the long run and promised that, after becoming a lawyer, he would return home to help run the family fisheries. Aware that his younger brother was neither adept at business nor enamored of it, Ilya knew he couldn't let his father down much longer. But he remained away for almost four years, rarely coming home during that time, even to visit.

Kolya hadn't been as lucky. Like Ilya's brother, he neither wanted nor enjoyed business. The idea of continuing his education was even less inspiring to him. Though he'd worked grudgingly alongside our brother Matvei for a few years, he was more than pleased when rumblings of war with Japan began in the first years of the new century. He immediately signed up for service and never seemed happier than when dressed in his smart uniform and wielding a weapon.

Once he found his calling, Riva began to eye Nikolai in a fresh light. Her daughter, Esther, was growing into a woman and needed a husband, and she and Kolya had known one another since childhood. It wasn't a secret that they would find excuses to be near one another whenever possible and I began to hear Mama and Riva whispering about the possibilities of a union. Almost three years older than me and much more out-going—even brazen—Esther was a perfect match for Kolya who also loved a good laugh, a good meal and, naturally, a good drink to go with both.

Ilya returned to Nikolaevsk, in 1905, in time for their wedding. Eight years my senior, I had never paid much attention to him. He was merely Esther's older sibling and my brother's good friend.

I was fourteen and this was my first opportunity to dress up and mingle with the adults. I remember Matvei having brought me yards of taffeta, a beautiful eggshell blue, from a recent trip to Kharkov. It made my eyes sparkle and Mama's dressmaker had sewn me a dress with a tiered skirt and three-quarter length sleeves. For once, I didn't have a huge bow in the midst of my back. I wore my first pair of heels, not very high but of a pale matching silk. The shoes weren't terribly comfortable, but I was so pleased to be treated as a young lady, I hadn't complained.

I'd walked into our families' shared courtyard the morning of the betrothal, eyeing the hoopah set up in the middle, surprised by the romantic visions that suddenly swirled in my head. I pictured myself walking down the river of white cloth that meandered toward the covered bower, imagining my classmate, Sammy Shimkin, standing beneath the canopy, waiting for me. Then all of a sudden, my dream was interrupted as I heard Matvei greeting Ilya, welcoming him back to Nikolaevsk at long last. The men were walking toward one another in the yard behind me.

I hadn't seen Ilya in years. He'd always been smart, but now, puffing on the pipe in his hand, he looked like an intellectual. I wondered if he'd become pretentious.

"Not too good for our little city here, are you, my friend?" Matvei asked as he clasped Ilya in an affectionate embrace.

"Not at all. It's grand to be home." The men stopped by the gate that separated our two properties. "But I do intend to set up that office in town for my law practice, as I told you I would."

"Besides working with your father at the fisheries?"

"Yes. And I've an idea to start my own gazette as well."

"Aren't you the enterprising prodigal?"

"Nikolaevsk is big enough to have two newspapers, representing different points of view, wouldn't you say?"

"Absolutely," Matvei agreed. "And I'd be happy to become a partner and help with the funding, if you need." I could tell how thrilled Matvei was that his old friend had returned. He was jauntier than usual. It made me happy to see my brother so exuberant. Too often lately he seemed bogged down with business problems.

"Excellent!" Ilya patted Matvei on the back, a pleased grin breaking out under his trim moustache.

"Especially now that we're going to be brothers-in-law."

"You couldn't invent a more ideal couple than Kolya and Esther, could you?"

"All we have to do is find you a beautiful wife and get you settled so you don't pick up and desert us again."

"Not so fast, not so fast. Let me look around a little, eh? Find my bearings." Ilya winked as he followed Matvei into the house. I caught him glancing in my direction as they passed. I turned away, but stopped when I heard, "Hold up! Who's this?" Ilya had broken away and was stepping toward me. "Not little *Lubachka*?"

I could feel my face flush as he grasped my hand and gallantly kissed it. Not exactly handsome in a dashing sense, there was an elegance about him. I nodded and he clasped me in an embrace. The scent of a musky cologne clung to his suit and also a hint of tobacco. He held me at arms length to look me over. "Well, you've certainly grown into a lovely young lady," he exclaimed. "How come you're not yet betrothed? Or perhaps I just haven't heard?" Ilya joked.

I giggled and shook my head. "Well, we will have to find you the perfect husband. A knight!"

Ilya turned back to my brother who was waiting and, as I watched them disappear, I felt like butter that has been sitting too long in the sun. All around, servants were bustling about, setting up benches for the marriage service and long tables for the reception that would follow. Because he was so much older, Ilya had always been more of a father figure, like my brother. Suddenly, I felt fluttery in his presence. Why was I blushing? Guests began arriving and Mama called me inside to finish dressing. I took a circuitous route in order to pass the room where Matvei and Ilya were conferring.

The ceremony was beautiful and the celebration had the fizz of sparkling cider. Musicians provided a variety of ethnic and regional fare, but also some more modern tunes. Sammy startled me by asking me to dance. My gaze was fixed on Ilya, making his way around the assembled guests, most of whom he hadn't seen in years. I didn't mind when he'd stop to chat with one of the men, as I guessed the subject was mainly business. But when a mother—or, even worse, a daughter—latched onto him, my breath tightened in my throat as I watched Ilya charm each and every one of them. Naturally, I had to dance with Sammy, though focusing on conversation with him was not easy.

How odd that, earlier in the day, I'd been longing for that

very opportunity, even secretly hoping that his parents might broach the subject of an engagement with Mama and Matvei, making the most of the nuptial spirit. All of a sudden, this idea filled me with terror. I needed time before any irrevocable measures were taken. I tried to steer Sammy into Ilya's line of vision. It wasn't difficult because Sammy was so awkward that he let me do the leading. But Ilya remained oblivious to my presence, happily laughing with his own partner, Iulia, who was clinging to him. She had just graduated *gymnazia* in June and was no doubt fearing she might become an old maid. I realized Ilya mustn't even consider me eligible for him, being so young.

A little later, I caught sight of Ilya alone, standing and filling his plate at the buffet table. I rushed over and slipped in next to him. "That's your mother's *kulibiaka*," I pointed out. "I'm surprised there's any left. Everybody agrees she's the best cook in all of Nikolaevsk." Why was I acting so bold?

"How I've missed her cooking," Ilya winked at me, "... eating always in my boarding house at school...rarely getting invited to private homes...."

"It must have been exciting, though...to be so far away. And for so long!" I sighed.

"Yes. But greater to be back here."

"Join me?" Ilya asked, nodding toward a gap in the seating at one of the long tables and leading me toward it with his free hand on my back. We sat down and enjoyed a brief bite and a bit of conversation, but we were constantly being interrupted by others coming over to welcome him home. Just as well because I couldn't concentrate on what I was saying. When the musicians broke into a tarantella, he cocked his head and asked if I liked to dance.

I was out of my seat so quickly I hoped Mama wasn't watching. Not that she could make me out from her position across the yard with her awful eyesight. But once in Ilya's arms, I hoped the entire crowd had their eyes on us. How I longed for Matvei and Mama or Simon and Riva to notice that I was no longer a child but a poised and elegant lady. The tarantella was boisterous and when it was over, we were both panting and laughing from exertion. "I just love to dance!" I blurted out as the music segued into a slower, romantic waltz.

"Well, then we can't sit down yet, can we?"

I shook my head and spent the next quarter hour in a trance. We were finally pried apart when Iulia's mother materialized with her eager daughter. "You mustn't monopolize our most eligible bachelor," she scolded. "Even if he is now your brother-in-law!" I wondered if that would preclude me from being eligible. Ilya, chivalrous as ever, bowed toward me and took my hand so that he could bestow another kiss on it. He then turned to Iulia and offered her his arms. I moved off the dance floor, suddenly aware that my shoes were pinching my feet. When Sammy tried to woo me back for another spin, I told him I needed to rest. I couldn't relax until Iulia finally relinquished her position to yet another candidate. At least there was more than one possibility, I told myself. There was still time before Ilya made up his mind.

Since that first encounter, I'd watched enviously from the perimeter, gauging Ilya's interest in one and then another prospect. He was always the perfect gentleman, escorting a girl to dinner or the theatre, often double dating with Matvei and his wife. Once, while the men were sipping drinks in our living room, I'd overheard my brother nudging him toward Mira or Iulia, extolling their virtues. It made me churn with frustration that it never occurred to either of them to focus on me. But try as Matvei might, Ilya never seemed eager to settle on anyone. He was consumed with building his various businesses and wasn't concerned about putting down roots.

Only after Ilya's father passed away did Riva join forces with Matvei and begin to pressure her son to settle down. Ilya had established himself by then and perhaps Simon's death had made them more aware of the fleetingness of life. By this time, he'd tired of Mira, Iulia and the others. Or they'd been married off.

Meanwhile, though Sammy Shimkin had clearly set his sights on me, I no longer had any interest in him. Next to Ilya, Sammy was a puppy. His earnest attempts at bringing me flowers or his shy insinuations that we walk together along the river only made me impatient with him for not being Ilya. Petulantly, I'd turn away, claiming to be busy or have a headache, feeling badly when I saw the hurt in his eyes, but unable to muster any enthusiasm regardless. Keen and ungainly, he had none of the finesse and command of Ilya. How strange that the authority I now bristled against had been part of Ilya's allure.

Esther's throaty chuckle when she saw how distraught I'd get at having to constantly find new excuses to avoid being with Sammy helped ease my guilt. After the wedding, she'd started living with us, and Esther and I had grown quite close. As a child, she'd always intimidated me, but the nonchalance and boldness she brought to our house made me admire her. I watched as she let Mama's critical looks and insinuations bounce off her armor of heft. Esther was the only person I'd confided in about my crush on Ilya. She understood my lack of enthusiasm for Sammy and actually thought her brother and I would make an interesting match. When she overheard Mama's intentions to agree to a Shimkin merger, her eyes lit up and her agile mind began to whir.

The next thing I knew, I was seated next to Ilya at the New Year's Ball in 1907 and he was looking at me in a way he never had before. That winter, it was suddenly me on Ilya's arm at the ballet or theatre, then sitting opposite him at his favorite dinner club afterwards. He introduced me to pink champagne cocktails that tickled my tongue and made my mind tingle. He took me on long sleigh rides where we snuggled under a heavy rug. Arm in arm, we skated across the Amur on Sunday afternoons, then gathered with friends for *borscht* and flaky *piroshki* at Keller's afterwards. Ilya showered me with handkerchiefs, a bracelet, leather bound books by Jane Austen. He made me feel like a princess as he blotted out the world and made me his primary focus. He seemed younger suddenly and I felt much older. We were engaged by summer and several weeks later, in front of our friends and families, under a canopy of trees ablaze in orange, red and gold, we exchanged vows and became man and wife. I floated through my days, incredulous at my fortune.

I had never believed this would come to pass. I sensed the rattle of whispering behind our backs from those who saw our union as a business deal, cementing the bonds between Nikolaevsk's two leading families. But I chose to concentrate on our mutual attraction. Ilya and I complemented one another, the final missing pieces in the jigsaw puzzle of our lives. And once Sammy married our schoolmate, Eda, everybody seemed the happier.

As I raked the brush through my hair, I looked around the room, grateful for my surroundings and comfortable life. Ilya was a good provider. Living under the shadow cast by Riva was the only flaw in my perfect gem. Because her husband, Simon, had died, Riva felt Ilya and I should live with her in his childhood home as was the custom of the day. Though she generously gave up the master bedroom and moved to the back of the house, my mother-in-law's presence prevailed in every fixture that surrounded me. It was difficult to relax around her. I could hear her footsteps outside our doorway late into the night and then her clattering in the kitchen in the mornings. She rarely intruded directly; she merely hovered constantly.

Nessia lived with us, too. Though generally unobtrusive, my sister-in-law was always complaining of a sniffle or indigestion. She and Riva were constantly in one another's company, confiding, conferring, complaining.

I had little desire to be the head of our domestic household, but I took offense when Riva stepped in to oversee the daily running of our lives. In one way, it was a relief, but it also usurped my control. And it gave Riva increased access to Ilya with whom she consulted endlessly on functional details and financial matters. Ilya had become the much desired prize in an increasing tug-of-war between mother-in-law and wife. And no matter that I held what I considered to be the trump card, I'd learned how difficult it was to cleave the fierce love between a mother and her eldest son. What had originally appeared as an ideal situation, was quickly closing in on me. I couldn't win no matter which route I chose. Either I'd have to run the house; or I'd have to be ruled by my mother-in-law. Neither one was an appealing option.

As our family increased in size, I spent long periods of my once carefree life weighted down with babies and their needs. Despite *amahs* and servants, there was less and less opportunity to be alone with my husband. I reveled in the festive evenings when I could get dressed up and step out with him to dinner or the theatre, but I had so much less energy left at the end of the day. After being pregnant and giving birth every year or two for a dozen years, I dreaded finding out that I was once again with child. Ilya clearly wasn't haunted by such a fate and, though he was working harder than ever, he seemed only more energized at night when we were alone in our bedroom.

As the years passed, I'd matured. Always the coddled baby of my own family, I'd gained responsibilities. From those, sprang opinions. Ilya didn't like to share his work problems with me, nor did he discuss the political or economic state of the world. He was happier to see me occupied with the organizing of balls and war relief, hosting teas and updating the family's wardrobe. But, as word of the turmoil that was fast encroaching upon Nikolaevsk seeped into our days, I'd become both interested and anxious. The more I got out of the house, the more I heard and the more I thought.

When I tried to talk to him, Ilya disregarded me, probably because he wanted to shield me. But I didn't want to be constantly shooed away. So, I balked. Which created friction. The chafing had been growing more and more irritable. There'd been so much discord between us during the past months that Ilya and I had begun to grow apart. Fortunately, I hadn't had the need to steal money or do anything foolish like Nora in the play. But it was no less frustrating to be simply unacknowledged.

Loud booms cracked the air like thunder. My eyes dove to the icicles, suspecting one had met its demise. But the sun continued to bounce brightly off the dangling spears. I dropped my brush and rushed into the kitchen where Riva was stirring a barley soup. Every carrot and potato, each morsel of meat and grain, was spinning in agitation, like my mind. Hot drops of liquid sputtered from the pot. Riva wiped them away with a rag, erasing any trace of their existence. I looked at her. "What was that?" I managed to croak.

She peered out the back door, seemingly untroubled. "Sounds like cannon fire. Coming from the fort." How could she be so calm?

"Chinnarakh?" I asked. "Those cannons have been de-activated for years."

She paid me no heed. "Just saying what it sounds like."

"Yumiko-san," I called, my voice catching as I ran to the nursery.

"Everything is alright?" she asked, getting up from the floor where she was playing marbles with Misha and Veronika. Across the room, Katya, with Viktor on her lap, rocked by the window. These days she preferred ministering to her live little brother than to her dolls. All eyes turned to me.

"Yes, yes," I lied, embracing our *amah* in place of gathering the little ones close, squelching my urge so as not to frighten them.

I returned to the hall, jolted every so often by another blast. Riva was standing by the telephone. She grasped the slender metal neck like a candlestick and held the bell-shaped receiver to her ear. "It's dead," she said. Could she be losing her composure? If I wasn't so frightened, I'd have been glad of it. The children and Yumiko-san watched from behind me.

Nessia hurried down the hall from her room, her face ashen. She ran past me to Riva who put down the phone and guided her daughter into the living room.

I shepherded my brood in as well. We huddled together on the divan. Yumiko-san paced with Viktor in her arms. Behind her, the large horn of our victrola leaned toward the window as if it were craning toward the noise. In the distance, the sky filled with smoke.

Rumors of unruly partisans infiltrating nearby villages had been assaulting our ears all winter. Word had reached us that a raffish, young leader, Yakov Triapitsin, was spearheading a campaign to spread Bolshevism across the country. He and his partner, Nina Lebedeva, claimed to be disciples of Vladimir Lenin, the Chairman of the Russian Socialist Democratic Party in Moscow. They professed to be bringing the revolution to Siberia; their aim: to spread equality among the populace. They had gone from village to village along the Amur from Khabarovsk northward, taking over the homes of peasants, emptying their larders and their supplies of ammunition. They conscripted local men to join their forces, under the guise of gaining food and riches. Those who showed reluctance were forced to enlist at gunpoint. Or they were simply shot. Now, it appeared, they'd reached Nikolaevsk. And the rumors were no longer hearsay.

Since Matvei's departure, this news had peppered conversations. Apprehension stalked me and I snapped at Ilya every chance I got, furious that he hadn't heeded my pleas to leave Nikolaevsk. He continued to assuage me, but a gnawing premonition nagged at my gut. I hoped that Matvei had made it safely to Japan. It had been three months and we still hadn't received word from him. We hadn't seen or heard from my brother Nikolai in several weeks either. He'd been home over the winter holidays but had returned to his post at Fort DeKastri soon after.

As church bells had rung in the new year, we'd attended a festive ball in the Amur Hotel, dressed in our finery and drinking and dancing until dawn. We'd toasted our health, prosperity and the promise of 1920—a new year and a new decade. With the Great World War swiftly becoming a memory, we hoped that the civil war in our country would fade away in much the same manner. But here it was the beginning of February and, like snow in the Spring, our optimism seemed to be turning into sludge.

Ilya rushed in, still in his outerwear. His cheeks were pink, his eyes a little too bright to be from just the cold. "The telephone and telegraph wires have been cut," he said.

"Are they going to shoot us?"

"No, Veronachka. They're not," Ilya said, giving his daughter a quick kiss on the top of her head. "Everything's going to be alright." He looked at all of us and it seemed to me he was trying to keep his voice light, but the cannon fire continued to go off in the background.

"Who are they?" Katya wanted to know.

"A bunch of unruly men who've gotten out of control." Ilya took off his coat and lay it over the back of the armchair. He squeezed in next to us and put his arms around Katya and Veronika.

"Is this a war?" Misha asked.

"No, *sinich*," he said as he ruffled his son's hair. "Just an uprising. A revolt." I knew he was saying this for the children's benefit.

As Ilya answered their endless questions, I got up, barely

able to contain myself from shouting, from damning my husband for his restraint in the face of impending disaster. But I knew I had to remain calm.

"I'm sure it will end soon," said Ilya. "Now why don't you go and have some supper. Yumiko-san?"

"*Hai*," she nodded. "Come, children." Riva nudged Nessia who followed them to the kitchen.

Once they were out of earshot, I spun around. Ilya was pouring himself a shot of vodka at the bar by the victrola.

"End soon?" I hissed. "What is going on? How can you possibly be so relaxed? Where is our army? Why are they not coming to our aid? And how is it that the cannons are working?" The questions burst from my mouth.

"I'm sure our troops are figuring out their next move. After all, they're on the other side of the fort and will have to get past the Reds before they can reach us." Ilya sounded defensive. "Colonel Vits will devise a good plan." He threw back his drink and poured another, not offering any to me.

"What about Medvedev? And the Japanese?"

"I'm sure everything will work itself out."

"Luba," Riva stepped in.

"Don't try to shush me, Mama. I am not one of the children!"

Ilya put down his glass and spread his arms to encompass us both. "Mama....Luba.... Please. As you can see, it's more noise than anything else." He maneuvered us back to the sofa. Riva sat, but I went to the window and stared out. "Think of it as a boy having a tantrum. These men want us to notice them. They don't know what they're doing."

"How can you say that?" I swirled back, practically pouncing on my husband. "They seem quite sure of themselves to me."

"I promise this will blow over," he said, holding his palms up, as if in surrender. "They can't have that much ammunition. Give them a couple of days." He slid his hands into his pockets, then withdrew them, not knowing what to do.

"A couple of days?"

He looked at me, then at his mother whose lips were smacked together in a frown directed at me. "They'll get tired of playing games and move on."

"You better be right," I seethed and stomped out of the room.

"Ilya says they've used up their ammunition," I said to Esther a few days later. We were in Marfa's Millinery, eyeing some fur hats. Marfa, the proprietress was circling us, trying to oblige. She reached into the window and removed several items from the display. The luxuriant skins beckoned to be touched and worn. Marfa offered the fox first but Esther pointed to the seal, which was practically the same hue as her hair. "I'll try that one. It's so soft." She stroked the fur and brushed it gently across her cheek before settling it on her head. "What do you think?" she asked me.

I stared at her. "Did you hear what I said?" She was admiring her reflection in the large hand held looking glass Marfa had offered her. Marfa also seemed more intent on the sale than on our predicament. She had an angular face and her silver blonde hair was braided into a fashionable twist. A fringe of bangs softened her appearance and took years off her age, which I presumed to be close to fifty. I'm sure shopping had fallen off that week and she was happy for our business.

Their nonchalance made me prickle. "Even if they have used it up, it still doesn't make me feel secure."

Once the cannon fire had abated, several quiet days followed. No one had come up with an explanation for how they'd been re-activated, but Ilya headed back to the office and convinced Esther and me to go into town for lunch and shopping. That was his solution for everything.

"They're just a bunch of scoundrels, thinking they can come here and disturb our lovely city," Esther said as she removed the seal hat and settled the red fox in its place.

"I've got just the thing for you, my dear," Marfa said to me, bringing over a black velvet hat with a demi-veil which she perched on my head, tilting it to adjust the angle. I shrugged her off.

"Disturb? They're not disturbing, Esther. They're threatening to take us over!" Marfa's eyes arced between the two of us. I could tell she was considering whose side to chime in on.

"That's never going to happen." Esther shook her head and pursed her lips so that her chubby cheeks became even puffier.

I handed my hat back to Marfa who looked at me questioningly.

"It makes me look like a dowager," I barked and she began to survey the room for something more youthful. "You are so like your brother, Esther. Are we done here? Can we please leave?"

"Alright. But which one do you prefer," she asked, the red fox in one hand, the black seal in the other.

"Take both, why don't you? I don't care. I'll wait for you over here."

I edged toward the doorway as Marfa took her place behind the counter. A wide smile spread across her pale face, revealing overlapping teeth. The smock she wore over her dress was threaded with needles that dotted her left shoulder strap as if it were a pin cushion. The ends of various ribbons and feathers poked their tails out of her pockets. "Would you like to wear one now or shall I wrap them both up?" How was it that I was the only one concerned about our future?

In the tight interior of Shu Sun Tai, Esther and I squeezed together on a bench at a small wooden table in the corner. She was wearing the seal hat and the beribboned box containing the fox concoction sat by her feet. It looked out of place in the noisy and crowded establishment. The humid air was pungent with flavor and speculation. Waiters scurried in the tiny space delivering bowls of steaming broth with *lo mein* topped with roast duck or pork. Using her fingers, Esther sucked the meat and fat off the bones. She then slurped the slippery noodles from wooden chopsticks, undisturbed by the tension of the past few days.

My appetite had abandoned me and I pushed my bowl aside. Esther was about to exchange my uneaten meal with her own empty dish when a commotion outside distracted us. The windows were clouded with steam so it was difficult to see anything. Through the slit of the doorway as it opened to let customers in or out, we glimpsed a crowd gathering in front of the Amur Hotel.

"Let's go," I said, selecting a handful of coins from my embroidered purse and laying them on the table. The Chinese proprietor frowned as he watched his restaurant empty out behind us.

The hotel was a cheerful building, white-washed with pale pink trim and large, lead paned windows that overlooked the boulevard. I noticed several businessmen peering down from their rooms. Overhead, pregnant clouds boded snow. The wind whooshed and the cold bit through my coat like the fangs of a snake. Esther and I pressed in closer, for warmth and news. But we couldn't get to the center because the circle kept growing.

"What's going on?" I asked the person next to me.

"Have you heard about the envoy?"

"Envoy? What envoy?"

"Sent here by that Triapitsin." The mention of the name I'd only previously heard uttered in whispers made me shudder.

"Here?" I said.

"When?" The conversation had expanded to include the people around us.

"To Colonel Medvedev."

"When? What for?"

"Asking for the citizens to surrender."

"Surrender?" Gasps of fear and bursts of anger broke out among the onlookers.

"No...."

"Yes. It's true."

"And he was executed."

"Executed? Medvedev?" My teeth began to chatter. I felt like the world was closing in on me.

"Really?"

"No. Not Medvedev. The envoy!"

The braying was louder than the livestock in the slaughterhouse and becoming overpowering. I felt dizzy.

"We should go," I whispered to Esther.

"Let's walk to Ilya's office," she said. I slipped my arm through hers in an attempt to turn my fear into defiance. The office was empty and neither Ilya nor Gennadi Richter, the printer, were on the premises. "Let's find Ivan."

We walked back toward the restaurant but there was no sign of our sleigh. I looked at Esther. "Where do you think—?"

"Let's look in the next street." She led the way. My steps quickened as I began to panic. We stalked up and down back streets until we finally spotted the coach and Ivan several blocks away. "There he is!" I practically screamed with relief.

"I'm sorry," Ivan said as he helped us up. "I couldn't get through the crowd."

"Have you seen my husband?"

He shook his head.

When we entered my house, the smell of tobacco overpowered us. The living room was abuzz with male voices. Esther went into the kitchen to see her mother, but I peeked my head in. Through the haze of smoke, I made out Mayor Karpenko, Colonel Medvedev, Major Ishikawa and a few other neighbors ensconced in conversation. The men looked serious as they gnashed on their pipes or cigars with their nicotine stained teeth, contemplating their situation. Glasses were scattered on end tables and several bottles of whiskey and vodka appeared almost empty. Ashtrays overflowed. Months earlier, I would have been pleased that these men were finally heeding the situation, but at this late date, their presence only heightened my dread. I had a sudden desire to hold my children and went in search of them.

An hour later, the men left and I tried to coax the details out of Ilya. He wouldn't say much. Only that this rebel leader, Triapitsin, had taken over Fort Chinnarakh and was asking the town to surrender. He'd dispatched an envoy to

Major Ishikawa who'd sent him along to Colonel Medvedev. Disgusted, the retired colonel had had the messenger shot. Now the partisan leader was asking for a delegation of men to come to the fort and discuss terms of surrender with him. Ilya was tugging at his moustache.

"I thought they were going to run out of ammunition and retreat," I whispered under my breath.

"So I was wrong. Shoot me, *Lubachka*." He removed his spectacles and rubbed his bloodshot eyes. His cheeks were sunken.

"I may not have to." When Ilya didn't comment on my sarcastic retort, the pit of dread in my belly welled up. "You're not going to go, are you?"

"Not by myself," he said.

"What if something happens?" My voice sounded shrill.

"What choice do we have?"

"Now that we've killed their envoy, why wouldn't Triapitsin kill you?" He looked at me, folded his glasses into his breast pocket and moved toward the decanter that held the whiskey. I stared at his slightly stooped back and reached toward him, but retreated before giving him a hug.

11

I paced the hall awaiting Ilya's return from the fort where he'd gone to confer with the Bolsheviks. The light from the gas lamp was enough to illuminate the passageway, but not bright enough to read by. We had electricity in the living room, but the remainder of the house had yet to be wired. I glanced at the phone that had been dead for days. We'd only had the equipment for several months and it, too, was a novelty. Even though there was a good chance Valentina, the operator in the telegraph office, was listening in on any conversations she connected, it was such a pleasure not to have to jot down a note and bother Ivan to take it. Or to have to put on coat and boots and trudge through the snow to deliver it ourselves. I picked up the contraption and put the black earpiece to my head, hoping beyond hope. "Hello! Hello! Valentina?" I spoke into the mouthpiece. Nothing. I slammed it down and the unstable hall table supporting it shook from the force. I checked to make sure I hadn't damaged the components. But that was the least of my worries.

Tired of being on my feet, I went into Ilya's study and collapsed in his chair. He'd been gone for hours. The leather surface was cold and the nail heads hammered along the armrests and sides securing the upholstery were even colder. There, on the uncluttered plain of his desk, lay Ilya's pouch of tobacco. I picked it up, squeezing the soft sac and inhaling the sweet woodsy flavor. I looked around at the thick leather bound law books of which he was so proud. A large globe stood in the corner by the window. I'd often twirled it on its axis until I could pick out Paris, London or other exotic locales that Matvei was visiting on its painted surface. Recently, I'd been poring over the distance between Vladivostok and Nikolaevsk. Every time sleigh bells jangled in the street, I rushed to the window.

The creak of floorboards made me rush back into the hall. I was doubly disappointed to find Riva pacing. To avoid her gaze, my eyes drifted to her swollen feet. They looked uncomfortably confined by her leather shoes. A black crocheted shawl hugged her drooping shoulders. Our eyes met, then darted away. There was nothing to say and she was the last person I wanted to comfort or be consoled by.

I returned to Ilya's den. His lingering scent taunted me. One of the things I loved most about my husband was the way he smelled. How he savored his imported Old English cologne! No matter how often they were laundered, his shirts and handkerchiefs retained his distinctive aroma. The first time he kissed me, leaning against a tree in the forest where we'd gone to forage for mushrooms, the air was rife with the musty odor from the selection we'd amassed in our basket. The fallen leaves on the damp ground under our feet also filled our noses with that pungent autumn scent. But when Ilya gently pushed me against the rough bark of the tree trunk and took my flushed cheeks in his gentle hands, it was the delectable blend of his fragrance, a little spicy, a little woodsy, that I will never forget.

Thoughts of our romantic early days tumbled into images of our more recent discord. All marriages had their trials, even under the best of circumstances. I knew that. But the tumultuous political events that we now found ourselves in the midst of was only eroding our relationship more rapidly. It was also making everything crystal clear. What if Ilya didn't come back from today's meeting? We needed to abandon our constant quibbling and maintain a strong front. I made a silent oath that if he came back safely, I would stand by my husband and stop finding fault with his decisions.

Bong...bong....The grandfather clock in the living room was calling out the hour. Could it be eight o'clock already? I checked the smaller brass timepiece on Ilya's desk to be sure. Next to it sat the malachite ashtray, given to him by Matvei on the occasion of Katya's birth because malachite was supposed to protect children. We'd lost our first daughter and we were not against good luck charms. In fact, we were both superstitious.

The ashtray was fashioned from a substantial block of the semi-precious mineral. I lifted it and searched the thin veins of differing shades of green that wove through the hard surface, hoping for an answer. It was heavy, but cool to the touch. I wanted to lay my aching head on it. Or hurl it at the wall. Or through the window.

"Luba..." I practically dropped it on my foot as I turned to find Ilya standing in the doorway.

"You're alive," I gasped and ran toward him.

"Of course I am." He hugged me lightly and let out a weary sigh. He turned his back and leaned against his desk, supporting himself on his hands. "I'm afraid the partisans are going to take over." I don't know what I'd been expecting to hear, but it certainly hadn't been that. I'd been sure Ilya would be able to negotiate some sort of peace. Perhaps a payoff and then a removal of troops. But this? I stared at him. "They're supposed to enter the city day after tomorrow. At noon." His voice cracked and he sounded on the verge of tears. I'd never seen my husband so vulnerable.

I sat in the armchair across from him and folded my arms across my chest, sitting there, dumbfounded, as Ilya continued.

"There's going to be a big parade and it's mandatory that we all attend. Triapitsin promises that life will continue as usual."

"You don't believe him, do you?" I shot back. I searched his eyes for an answer, but he avoided my stare. I was torn between proving my husband wrong and willing him to soothe me.

"No. I just don't see it." Ilya began to pace, like a caged tiger.

"Don't you think we should stand up for ourselves? Put up some resistance?" I was trying to make sense of our situation.

"Yes. That's exactly what I think. But without the Japanese forces to back us up, our hands are tied." He stopped in front of me. "Our good friend Ishikawa-san refuses to come to our

aid," he ranted. "Us...his Russian friends." Ilya was referring to the leader of the Japanese Occupational forces, Major
Ishikawa. "With all his troops, our city would stand a decent
chance against those barbarians. But without them..."

"Can't you talk some sense into him? Or Triapitsin? Make
an agreement? That's what you're so good at..."

Ilya said nothing; just pulled out his handkerchief and
rubbed his eyes. Then he wiped the lenses of his spectacles
before stuffing the linen square back into the pocket of his
tweed jacket.

"I still don't understand how they managed to take over
the fort and activate the cannons," I said. "Did you find anything out?"

"Somehow Triapitsin and his men were able to elude both
the Japanese and the White troops guarding the city." Ilya ran
his hands over his close cropped hair, so thick it was like the
curry comb Ivan used on the horses.

"But Chinnarakh's been abandoned for years. Didn't you
say that the cannon locks were buried back in 1905? After the
war with Japan ended? How could they be working?" Now
it was me who was pacing. I felt a surge of boldness as the
situation was becoming clearer and firm action was required.

Ilya slumped into his chair behind the desk. He removed
his pipe from his pocket and emptied the bowl into the ashtray,
then re-filled it from the worn leather pouch. Using his thumb
to compress the tiny, dried flakes, he struck a match and puffed
in and out, igniting the tobacco. His passivity was beginning
to irritate me.

"Triapitsin managed to find men who knew where the
locks had been buried," Ilya said. "They dug them up, re-in-
stalled them and rotated the guns around to face the city."

I tried to picture this. Fort Chinnarakh had always been a landmark on the horizon, a gray stone structure that graced the end of an isthmus that jutted into the Amur several miles above the harbor. It had been built to protect the city during the Russo-Japanese War in 1905. I remember when it was being constructed, I was still a child and I was visiting Father's fisheries with him and my brothers in the early hours of dawn one morning. The sun rising behind it gave it a luminescent glow. Years later, after the war ended and the fort was abandoned, we only thought about it when we rode to our *dacha* every summer. Misha would glimpse it in the distance and always asked if we could visit. We never did. And now it was overrun with soldiers. And they had activated the cannons.

"What's he like, this Triapitsin?" I asked, trying to fill out the gaps in my mind.

"A young hothead from Irkutsk," Ilya casually described him. "Spent the last half dozen years in and out of prison." My eyebrows arched questioningly. "For inciting factory workers to rise up against their owners and bosses." Ilya peered into the bowl of his pipe as if he could garner information from it. "Made his way across the continent to Vladivostok." He took a puff before continuing. "There, he managed to convince Nina Lebedeva, one of the principals of the Bolshevik movement here in the East, to spearhead an assault on Nikolaevsk."

"But...why Nikolaevsk?" I asked impatiently. I walked over to the window and knocked into the globe, setting the large orb spinning.

Ilya shook his head and shrugged. "It's a beautiful city."

"And she?" Questions kept popping out of me. I was searching for a clue as to how to deal with our dilemma.

"They say she's a Jewess."

"What makes you think that?" I turned back to him.

"Well, when you see her, you'll understand."

"Isn't that good for us?" I ventured. "That she's Jewish?"

"I hardly think she wants to advertise her background. No doubt that's why she linked up with this Triapitsin. He's her polar opposite. Sandy hair, pewter eyes, he's Russian through and through. The man possesses a combination of fearlessness and charisma. And he's young. Still in his twenties, I'd wager. Younger than her."

"But how...Did he...?" I didn't know what I was trying to say.

"He must have charmed his way into Lebedeva's life and bed the same way he woos his followers." I tried to imagine this uncharacteristic duo, what their lives were like and how they were going to affect ours. "He knows how to talk to the common people because he's one of them." I looked at our country splayed across the round surface in front of me and, as Ilya continued to speak, with my finger I traced Triapitsin's journey from Irkutsk to Vladivostok to here. "The good news," he said, " is that his army are not trained soldiers at all. The bad news is that they aren't even angry peasants who might have a right to fight for more..."

I looked at him questioningly.

"Most of them are scabbards and drunks," Ilya explained. "The dregs of society who have nothing to lose by following him."

I took a deep breath. I abandoned my geography and gave the world an angry slap. Its base began to wobble. I pressed my hand down quickly to steady it. "What does this all mean? What is he asking?"

"He's demanding that we, the White population of Nikolaevsk, surrender all weapons to the Japanese and allow the Bolsheviks to enter town peacefully. If only Ishikawa were to refuse and stand with us—"

"Why won't he?"

"Triapitsin showed the major a telegram from his superior in Tokyo, instructing the Japanese troops to remain neutral. I know that Ishikawa-san is divided about what to do; but in the end, he opted to follow orders."

"And Colonel Medvedev?"

"He's as angry and frustrated as I am. But neither of us can sway the major. He's signing his own death warrant, I told the colonel, who agrees. But what can we do?"

"We still have a day. Isn't there somewhere we can go? To your sister up in Kerbi?"

"Guards are posted all over town. We couldn't get our whole family out. And besides, who knows what the situation is like in Kerbi?"

Ilya and I stared at each other across the room, in silence, as this last detail sank in. I reminded myself that we had to stick together. I watched the curls of smoke swirling around his head. I felt like I was swirling, too. Again, visions of the citizens of Paris storming Versailles and the guillotine flashed before my eyes. The French Revolution had made quite an impact on me. I'd studied it in school and read an account by the French author, Alexandre Dumas. The fact that we might be living something similar was too horrible to think about.

Ilya stood and walked toward me. I reached for my husband, burying my face in his shoulder. "Oh, Ilya..." I wanted to comfort him. And be comforted. But when he wrapped his arms around me, it elicited a surge of anger rather than re-lief. I pushed him away, then brought my fists down on his chest. "Ilya, why didn't you listen to me? I told you we should have—What are we going to do?"

Tears streamed down my cheeks. I reminded myself of Veronika, known for her temper tantrums. Suddenly I stopped, aware that I'd just broken my promise that if he came back alive, I'd support him, no matter what. Ilya just stood there, accepting my beating as if it were his due. I cursed myself for letting my anger and fears override my love. This only made me break down more. When I was finally spent, Ilya allowed me back into his embrace.

The following morning, a town meeting was called to resolve how the citizens should react to the Red leaders' demands. Naturally, it was only attended by men. When Ilya returned from it, he conveyed that the consensus had been for the Whites to submit to the Reds.

"Submit?" I'd asked Ilya upon his return. "You mean surrender? It makes it sound like we're at war with these peo-ple. We haven't attacked them. Why would we surrender?"

"They're offering us an out. If we let them enter Nikolaevsk without a fight..."

"But—"

"There are four thousand of them, Luba. All men. We are men, women and children—without protection from the Japanese. If we don't submit, the partisans will move in and sabotage us. This is to prevent them from overrunning the city."

"But that's exactly what they are doing. Shall we allow them to overrun us without a fight?"

"You know that's what I've been saying all along," Ilya

conceded. "But no one will listen to me." He slumped on the sofa, like a deflated balloon.

"Ah, so now you see what's it's like to not be taken seriously." I couldn't help myself from lashing out at him. My vows of support were evaporating as rapidly as events were overtaking us. Ilya was silent. "What happened to your being able to talk to Triapitsin because you're both young? All your legal expertise and charm don't seem to be getting us anywhere." I hated myself for being so blunt, so accusing. But I was ready to jump out of my skin. The noose had tightened and I couldn't see a way to avoid our hanging. I looked at my husband, his easy smile frozen into a grimace and his smooth, wide brow carved with tracks of worry.

12

We awoke to the news that Colonel Medvedev had shot himself in the night. It was a clear, cold day, the last of February. In fact, it was leap year. Might that have something to do with our bad luck, I wondered. The sun smiled brightly from the heavens and it seemed too beautiful for the horror we were facing. Ilya and I were dressing for the mandatory meeting of citizens in the town square. I felt like a puppet whose master was orchestrating my movements. I couldn't focus. I pulled on whatever was close at hand, not caring how I looked. Ilya, naturally, was scrutinizing every detail of his appearance, brushing his hair, trimming his moustache, straightening the knot on his ascot. We weren't going to a ball, I wanted to remind him.

He'd suggested we walk to the square rather than drive up in a sleigh. I could hear my mother in the hallway. Esther was going with us, but Mama would remain with Nessia, the little ones and the *amahs*. She claimed she was too old for this nonsense. Riva, on the other hand, was bundled and by the door wrangling everyone into position, the general of her own small army. I kissed the children and set my jaw against Riva's orders, reminding myself who the real enemy was.

People making their way toward the town center filled the roads. The snow was packed down and easy to traverse. Shouts could be heard from the harbor to the square. It was Sunday and the church bells from the cathedral pealed. Morning mass had ended and the congregants were spilling through the cathedral doors as we arrived.

A platform had been erected in the center of the quadrangle and benches were set up behind a podium. In front of the stage, large wagons guarded by taciturn soldiers carrying bayonets were stationed. As people filled the square, we were herded toward the wagons and ordered to deposit any rifles, guns and ammunition. Ilya had only a handgun and he'd left it behind in our house.

"Weapons?" Ilya said innocently as we filed by. The partisan who'd accosted him gave off a sour loamy odor. "I don't keep any." When the ruffian stared at him questioningly, Ilya retorted. "I've never had need of weapons." This made the partisan snort.

We found a place in the gazebo where, in warmer months, a band usually played on Saturday nights and Sunday afternoons. I recalled those happy days when Ilya and I would stroll arm in arm, sip cool drinks sold at kiosks and laugh and dance with our friends. But today the square stood barren and forbidding.

As the clock struck noon, more rebel troops arrived. Like a

barrage, unruly and unkempt hordes of men marched along the thoroughfare. It was difficult to see over the heads of those assembled, but I caught sight of banners denouncing the Whites as "Skunks" and "Enemies of the People," and others proclaiming "Down With International Plunderers!" carried aloft. The magnitude of people was difficult to absorb. It reminded me of news clippings I'd seen of the Tsar and his subjects. The march on the Winter Palace when so many innocents had been slaughtered by the White Army. I shuddered. I couldn't avoid these recurring thoughts. Behind the partisans, Triapitsin and Lebedeva glided in on a sleigh, waving at those who lined the streets leading from the wharf, as if they were royalty,. If only these invaders would meet the same end as the poor Tsar, I thought to myself. I caught sight of our friends Sammy and Eda Shimkin as they walked in our direction. We embraced numbly, then stood arm in arm, as our newly proclaimed leaders mounted the platform.

Shivering, I studied the pair of conquerors on their throne. Ilya was right in his description of them. Triapitsin was definitely not as old as his partner. Though small of stature, he exuded confidence like an ember of coal emits heat. He looked so young and handsome it was difficult to believe he was the calculating mastermind responsible for all our current troubles. He didn't look capable of such despotism. The woman at his side was much more menacing. Her black eyes, as impenetrable as shale, were hawklike as was her beak of a nose. A dangerous current galvanized her. I imagined it was she who was silently directing from behind. Like Riva and the way she was able to influence Ilya.

The words from the podium raced past my ears like bullets. I tried to tune them out, but the context of the speeches couldn't be ignored. They reiterated the messages on the banners slapping in the wind: "Long Live the Russian Federated Soviet Republic!" Around us, the stern façades of the synagogue, mosque and cathedral hemmed in the mayhem being created by this man called Triapitsin and his co-conspirator, Nina Lebedeva. Several military officials were also on the dais. It was announced that the administration of the town was being transferred to a temporary Executive Committee. Strangely, the members of this new committee didn't include any townspeople and seemed to have been organized ahead of time. The head was a man named Zhelezin, a furry mammoth ensconced by a thick, bushy beard.

"Can you imagine? He's nothing but a schoolteacher from Bogorodskoye Village!" Esther whispered as he got up to speak. How she knew this, I had no idea.

"Yes. What kind of qualifications does that give him?" Riva sneered.

None of the other Reds were any better suited to lead. One was a clerk from a nearby village; another had previously worked in a textile company, and one was a complete unknown. Yet they now had titles of "Secretary," "Manager" (of the Town and District Economy) or "Commissar" (of Finance; or of Provisions). Triapitsin had dubbed himself the Military Commissar. How had these men managed to become so prominent? By overrunning villages and stealing everything in sight? Is that what they were going to do to us? Here?

Endless speeches were given by these men, proclaiming that all private businesses were being turned into cooperatives and everyone was required to work together for the good of the People, making clothes, shoes...whatever was needed. I peeked at the mob. I saw a woman nodding her head, a man smiling. We were surrounded not only by our neighbors, but also by workers and peasants. The general mood was one of frenzied hope and excitement. To me, their jubilation was repugnant. How had their revolutionary attitudes escaped our notice before now?

"The newspaper will now report unbiased facts and events," we were told. Esther was clucking her tongue and I noticed Ilya flinch.

The wind grew fiercer. I nestled into my husband's embrace, trying to eke out every ounce of comfort. My anger had temporarily subsided, overtaken by my need for solace. The faces of our neighbors and friends were as panic-stricken as our own and everyone avoided making eye contact. It was as if we were embarrassed by our fears. Finally, after what seemed like days, we were permitted to disperse and return home. The chanting echoed behind us.

How I wished Matvei were here. Or better, that we were with him. In Japan. Far, far away from the escalating terror. With no appetite and exhausted from the long day, we went to bed early. I tossed and turned and clung to Ilya, unable to fall asleep. Visions of the day's events clogged my mind.

I finally drifted off but was awoken by a heavy banging in my head. Only it wasn't in my head at all.

Part Two

13

---

*I*was rummaging through our stores for food to feed our captors. Since Ilya's arrest and the arrival of the partisans three days before, Riva, Nessia and I had been in charge of putting together meals for the men. It felt as if a constant party were in progress.

A vast space underneath the house, the cellar was incredibly cold. In summer months, the ice man would deliver large blocks covered in sawdust to help keep everything cool, but in winter there was no need for that. Usually so organized, the place, like our lives, was in an uproar. Crates, barrels and cans formerly stacked neatly along the perimeter had been moved, opened and rutted through. Many of the sides of smoked salmon and sausages that hung from the rafters along with ropes of garlic, bouquets of onions and sprigs of assorted dried herbs, had been torn down. The wooden root vegetable hampers lined

with tin and filled with turnips, beets, parsnips and rutabagas
and the bins of flour and grains lay uncovered. Not only were
we women coming down daily for supplies, but the soldiers
felt they had the right to intrude any time they had a craving
for a snack. Bags of coffee beans and loose teas, elegantly
wrapped boxes of *sembeh* and cans of sardines and herring
were strewn about rather than stacked on the shelves next to
glass jars of pickled carrots, beans, beets and cucumbers that
had come directly from our garden. All this bounty and order-
liness was the result of Cook-san's hard work and I felt a pang
of loss as I thought of him. My mind instantly shifted to Ilya
and Esther and I wondered what they were eating in prison. I
felt so helpless surrounded by this abundance, knowing they
were locked away. Apples and pears were packed in straw
and Cadbury chocolates spilled from boxes. Crates of wine
and vodka lined one wall but were already severely diminished. Sacks of rice and kasha were sprawled in heaps. I cut
down some of the sausages, filled my arms with vegetables
and stumbled up the ladder to the kitchen, trying to figure how
I might transport some of those goods to the prison.

With Nelibuov and his men in our home, Triapitsin and
Lebedeva in Matvei's house and other leaders ensconced in
neighboring abodes, it was hard for anyone to find a ray of hope
to cling to. These peasants and school teachers from nearby
districts were now Triapitsin's trusted commissars, dictating
the law; and we and our former servants worked for them.
The new, self-appointed officials slept in our rooms and entertained themselves in our living room most evenings. I could
hear the music and laughter as I lay in bed at night. I used to
fall asleep to the howling of the lone wolves that prowled the
hills outside town, their baritones sometimes augmented by

the tenors of foxes. Their mournful cries were much more suited to our present situation than the revelry echoing from the front of our house. I prayed that the merrymaking would remain out front, and not encroach on us.

Time passed like the unvaried ticking of a clock, the repetitiveness almost reassuring. But what was going on in the prison? And how were we going to save our loved ones and avoid being taken in ourselves?

Each morning, Riva, Nessia and I were expected to awaken before dawn to prepare fresh bread and breakfast for the men. Not only did we cook, but we were also required to serve and clean up after them. Once they were sated, we were allowed to consume whatever remained.

Yumiko-san rose with us and took the children for their daily walk to gather eggs for the men's breakfast. Most days, Misha accompanied Nessia to the barn to milk the cow. Yumiko-san always managed to sneak back an egg for the boy in her apron pocket. I was carrying a bucket of waste out the backdoor, taking it to the coop to feed the chickens, when I heard Misha crying, "No, Yumiko-san. Please. I don't want any!" His *amah* was holding a delicate oval, about to pierce the shell with her hairpin, but he was trying to stop her.

She wouldn't listen. He looked helplessly at me. "You need strength, Misha-chan. Drink it," his *amah* said as she handed it to him, prodding him to suck out its contents. I knew he was thinking of the egg that Baba Riva had cracked into a bowl several months before. Though the buoyant orb had sat proudly in the center of its cloudy environs, the yolk had been a mottled grayish blue. It had looked like the veined eyeball of an old man.

"What's that?" Misha had asked and his granny had shaken

her head nervously, as if it were a bad omen. She'd insisted it was nothing. Still, she'd thrown the egg into the yard and hadn't used it in her baking, or even for the chickens. Since that day, Misha told me he couldn't help wondering what was inside the eggshells he was supposed to drink down, a treat he used to love. I couldn't blame him. As for me, I wondered why my superstitious mother-in-law hadn't heeded the portent.

After breakfast, we women prepared the rest of the day's meals while Yumiko-san tended to the little ones. Riva, in her element when near a stove, instructed Nessia and me in everything. I'd never shared my mother-in-law's ardor for cooking and since Ilya and I had moved in with her after Simon passed away, the kitchen had become my least favorite room in the house. I was aware of my mother-in-law's disappointment that I didn't covet the opportunity to learn from—and work alongside—her in the preparation of the family's meals.

Though Cook-san was more than able to handle everything on his own, Riva loved to oversee his work. I knew she genuinely enjoyed the activity, but I suspected there was also an element of wanting to remain in control. I neither longed to create meals nor to spend extra time in Riva's company, listening to stories of her difficult past or receiving counsel on how to best care for her beloved son. How ironic that now, here I was, not only helping—but depending on—her as, together, we tried to figure out how and when we would ever see our prince again.

As a young girl, I'd often wandered into the kitchen to watch Vasya, our family's cook. The room always exuded an enticing odor, whether it was the hearty scent of fresh bread, the sweet suggestion of a *babka* in the oven, or the mouth-watering combustion of some soup or meat slowly evolving into our midday meal. I'd silently watch as Vasya concocted all sorts of delicacies. Often, he enlisted my aid, handing me some dough to knead or some cream to whip while he scurried about preparing the family's meals. His hands were arthritic, but his bony fingers flicked through their duties like a concert pianist.

One of my favorite pastimes was helping Vasya make *pelmeni*. Not only did I love to eat the little meat-filled crescents which were served in broth, I almost enjoyed the creation of them more. Vasya would roll out the dough until it was thin and satiny, like cloth, but with enough body that when he flipped the entire sheet over to roll out the other side, it wouldn't tear. When he was perfectly satisfied with its consistency, he would pull over one of the high wooden stools and help me up on it. He'd hand me a small shot glass to use as a cookie cutter and I'd set to work.

When I was really young, I used to make all sorts of designs in the dough, cutting out circles haphazardly, creating faces or abstract patterns in it. As I grew older, Vasya showed me how to be more efficient, eliciting as many perfect discs as I could, one next to another, so that very little dough was left over. When finished, the sheet looked like a moth-eaten blanket. Several columns of the stacked coins teetered on the table. Sometimes I pretended to be a bank teller; other times, a savvy gambler at the roulette table. I'd gather the leftover dough, squeeze it into a pliant ball and Vasya would iron it out with the rolling pin so that I could repeat the cutting process until nothing remained.

While I was incising the dough with my glass, Vasya prepared the filling, a mixture of ground meat, beaten with an egg, to which he added a touch of rice vinegar, soy sauce, pepper and a pinch of fresh or dried parsley. He'd bring over the bowl, along with another stool, and, side by side, the two of us would sit, taking a wafer of dough, placing a lump of filling in the center of it and folding the discs in half, pressing the dough firmly shut with our fingertips. The half moon shapes were the perfect size to pop into our mouths once they were cooked in a simmering broth. Sometimes, we made *varenyaki*, larger dumplings, which Vasya fried in oil. Unlike the tender boiled mouthfuls, those were crunchy and succulent, more like Chinese *gyoza*. Whether large or small, both were fun to make and scrumptious to eat.

We always made much more than needed and Vasya or Cook-san would dole any extra soup and *pelmeni* into copper bowls to freeze. Once they turned solid, they would wrap individual portions in burlap and store them in the cellar. When anyone would go on a trip in winter, they'd tie the portions to the runners of their sled and the bundles would get dragged through the snow, remaining frozen until the traveler reached his destination.

I thought of Matvei and recalled those days as I now stood next to Nessia, performing the task I knew by heart. Riva expertly rolled the dough like Vasya once had, then handed it over for us to perforate and fill. The pleasure I'd once taken in preparing *pelmeni* was absent now, knowing who was going to consume the products of our labor. But the simple rote of the activity was meditative. We still made huge batches but now everything disappeared into the hungry gullets of the Reds. There was barely anything left for us, let alone for freezing.

Plucking chickens was another daily task. Thankfully, Riva hadn't forced Nessia or me to kill the birds. She did that herself. But we were forced to remove the feathers which we saved in a basket to be used later to stuff new pillows. Working under Riva's tutelage, I wondered if my mother-in-law felt a sense of satisfaction that she'd finally gotten me into the kitchen.

While we perspired over the stove and sink, paring vegetables, grilling meats, washing linens and churning butter, the interlopers roamed through our house, acting very familiar with all our belongings. I no longer had access to my bedroom, nor my things, except for the scant few I'd been able to move to the nursery. I assumed the men had divided the rest amongst themselves to share with their wives and women.

Our family wasn't allowed to use the living and dining rooms, unless it was to set the table, empty ashtrays, sweep up or clear dishes. I felt as if I worked in a hotel. A rhinoceros of a man, his thick jowls laced with veins that made his skin seem like glazed pottery, spent hours reclining on the living room sofa. The scrawny soldier with the cobweb beard loved to sit at the piano any free moment he could. Whenever I was in the vicinity, he'd strike up a sentimental tune, as if to apologize for the behaviour of his comrades. The men leered at Nessia and me when we served their meals and their suggestive remarks made me shudder. The looks weren't as unbearable as the taunting allusions they made as to what life must be like for Ilya, Esther and the others. When one of the Reds walked in wearing Ilya's coat with the sable collar, something in my brain exploded. If Ilya's coat was here on this man, how was my husband staying warm in prison?

My mind was no longer clear or rational. I was flooded with memories and overcome with fear. What were the

conditions like in jail? The food? The beds? I didn't want
to think past these everyday basics to subjects like the
treatment of those incarcerated. I couldn't bring myself to
venture into the arena of questioning and torture. I merely
expunged those thoughts and focused on my chores. My ears
were constantly peeled to any conversations that might per-
tain to what was going on in the jail. But I knew I had to do
something. Quickly.

Nelibuov had taken over Ilya's study. He loved to sit in
my husband's favorite chair, the one with the brass nail heads
along the seams. A pewter mug was stationed on the wooden
desk, not on the ink blotter where Ilya would have placed his.
It was probably eating circles into the veneer. I could feel
the mark as if it were branding me through my skin. He'd
also subsumed Ilya's wardrobe and when I saw him in Ilya's
clothes—especially his smoking jacket or the paisley robe that
Matvei had bought him in London—I could barely restrain
myself. But at least those items had been absconded from his
armoire—not stolen off his body.

Even though Nelibuov was broader than my husband, he
crammed himself into his new finery and paraded through the
house like a fop. The sight pained me, but I was relieved that,
despite his bluster, Nelibuov seemed content to merely trans-
pose himself outwardly into the man of the house. By some
stroke of luck, he hadn't made good on his threat that I should
remain in the master bedroom with him. Despite his hatred
for us Whites, I sensed a latent admiration for Ilya, a gratitude for his legal defense. Perhaps even the slightest twinge
of guilt at the turn of events. Though stern and commanding,
he restrained himself from being outwardly cruel to us, as he
sometimes was with his soldiers. I imagined that somehow

Ilya's code of ethics was embedded in the weave of his shirts and jackets and was invisibly being transferred to the new owner.

Inspired by his semi-civility, I decided to lure Nelibuov into helping me. Carrying a plate of fresh *blini* smothered with sour cream and caviar into the study for a late morning snack, I placed the dish in front of him. "I thought you might like a special treat," I said. His scowl at being interrupted quickly transformed into a grin of delight and he dug into the treat with gusto. No "thank you" emerged from his lips. I stifled the urge to remark sarcastically and simply asked, "Is it good? I hope you're enjoying it." He answered with a satisfied grunt.

Emboldened by the fact that he hadn't rudely dis-missed me, I ventured into more volatile territory. "I was wondering....Seeing as how my husband saved your life..." Nelibuov struck me with a fierce glance. "I thought you might be willing to speak out on his behalf. To Triapitsin and Lebedeva."

"There is nothing I can say."

I wanted to contradict him. Instead, I held my tongue. "Could you at least find out for me how he is? If I could may-be visit him in prison?"

Nelibuov had wolfed down the *blini* and was wiping the remnants of sour cream from the plate with his finger. As he licked it clean, he fixed me with a stare. After a moment, he replied. "We'll see."

"Thank you," I said as I removed his plate and backed out of the study as rapidly as I could. I peeked through the slit in the doorway, watching him lean back in Ilya's chair. Might he really help me? He certainly owed Ilya an enormous debt.

Now that he had stepped into the shoes of his own liberator, perhaps he could afford to show similar mercy.

We weren't supposed to leave the house, but on the fourth day, things were particularly tranquil. Maybe I could reach Mama, if her home was equally quiet. There was a guard in the yard so I decided to walk around the block. As I approached the house where I'd grown up, I was taken aback as Matvei's sleigh came to a halt practically in front of me. I leapt toward it. Then, realizing that Matvei could not possibly be in it, I quickly sought refuge behind a tree, hoping to remain unnoticed.

"Your ladyship..." I overheard Commander Triapitsin croon as he descended and offered his hand to Nina Lebedeva.

"*Comrade*, Yakov," the woman corrected him curtly. "Comrade. We are all equals." I laughed to myself at this absurdity.

"Of course," Triapitsin smirked as he bowed his head and clicked his heels in jest. He himself seemed aware of the irony. "And that's why we are staying here and the rest of our troops are scattered in the less desirable homes in town, right?" he asked with a sly wink. He was wearing Nikolai's camel hair coat and I could see she had on Esther's favorite mink with the new seal hat. I thought fleetingly of the day we'd bought it; and then of many others Esther and I had spent together. As he surveyed his surroundings, Triapitsin's eyes glinted. They were so close. I prayed that they wouldn't turn and see me. Fortunately, they seemed quite wrapped up in their new home.

Nina brushed her comrade aside and stomped up the walk toward the entrance. There was no doubt she felt this elegant manor rightfully belonged to her, but she lacked the finesse of a society woman.

"*Ninotchka*," Triapitsin called after her, but she strode inside without waiting for him. He directed the driver to pull the sleigh around to the back. Adjusting his holster, Triapitsin followed on foot. I wondered what the young leader saw in that bossy wench. He might be evil, but he certainly was handsome. She, instead, was swarthy and charmless.

Perceiving this wasn't a good time, I hurried home. Before going in our back door, I peered over the fence to Mama's yard and noticed that woman, Lebedeva, emerging from the back door of the house. Still wearing Esther's coat and hat, she looked not unlike my sister-in-law from a distance. I seethed at the sight.

Suddenly, from out of the cottage in the yard, Tolya bolted, calling, "Mama! Mama!" his shouts growing more and more feverish as he ran toward the fur clad figure. Before Lebedeva had time to turn around, Tolya had taken hold of her from behind and was gripping her tightly to himself. "Oh, Mama!" the boy cried, "I thought you were gone forever!" I winced at the yearning in his voice and, without thinking, made a move in their direction. Aware that my presence would only exacerbate the situation, I held my breath and crouched behind the chicken coop, watching from there. Shocked and disgusted, Lebedeva extricated herself from the clutches of the hysterical child.

"I am NOT your mama!" she hissed at him. "And she is gone...FOREVER!" The venom in her voice struck right at my core.

"No! No!" he cried, about to pound his frail fists into her staunch ramparts. Luckily, Sophie had followed her brother out of the cottage. She grabbed him with all of her wiry five-year old might and tugged him back so his flailing wrists flung only at the air.

Hearing the commotion, Mama, an apron covering her front, ran into the yard. At the same time, rounding the corner of the house came Triapitsin with Zhelezin, their heads bowed in conversation. I froze in panic.

"What's going on?" Triapitsin demanded as he absorbed the scene.

"This rascal...this urchin..." Lebedeva pointed at the shivering boy. "He tried to assault me...! He should be whipped... shot!" The words spewed from her mouth, a fountain of fury.

"No!" Mama exclaimed as she waddled through the snow and gathered her grandchildren in her outstretched arms.

Lebedeva turned on her next. "You again...eh?"

"He only thought you were our mama," Sophie boldly spoke up.

"Moment, *Ninotchka*," Triapitsin interceded. "He's just a boy."

"A White," Zhelezin modified with revulsion. "And a Jew. We don't need more of them...!" He reached for his revolver.

"He wanted his mother....Come, let's go back into the house," he told Lebedeva and Zhelezin. "You," he addressed Mama, "Calm those youngsters and get back to work. Understand?" She nodded thankfully and ushered the children back into the cottage and out of harm's way.

I stared at the scene, my ears ringing, not really sure if what I'd just witnessed was real. Suddenly, a woman appeared in the kitchen doorway. I recognized her as Oksana Dimchin, a peasant we knew from the market and also from our summers in Mago. It was her husband, Iosef, that I'd seen at the prison.

Oksana was a good-natured soul with children and a mother of her own and I'd seen her patience caring for them in the past. To know she was working with Mama was a relief.

The following evening, as I carried a platter of sliced cold meats for the men's supper, I overheard them talking about my brother, Nikolai. I suspected their intention was to bait me, so I didn't let my interest show. But my body stiffened in anticipation of the news I feared they were about to deliver. It was worse than anything I expected.

"Yes..." guffawed one of the men, "he was on his way from Fort DeKastri. To deliver a packet to Colonel Vits. There were three of them, slinking across the ice, trying to reach the cover of the woods without being discovered. But we outfoxed them, we did!"

I busied myself to have an excuse to remain in the room. A young man with long limbs demanded more bread. I rushed toward the kitchen but hid behind the doorway to intercept the news. My heart pounded so loudly I was afraid they could hear me.

"Didn't have much in the way of rubles on them—though we relieved them of any they had...Kept Lury's wallet here as a souvenir. Nice leather, no?" The voices overlapped as I puzzled to discern who was saying what.

"You didn't let them off, did you?" another voice burst into the conversation.

"What...do you think, I'm a woman?" It was the first man again, laughing at his own joke. "Of course not. We shot the others, but I gave Captain Lury the honor of wallowing in his fear, then dying more slowly, courtesy of my bayonet blade."

The grain in the wooden paneling came alive. The knots

and lines in the pine wavered and spun. My good hearted, fun-loving brother. Who'd always been able to befriend noble and peasant alike. He may not have had a head for business, but he could seduce a weasel. How could these beasts be so callous to another person's pain? I ran into the kitchen and heaved into the wash basin. The man's laughter resounded in my ears. Nessia and Riva hurried over. In between gasps and sobs, I spewed out what I had just heard.

"*Lubachka*!" I heard from the other room. "Where is our bread?" Riva seized a loaf and sliced it crudely. I took the basket and practically threw it into their midst. The men snickered. There were one or two who occasionally interrupted the others and showed a little humanity, but it was difficult to get a sense of these soldiers because I was always too afraid to look up and meet their glances—kind or evil.

I wondered if Mama had heard the news yet. How would she take it? Always boasting about her wonderful sons, "*Matvei this*" and "*Nikolai that,*" this would be an horrific blow for her. The fact that Oksana Dimchin was with her was only slightly comforting. In the cramped confines of our kitchen, I assimilated these details, not wanting to accept the account. Perhaps it wasn't even true and they'd made the story up just to torment me.

———

An hour later, I walked into the hall on my way back to the nursery. As I rounded the corner, I froze in my tracks. "Misha!" I shouted, running toward him. "What do you think you're doing?"

At the other end of the corridor, my son was grappling

with a bayonet almost as long as he was tall. He was standing between the folded legs of the lanky soldier whom I'd noticed at the dining table. He hadn't been directly rude or mean to me, but I had heard him boasting to some of his buddies, trying to act tougher than he probably was. At the sound of my voice, they both turned and the nose of the weapon pointed directly at me. They shifted their aim away and I lunged forward and snatched my son from the man's clutches.

The Red, who only moments before had been quite friendly and attentive to Misha, immediately altered his focus, forgetting about the boy in an instant. "Why don't you step over here and let me teach you a little about rifles?" he offered. "I'm Igor." He extended his hand. His deep blue eyes, the color of the Amur in summer, probed me provocatively. I dragged Misha toward the nursery, ignoring the Bolshevik's boorish tone and offer of friendship.

"What do you think your father would say if he saw what you were doing just now? Well…?" I bore down on the boy right there in the hallway, livid. "Do you realize these are the men who've captured him and are keeping him hostage?"

"I'm sorry, Mama. He told me his name and he was being nice to me. Offered me a caramel. He was showing me how his gun works. I thought if we became friends, maybe he'd help us free Father." Misha was so earnest. How could I scold him? Hadn't I felt the same way when I'd spoken to Nelibuov and when I'd offered the young soldier at the prison the sausage the other day? Wasn't that why I was planning to return there? In the hope of encountering him again? He had seemed so innocent himself. I truly believed he might help me. He certainly wouldn't harm me. And maybe Iosef…!? But the others….

"It's alright, sinich…" I hugged my son close and kissed

the top of his tousled head. "It was a good idea. I was just frightened that he was going to hurt you..."

Misha wrapped his arms around me and hugged me back. When we entered the nursery, I delivered him into Yumiko-san's capable hands. Her face was ashen, having just realized the boy wasn't there. My mind suddenly returned to thoughts of Kolya. I dropped onto my son's bed and buried my face in his pillow.

"Please don't cry, Mama." Katya was standing over me, caressing my hair to soothe me, as if she were the mother. I pulled her to me, needing to feel her closeness. But my thoughts and fears I kept to myself.

"The children need fresh air. What good does it do to keep them cooped up in here?" I was jolted back to reality by the sound of Riva demanding Nelibuov allow them to go outside. "You've got guards. They're not going to run away."

"Alright, *Babushka*. Alright. Take them out," he relented in the face of her onslaught.

Without another word, she slipped into the room and told us all to bundle up. "He didn't say anything about us not being allowed out with them," she whispered to me. We hurried into our coats and mittens before he could stop us.

The snowdrifts were high and the wind gusted. But we were accustomed to this weather. We had a large yard. I looked at the stump on which Cook-san always chopped wood and where he decapitated his chickens and saw the large hatch-et poised like a sentry, its blade in the wood and its handle erect. On the other side of the fence near the chicken coop was the cabin where Mama, Sophie and Tolya were confined. I peered over and suddenly saw them coming from around the back, near their wood pile. Arms weighted with kindling, they were stumbling toward the cabin door. "Mama!" I shouted, then looked around, hoping I hadn't been heard. It was the only time I'd seen Mama except for when Tolya had assaulted Lebedeva the day before; but she hadn't seen me. When nobody seemed to be paying attention, I inched my way toward her. Catching sight of me, she threw down her logs and approached me. I reached out to hug her over the low fence. We tried not to cross the properties but got close enough to talk. "Are you alright?" I asked.

Meanwhile, without even thinking, Sophie and Tolya ran across the divide and joined their cousins who were sliding down the huge mound of snow that Ivan had built for them at the beginning of the season. They climbed up one end of the hill, carrying a shiny leather skin, which they used as a sled, to glide all the way down the other side. Misha started a snowball fight. Sensitive Tolya wasn't much of an opponent. His little sister Sophie was a more resilient competitor. Unafraid of the cold or of getting hit, she gamboled about like a boy. Veronika also delighted in such games and threw herself into the game with abandon. Katya seemed to be pretending that she was too grown up to join in the silly activities. I worried about the way the men looked at her and kept my eye on the girl. Wrapped in thick layers, she looked more childlike and less alluring. Finally, the children's giggles and smiles proved too enticing for her to ignore. I sighed with relief.

"Do you have any news of Esther and Ilya?" Mama said.

I shook my head and decided not to mention Nikolai. "How are they treating you?"

"Don't ask," she said. "They're savages. Especially that Lebedeva."

"I know." I told her how I'd watched the scene with Tolya and how relieved I was that Triapitsin had let the boy go.

"He's not as bad as she is," Mama went on. "But neither of them are a picnic. They strut around the house in Nikolai and Esther's clothes and jewelry. He found Papa's ebony cane and now he uses it as a walking stick. They think they are to the manor born and demand to have *pirogues*, *pelmeni*, *Kulibiaka* and *blini* every night."

I nodded knowingly. "I saw Oksana Dimchin. Is she working there with you?"

"Yes," Mama nodded. "Thank goodness. She's a godsend. But I don't think she's having an easy time of it."

"Are any of us?" I confronted her.

"Well, 'their honors' throw parties every evening after dinner. Women and girls—some whom we know—are brought in for 'questioning.' The 'interrogations' take place behind closed bedroom doors." I flinched at the thought. "Often, the suspects are re-questioned night after night." Hearing my mother's familiar sarcasm as she described the scene made me realize how much I missed her. I knew Nelibuov and his men frequently headed across the yard after eating and for that I was humbly grateful. "I don't know what to tell the children," Mama went on. "Tolya cries himself to sleep every night. He misses Esther so." Should I bring up Kolya, I wondered again. Before I even had a chance, I saw Mama's eyes light with fright at something behind me. I turned to find Igor, the soldier from the hall, approaching, bayonet in hand.

"What are you doing?" he demanded.

"Just...uh...talking...to my—" I turned to hug Mama, but she'd already turned back to her cottage. "Come along," the Red ordered. As I followed him back to our house, Sophie and Tolya ran past.

"Help your Granny with the wood....With everything..."I whispered, not knowing if they heard me.

My own children were exhausted from their running about. It wouldn't be difficult to get them to come in and take a nap or read a book quietly. "But first," Igor barked at them, "Bring in more wood for the oven." They looked from him to me and back, and then ran off to obey.

14

On the morning of our sixth day of occupation, I sensed a change. Looking out the window, I saw that it had snowed during the night. The trees, the neighboring houses, even the coal black cannons in the driveway were cloaked in cottony sweaters. How could such purity harbor such evil? The magical wonderland was so beautiful that, for a moment, I wondered if the frightening circumstances of the past week hadn't been a dream. I glanced around the nursery, filled with my sleeping children, and reality toppled into my consciousness.

I roused myself for my morning chores, going through the motions in a state of inertia. My family seemed to be growing used to our situation. No longer expecting to be treated with the respect we were accustomed to, we were becoming inured to the scorn of our captors. Everyone fulfilled their duties and remained unobtrusive so as not to raise the ire of the Reds. Still, the days stretched out endlessly.

I tried to decipher how much the children were taking in. I could see they were growing bored and irritable. Tempers sporadically flared and frustrations erupted in squalls of tears. They were puzzled by everything. They didn't understand why their mother, aunt and grandmother had moved into their bedroom. Why these strange, dirty men were in our house, ordering everybody about. They were stunned to see the grown-ups driven to work at tasks they'd never seen us do before or get berated for not acting fast enough. Most of all, they wondered where their father was and when they'd see him again. Yet they instinctively behaved better than one would expect from those so young. I looked at them, unbelieving at how well they'd been holding up.

It wasn't my absence that put the children on their guard. Yumiko-san had always been in charge of them and Riva ran the kitchen while I frequently went out to visit friends, shop in town or spend evenings with Ilya. They were used to my truancy. It was the change in my demeanor that made them vigilant, I suspected. I'd always been care-free and happy, laughing all the time, eating chocolates and worrying about my appearance.

When I passed the hall mirror now, even I didn't recognize the stranger there. Replacing the spark in my eyes was a dull glaze. My thick hair that Ilya loved to run his fingers through had overnight become flecked with gray. It hung drably about my shoulders. It was as if I were using my long tresses as a shield to hide behind. The last thing I wanted in our current situation was to look alluring, so I no longer even brushed it. That way, the tangles and wisps, flying in every direction, acted as a deterrent to all those leering glances. But I could see my children wondering where their mother had disappeared. I didn't want to question why the men had been leaving us alone. I suspected Nelibuov had a hand in it. As much as he reveled in his new home and position, I sensed a hint of guilt in his gray eyes.

Misha, Katya and Veronika were old enough to be put to work. They were often relegated to various duties such as sweeping the ashes from the large stove and adding fresh kindling. The main hearth was located in the dining room, but it adjoined similar ceramic tiled structures in the living room, hall and Ilya's study. When filled with wood, the tiles absorbed the heat and relayed it to the other outlets, thereby keeping each room warm and toasty. A very economical solution.

The children's least favorite chore was cleaning the commode, but Katya pointed out how lucky they were. "Imagine if we had to empty the chamber pots like Yumiko-san and Nessia!" This elicited a nervous titter and a mutual "Ewww!" from her younger siblings.

―――――

I yearned to get away from the house, to return to the prison, to be in touch with neighbors, to find out anything I could. But with all my housekeeping duties, my absence might raise a flag. I kept waiting to receive some news from Nelibuov, but he was constantly surrounded by his men and unapproachable.

On Sunday, exactly a week since the rally that had abruptly overturned our lives, the partisans enjoyed a sumptuous afternoon meal courtesy of us. Clearing the table, I overheard

Nelibuov saying that he would be away for several hours. I rushed into the hall where he was putting on his coat and hat.

"I don't mean to interrupt....But have you had any news from the prison? Have you been able to speak to Comrade Tria—?"

"I have no news," he cut me off. But before walking out, he grudgingly added over his shoulder, "I'm working on it."

The door slammed shut and, in his wake, the men that remained in the house became like children once a parent's watchful presence no longer hovers. Nelibuov's pock-marked assistant immediately sent two men to the cellar to retrieve extra bottles of liquor and wine and soon the Reds were toasting their newfound fortune on the other side of the wall from me. By the time we'd washed the dishes and I'd set the table for a light supper, their merriment had subsided. I peered into the living room where ten men lay sprawled, asleep—on the sofa, in chairs and even on the floor, fatigued from their hijinks. Only the thin piano player who could never seem to get enough of our instrument remained awake. As his spindly fingers caressed the keys, he evoked a mournful folk tune that made me think of Ivan and his constant singing.

This could be my chance. I rushed to the nursery, which was thankfully empty, and retrieved a jade pin I'd never liked from under the stack of diapers. I stuffed it near my bosom. It was cool against my skin. I arranged my blouse to be sure that there was no evidence of its presence.

In the kitchen, all was still. I could hear the shouts of the children running cheerfully in the yard and see the silhouettes of Riva and Nessia standing by the barn, whispering and watching. A guard I didn't recognize smoked lazily in the shadows, not paying much attention.

Without a word, I grabbed a basket from a stack by the back door and hurriedly filled it with the most enticing items I could find in the larder—wine, sausages, sardines, soda crackers. All was still quiet. Did I dare do this? I put on my boots and coat and my thick red scarf. What was I thinking? The scarf was like a beacon that would surely draw notice. Shaking my head, I ripped it off and replaced it with a brown one, then pulled a knit hat down low on my forehead, making it harder to see who I was. I peered through the window, calculating if I could sneak out without being seen. Did I dare go out the front door? It was more blatant, but I was pretty sure it was unguarded. I decided to act with confidence, hoping it wouldn't arouse suspicion. I held my breath and turned the knob, half expecting to be pounced upon. I'd been right. There was no one out front. I straightened my shoulders and walked defiantly away, hoping my pace would help warm me against my fear and the biting cold.

The snow the night before had cleansed the city, erasing footsteps, tracks—all evidence of infiltrators. Into this white desert, I ventured. Bare branches wore thick coats of snow and the beauty of the black and white latticework against the blue sky made up for the precarious conditions. I was hoping to enlist Eda Shimkin for support. I was thrilled that there were no partisans on her lawn as I approached and was about to turn in at her gate when I glimpsed some shadows moving at the side of her house. I turned away and picked up my pace. I heard male voices calling farewell and hoped that whoever it had been hadn't seen me or been curious enough to follow. But the crunch of heavy boots in the snow gained on me from behind. I pushed onward, resisting the urge to turn back for a peek. In my haste, I slipped. Before I could get my bearings, an arm reached out to help me up.

I immediately recognized the face under the square hat, the cobalt eyes piercing into me. It was Igor, the partisan who had been showing his rifle to Misha in our hall. Since the incident two days ago, I'd noticed him, watching me, though he hadn't baited me with words. Usually, he was the guard who worked outside, patrolling our yard. He'd probably sneaked off from his post as well. If he hadn't been the enemy, I might have conceded that he was attractive. Misha had told me that he'd offered him candy and treated him nicely. Perhaps he had a son of his own. Unlike many of his compatriots, his face was clean shaven, displaying a chiseled bone structure. Maybe he was too young to grow a beard. He didn't stink like most of the others, but his teeth looked like a fence in disrepair, the individual slats overlapping and falling in different directions.

"Thank you," I mumbled as he helped me up. I brushed the snow off my coat. "It's slippery." I tried to make conversation to break the awkward silence.

"W-where are you going?" Igor asked, sounding nervous.

"To buy more supplies. Captain Nelibuov is aware that I'm out," I lied. I felt guilty even though there was no reason I had to explain myself to this man.

"Is that the only p-place you're headed?" he inquired further. He was almost friendly. He wasn't nervous, I realized. He had a stutter. Not knowing how to answer, I muttered some sounds under my breath and hoped he wouldn't ask me to speak more clearly. "We're running short of supplies," I added a moment later, in an attempt to change the subject.

"M-maybe I can help you carry everything b-back." Funny how I'd never noticed his speech defect before. Perhaps that was why he always acted so boastful: to look more bold to his compatriots. It made me feel a little sorry for him.

"That's very kind of you," I answered, half truthful, half sarcastic. Obviously, I couldn't stop and pick up Eda anymore. I didn't want her to get into trouble. And it wouldn't look good if I was seen consorting with friends. So, I continued on, my escort beside me. His strides were longer than mine, so either he had to slow down or I needed to speed up. I chose to maintain my pace, thinking maybe he'd leave me in his wake. No such luck.

Each time I walked through the downtown business district, I was further shocked by the change. The streets, once populated by our friends and neighbors, were now overrun with people I didn't recognize or had only seen on the other side of a counter. Posters proclaiming Lenin as the country's saviour and Bolshevism as the cure to the White menace were plastered on lamp posts and doors. The windows of shops no longer advertised their wares. Where delectable chocolates had once been temptingly displayed and ledgers, fountain pens and inks artfully arranged behind clean glass windows inviting passersby to wander in and purchase them, slogans now hung or were painted on the dirty glass storefronts. Factories had been set up in the library and hotel and the middle and lower class citizens who'd been enlisted to work in the various cooperatives were occupied sewing clothes and making shoes and boots for the army. I scanned the faces for Ivan or Cook-san or anyone I might know. How would they react to me if we met under these circumstances?

Kunst & Albers, previously our lavish shopping emporium, was now the site of the local Tribunal, announced a sign above the awning. Red guards were posted at the entrance. Reluctant men and a few women were being led up the three steps and inside. "For questioning," I overheard a bystander whisper to his mate.

Smaller shops like Marfa's Millinery had been emptied of their inventory. As I passed, I could see through the windows, now void of displays, that a long table filled the little boutique and perhaps a dozen women were seated around it, making hats of a more utilitarian style than Marfa's usual creations. Working even though it was Sunday. Marfa was leaning over one woman, instructing her in what was apparently a new trade.

Soldiers bearing weapons were everywhere

"Am I w-walking too quickly?" Igor asked.

"No," I said.

We continued to make small talk. There was a strange tension between us. It almost reminded me of similar walks with Sammy Shimkin, as he tried to court me on our way to school. I didn't understand why he was being so amenable. Perhaps he was actually a good person after all. I started to feel more comfortable in his presence and wondered if I dared broach the subject of Ilya and my desire to get into the prison to see him. If he were to accompany me to the jail, perhaps I could get past the guards there.

At Shimada's Dry Goods Store, he asked, "Is this where you're g-going?" I didn't know whether to nod or mention Ilya, but before I could utter a word, he pointed out, "It appears that your b-basket is already full. P-perhaps you were headed elsewhere?"

I clenched my teeth and reddened. Igor stared at me, then took out a cigarette and lit it. I made a swift decision to tell the truth. "Actually, I was hoping to go to the prison to try and get some information about my husband. I was wondering..." I tried to appear nonchalant, "Do you know any of the guards there?"

He was leaning against a post, relishing his smoke. "I m-might. Why do you ask?"

"It's just that my husband...and sister-in—"

"Ah...your husband," he cut in. "You m-miss him, don't you?"

What a stupid thing to say, I was about to snap at him; but I controlled myself. "Yes, I do."

"And what would the g-guards do to help you...?"

"I just want to see him...talk to him...get him word... Could you help me? Please?"

He dragged out a final lungful of smoke and tossed away the stub. "Supposing a guard were to help you?" He reached for my basket. It was so cumbersome I was happy to hand it over. "I'm sure he would want to be p-paid in return..." He began to poke through the contents.

"Of course. I would pay him gladly."

"You would be willing to—" He raised his eyes to meet mine.

"Yes, yes. I have a little money...some meat...That's what's in—" I indicated the basket.

"And if I w-were to help you...?" he whispered, leaning in to make sure I heard exactly what he was saying.

I recoiled as his intentions dawned on me. Could I—Would he—Did I even have a choice? My brain started clicking away like the telegraph in the post office in town as I tried to figure out what to do. In that moment, I realized that he'd steered me down a deserted side street and maneuvered me into a doorway. He let the basket fall to the ground and pushed me against the wall, leaning in to kiss me.

I was repulsed. Terrified. But I thought maybe a kiss would mollify him. Igor grunted with pleasure as he loosened my collar and pulled at the buttons on my coat, all the while hungrily navigating my face and neck with his warm, wet mouth. And those jagged teeth. There was nobody in the vicinity and even if I'd screamed or protested, who would have challenged this man in favor of me?

I shut my eyes tight as his fervent hands grabbed at my breasts. Suddenly, his roving fingers neared the pin I'd stashed away. Should I offer it to him instead of myself, I wondered; then decided not to lose both. Afraid he might encounter it, I shifted a little so that he wouldn't rip my garments and come across it. I could feel the sharp prongs of the setting pressing into my skin. The brute lifted my dress and, groping at my underthings, he pushed me harder against the wall. I tried to scream, but he clasped his hand over my mouth. I tried to get away, but he was too strong to fight off. And he was armed. I sunk into the softness of my coat, thankful that it cushioned me from the frozen façade. I tried not to think about what was happening.

As his urgency increased, I grasped his neck. I wondered if I had the strength—and daring—to choke him. He mistook my grip for passion. Grinning slyly, his tobacco breath blew across my cheeks as I turned away from him. When he'd concluded his assault, he stepped back and smiled, satisfied. I quickly pulled myself together. I wanted to run, but he restrained me. "Don't forget your g-groceries." His piercing eyes glinted as he handed back my basket.

I remained in the alley, dazed and furious, but thankful of the solitude, grateful for the bitter wind that whipped about.

It was so numbing I hoped it might eradicate the filth that had besmirched me.

I walked in the direction of the prison, but the mobs outside were larger and louder than before. I went around back where I'd been lucky the other day. It was getting dark but I noticed two guards immersed in conversation. One was Iosef Dimchin. Heaving a hopeful sigh, I approached.

"Iosef..." I called out.

"You know her?" asked his partner as I ran forward. He nodded and came over.

"Oh, Iosef, I have to see my husband. Is he—?"

"Yes, he's here." His tone was as vacant as my mind.

"Can you—is there any way...?"

I could see him mulling over what to say.

"Please. I'll pay you. I'll—" I started to reach into my blouse for the pin.

Iosef put his hand on my arm to stop me. "There is no need. Let me think..." Finally, he whispered, "Perhaps it's a good time right now. The commissars are all enjoying their Sunday dinners and day of rest elsewhere." I nodded recalling the passed out soldiers in our living room. "And it's practically dark. But they may return at any time."

"Just for a moment. Please."

"Follow me. I will try to sneak you in."

"Anything," I said.

We walked up the knoll and entered the stone structure. Iosef led me down a dank hallway. The floor was dirt and the smell was putrid. We passed a row of closed doors behind which I could detect faint cries and moans. I tried to block out the sounds and not think too much. In a small office at the end of the corridor, Iosef sat me on a chair and promised to return in a moment. There didn't seem to be anybody about. Only the prisoners in their cells. I hugged myself and tried to stop the chattering of my teeth. What if Triapitsin or Zhelezin were to come in and find me there? What would I say? I could only imagine what they'd do to me.

The jangle of keys made me hold my breath. And then a scrawny old man, barefoot and dressed in undergarments, limped in. His face and arms were bruised. It took me a minute to realize that this was my husband. "Ilya...?" I cried and rushed to hug him. He winced. Though he'd only been holed up for a week, he was a shrunken man. Tears were falling down his gaunt cheeks. His beautiful green eyes were practically swollen shut, the whites of the half-opened one now blood red.

"Luba..." He looked so pitiful, I cringed. Quickly, I shrugged off my coat and wrapped it around his bony shoulders. Surprisingly, it fit him. I quickly unraveled my scarf and wrapped his frozen extremities in it.

"Are you alright?" he asked. "The children? Mama?"

"We're okay. What about you?"

"Oh, Luba! Can you ever forgive me? My stupidity...?" He was shivering and sobbing.

I covered his lips with my fingers and then with my mouth. He shrunk back in pain and I noticed that several of his teeth were missing. "I love you," I said, realizing I was not going to get any answers from him. "Are you—Have they—?" I couldn't get the words out, probably because I didn't want to hear the reality spoken aloud. The ill treatment of the prisoners was more than obvious.

"The Japanese," he said. "Are they going to come to our aid? Do they realize...?" His words sounded funny as the came out distorted by a lisp.

"I don't know." I shook my head. "I don't know anything."

"Can you—?"

Iosef stuck his head in the door, looking nervous. "I'm afraid you'd better leave now. I see lanterns approaching at the end of the road. The commissars often return in the evenings."

Ilya and I clung to one another. He started to give me back my coat.

"No..." I told him. "You keep it. And here's a little food, too." I shoved the basket into his arms and then looked at Iosef, as if for permission. I reached out for one more embrace and then Ilya hobbled away with Iosef's support. "Esther..." I called after him, realizing I hadn't even asked about her.

I had never felt so lost. So devoid of hope. With my skin still crawling from Igor's recent assault, I confronted the fact that the man on whom I'd depended, who'd loved and bolstered me, was evaporating before my eyes. I had never wanted to be forceful like Esther. I'd always submitted to my husband. But when Ilya looked back at me, his eyes like hollows in a tree, dark and vacuous, I sensed that my days of relying on him were past.

Iosef escorted me out the back. "Please, tell me what I can do. How can I get my husband out of here? I'll do anything," I said. "I've got—" I started to dig into my corset for the pin I'd hidden there.

Iosef put his hand over mine and shook his head. "There is nothing. These men are heartless barbarians. Even peasants like myself fear for our lives. Any moment they can turn on us." We were outside and I was shivering in only my sweater. "Take my coat," he insisted. Neither of us had any words. "Thank you," I muttered as he let me out the gate.

I hurried through the dark, silent streets, my mind a tornado. How would I convey the news to Riva when I got home. I couldn't lie. But I didn't think I could articulate what I'd experienced. The futility that was so obvious. As it turned out, one look at my face and Riva grasped the unspoken.

15

A few days later, I was awoken by Yumiko-san scooting the children away from the window. Gun shots pinged the air. They were coming from across the courtyard.

"What's happening?" I asked

"Soldier shoot squirrel and rabbit. Hunt for dinner," she said. The children looked skeptical and with one glance out the window, I understood. Two corpses lay on the ground. I could swear that one of the victims was Gennadi Richter, the printer. He looked like he was still wearing his apron and visor. I swallowed my shock and turned away, shaken to my core.

We'd heard that, besides the courthouse downtown, there was a second Tribunal that convened in the dining room of my old home. The accused were brought in daily and supposedly given a fair trial for their crimes. Since these offenses were generally trumped up in the first place, that was an oxymoron. It was a rare captive who would get released rather than taken directly to prison or executed out back.

I wandered through the house and my work in a blur. Between my worry over Mama and what was going on in her house with the Tribunal and the other "interrogations," my dread of what was happening in prison, not to mention my fear of confronting Igor again, I could focus on little else. The young partisan's blue eyes followed me around every corner. I avoided being left alone. He hadn't made another move, though as I was filling the samovar with kindling that morning, he asked me to meet him in the barn, saying he might be able to get a message to Ilya. I wanted to believe him and was almost willing to pay the price. But I didn't. Believe him. He was only an underling and had not even come through after his assault on me. I knew I had to work quickly. Ilya had looked like he was already practically gone. That would mean....I'd need the help of someone more powerful. Triapitsin. Nelibuov. It was hard to admit to myself that I was having these thoughts.

I considered Nelibuov. He was clearly the cock of our roost, strutting about and ordering his underlings to do as he bid. But despite hints, he had done nothing concrete to help me so far. As I thought about Triapitsin and how I might capture his attention, I was caught off guard when Nelibuov suddenly sent me on an errand. He had a craving for more caviar and there was none left in our cellar. I slipped out when nobody was looking and walked as swiftly as I could, taking a different route than usual, just in case I might be trailed.

When I reached town, I made a point of walking by the

printing office where Ilya would head each week to receive his first edition of *The Amursky Liman*, hot off the presses. The place wasn't silent. But the gazettes being peeled off now voiced the propaganda that electrified the city. As I passed, I peered in, desperately hoping to glimpse Gennadi Richter in his ink smattered apron, presiding over his men. He wasn't there. I felt as if I'd been struck by a stone. For a brief instant, I was happy Ilya wasn't witnessing all this. But what he was undergoing was much worse.

I was so busy taking in the transformation of our city and trying not to stand out that I didn't recognize Ivan, our coachman, as he emerged from the print shop with another man. Both carried stacks of newspapers on their shoulders.

"*Gospozha* Kap—" he started awkwardly.

"Ivan...!"

"Comrade..." Ivan's partner corrected.

"Are you—?" Ivan ignored his sidekick.

"No fraternizing with the *burzhui*. We must get these papers to headquarters right away."

I looked over my shoulder at Ivan as he disappeared in the opposite direction, then scurried on toward Shimada's. Mr. Shimada was standing behind the counter. His abacus lay next to the metal box in which I knew he kept his money. There was a pencil beside a pad of paper covered with sums and crossed out figures. His usually cheerful manner had been replaced by somberness. He nodded as I entered, but couldn't seem to find words for a conversation.

The formerly overstuffed store seemed diminished, devoid of most of its contents. After a mere week and a half, it appeared to be going out of business. The space had become a neutral meeting ground where those not yet incarcerated could exchange information and commiserate. Because it was run by a Japanese, even though the proprietor considered himself Russian, the Reds couldn't really get out of hand in there. The Japanese were not yet considered Enemies of the People. But there was little activity at that moment. Just a few women in the back whispering among themselves; faces I recognized, but none whom I considered real friends.

"Any news?" I asked, hoping for something. Anything.

They muttered their own horror stories of captured loved ones and confirmed that arrests continued to mount. All over town, in the dark of night, every night, that dreaded knock was heard on doors as Bolshevik soldiers, bearing unauthorized warrants, rounded up more men from each home. Slowly, the entire male population of Nikolaevsk was being herded into the already overcrowded prison. If only our men had attacked when we'd had the chance. Even if the Japanese had refused to stand by us. With each passing day our chances were shrinking. Right before our eyes, our city and our lives were trickling away.

Japanese troops were still visible around the city, though less so. They guarded their barracks and the area around them, but they didn't seem to move much from there. They remained aloof, mingling with neither the Whites nor the Reds. Perhaps their avoidance was a result of shame. Although the Japanese were only supposed to be a peace-keeping force in Nikolaevsk, how could they remain neutral under these circumstances? That was the question on everybody's mind. Were they blind to the fact that Triapitsin was a liar? A disastrous threat to us all? When were they going to wake up and do something? All we women could do was stand helplessly by and share our fears of what was to become—*what was becoming*—of Nikolaevsk.

I filled my basket as quickly as possible, searching the shelves in the ice box for tins of the precious roe Nelibuov had sent me for. "Is there no caviar, Piotr Nikolaevich?" I asked Shimada-san. He shook his head and looked as worn out as I felt.

"They've taken it all," he said and my face paled at the thought of having to return without any.

"None? Do you know anywhere else I might find some?" It was clear he didn't.

"I will put this on your account, *Gospozha* Kaptzan," he told me, referring to my other goods. "No need to pay now. There is enough to worry about, yes?" I thanked the gentle man whom I'd known since childhood. He seemed ashamed that his countrymen were doing nothing to aid the citizens with whom they'd shared so much history. I wanted to reassure him, but could think of nothing to say. I left him standing in his hauntingly bare store.

I rushed across the street to Kunst & Albers, then realized the site had been transformed into a military Tribunal and barracks. Frantic not to return empty-handed, I continued up the street to the German cafe. Herr Keller was always very nice to me. Perhaps he could help. But it seemed the entire town had been depleted of the precious delicacy. I racked my brain to think of a substitute.

I looked around, hoping for an inspired idea. I was surprised at the traffic on the boulevard. Partisans—on skis or on horseback—weapons hanging from their shoulders and threatening glares on their faces or simple peasants scurrying on their way filled the streets and sidewalks. I tried to avoid looking at people, but felt them peering at me from under fur-lined caps and coats, many of them stolen from us. There were few people I could identify because most Whites stayed indoors, cowering out of sight.

By that time, it was growing dark. I knew I should be home helping to prepare the meal, but since I was already late, I decided to take another risk. Possibly there were extra stores of caviar in Mama's house. Through the window, as I neared, I could see Triapitsin, Zhelezin and Lebedeva seated at the dining room table. Because it was pitch dark by now, I knew they couldn't see me so I crept closer to get a better look. The table had been set in an attempt at elegance, using our crystal, silver and linens. Empty bottles of wine and vodka lay scattered like fallen bowling pins. Red splotches stained the linen, the result of carelessness. I wondered where the rest of the partisans had disappeared to. Lebedeva picked up the silver bell and I could see her ringing it furiously to summon the servants. Oksana Dimchin came running in. I prayed Mama wouldn't follow.

Triapitsin held up an empty bottle and indicated that he wanted more. Moments later, Oksana returned with another. Did I dare sneak in the back door and ask about the caviar? Hopefully, the partisans would never know of my presence. And if they did see me, perhaps I could turn it into an opportunity to plead on Ilya's behalf. They could have our houses, our belongings. If only there was some way to convince them to let us go. Away. Anywhere. We could leave Nikolaevsk to them. My reasoning was absurd. I was like a child trying to catch soap bubbles without letting them burst.

I crept around the house and peered into the kitchen. Mama was standing over the oven removing a *pirogue*. I quietly pushed the door ajar.

"What are you doing here?" she asked, looking around nervously. As I explained my dilemma, Oksana came in. She ushered us both into the coatroom where it was a little safer to speak.

"I just overheard them talking," Oksana whispered. "Triapitsin's fed up with the Japanese refusing to surrender their arms. He's giving Major Ishikawa an ultimatum: to surrender their ammunition by midnight tomorrow. If they don't lay down their arms peacefully, he's going to attack the 'yellow skunks,' as he calls them. They're as bad as the *burzhui*, he said."

Maybe there was a ray of hope at last. If the Japanese would attack, the prisoners could be released to help fight the Reds. Oksana filled a small container with caviar for me to take home. I thanked her for that and the news, hugged Mama and ran across the yard. Dinner was over there, too. I heard Nelibuov had been furious at my absence. But when he came looking for me and saw the container of caviar I held out to him, his grimace turned into a grin and his anger waned.

I told Riva and Nessia the news about the Japanese. The following day, from what we could overhear, word had begun ricocheting through the ranks as well. Tension ignited the atmosphere. Everyone felt a change was imminent.

Before going to bed that night, the 12th of March, Riva instructed us to remain in our clothes. She distributed some apples, dried salmon and chunks of bread to stash in our pockets. Our coats were brought into the room, rather than left hanging by the back door.

"Where's the rest of the jewelry?" I asked.

"Yumiko-san and I have sewn it into our coats and clothing.

A little bit here, a little there..." Ever the strategist, I thought, once again impressed by her ingenuity.

The air sizzled with the hope that we'd soon be reunited with Ilya and Esther. No one knew how this would be accomplished, but we were delirious with expectation. The soldiers in our house were also a bit delirious—they, from vodka. There was so much noise coming from the front rooms that it was difficult to get the children to sleep.

———

Sure enough, shortly after our clock chimed twelve, explosions and gunfire broke out in the streets all around. Screams could be heard outside and movement in the hallway. Riva jumped out of bed. "Wake up!" she whispered urgently. "Come quickly. Quietly. Take your blankets, coats and shoes..." She put her ear to the door. The footsteps and shouts in the hall were receding. On her face I could read calculations cascading through her mind. Like a chess champion, she must have been figuring out our next move...and the ensuing ones.

The children were groggy and bewildered. Yumiko-san carried Viktor and I helped the other three children out of their beds, reassuring while also warning them to remain silent and do as they were told. Veronika grabbed Oleg and tucked him into her coat. Katya glanced at her doll collection longingly. I nudged her toward the door. At the last moment, I reached out and picked one of the dolls off the bureau. I handed it to her as we crept out of the room. Riva was in front; I brought up the rear. A strong smell of smoke pervaded the hallway and the house shook with every blast. We headed toward the kitchen.

The house appeared to be deserted. This was unusual, but

a blessing. There were always several soldiers camped out in the living room, drinking and playing cards, or eating in the kitchen. Now, all of them seemed to have fled, engaged in the combat. Through the windows, flames flared and the gunshots were louder than ever. I could distinguish the terse clip of Japanese from our familiar Russian as soldiers called to one another outside.

I cracked the back door open a sliver and peered through. I wondered how Mama, Sophie and Tolya were faring, but Riva pulled me away from the door.

"We can't go out there. Nobody must see us..."

"But Mama..."

"Perhaps they'll make their way over here," Riva said. "We cannot arouse suspicion. We'll look for them in the morning." She steered me toward the cellar and lifted the wooden plank in the floor that led underground.

"What if the house catches fire?" I asked.

"We should be safe below." Riva went first. As deftly as possible, we climbed after her. It was dark and the only light came from two lamps which Riva and I held. I prayed they wouldn't go out. Yumiko-san descended last. She handed Viktor, who was asleep, to me, then replaced the lid over our heads so that no one would suspect we were down here.

Our stores had been greatly reduced of late but we wouldn't starve there, though we might freeze. We spread blankets on the ground and wrapped ourselves in our coats. Never had the fur lining felt so reassuring against my skin. Gunfire continued to explode above ground, blasting with more force from time to time before becoming muffled and fading into the distance.

"Finally...the Japanese have decided to take action!" Riva commented as we settled in for the night.

Part Three

16

I woke up, huddled against a barrel in a corner of our frigid cellar. The oak staves were rough and the metal hoops that bound them chilly against my cheek. Viktor was wrapped in a blanket on my lap and Misha nestled in the crook of my arm like a bear cub. I held them both close. Sacks of rice had become mattresses for Nessia, Yumiko-san and the girls. Riva was already awake, poking around, taking stock. Our inventory, meant to last all winter, had sharply dwindled during the past two weeks, having been used as fodder for our "guests."

Noticing I was up, Riva said, "We need to take as much as we can with us."

"With us?" I asked. "Where?"

"We can't stay here. Besides how cold it is, the Reds will soon be back and they may not be looking for us as servants anymore...."

I swallowed hard. "What do you suppose happened out there last night?"

"Clearly the Japanese attacked rather than folding to Triapitsin's ultimatum. But how much of a victory they garnered is anyone's guess. If the partisans are still in control..."

I gently extricated myself from Misha's sleeping body and joined her. She was stuffing strings of sausages and tins of fish into burlap bags and supplementing them with apples, pears, nuts and chocolate bars. "No rice or grain—nothing that needs preparation."

"What about these?" I indicated the shelf with the jars of pickled vegetables and preserves.

"Too heavy," Riva whispered.

It infuriated me that she was right. "Let's at least have some now, before we go," I said. I opened a jar of beets and drained the liquid into my mouth, wiping the purple water that dribbled down my chin with the back of my hand. When only the solid contents remained, I dove in with my fingers and pulled out the slippery chunks.

The house was eerily silent. The rest of the family awoke and I opened more containers. "Come, children. Eat," I urged, not wanting to mention that food might soon become a rarity. I wooed them with some peas and carrots, offering them the sweet juice to drink first. I poured the orange and green pieces into their cupped hands and offered little Viktor a few in my palm. He grabbed at them with his chubby fists. After a few bites, Misha and Veronika scurried over to the crate of chocolates and dug in, tentatively at first but with more gusto when nobody admonished them. They were bewildered and giddy.

"Have an apple with that," Nessia offered, handing each a rosy, red globe. The children bit into the crisp fruit, slurping the juice that squirted out as they devoured their picnic. Chocolate and apples were what they used to find on their pillows each night at bedtime, a treat that had ended with our current situation.

While the children were eating their fill, Riva held the ladder for Nessia who climbed up, carefully lifting the ceiling plank just enough to hear if anyone was around; then, a little more so that she could peek out.

"*Nu...?*" Riva asked. "What do you see?"

"The kitchen's deserted," Nessia reported. "It's very smoky."

"Maybe this is a good time to go. While nobody's around."

"Where are we going?" Katya wanted to know.

"Maybe we can stay with the Sharpovs," I suggested, thinking of Andrei and Iulia's house close by. Andrei had been arrested the first night; but we had no idea what our neighbors' circumstances were like now. Were they still free? Were partisans living in their homes, too?

"Or the Avshalumovs," Nessia added.

"Perhaps." Riva said. "But we need a better place than here."

Our pockets and satchels bulging, we crept out of the cellar. As soon as we'd gotten upstairs, I ran to a window and glanced across the courtyard. It looked like flames were spitting through the windows of Mama's house. Fire! I panicked. "I've got to see if they're alright," I said thinking only of the possibility that Mama might be trapped.

Riva tried to restrain me but finally relented when she saw that I was determined. "Be quick." She backed the others into the coatroom off the kitchen where everyone grabbed extra hats, boots, scarves and mittens.

As I approached the cottage, I could see that the Miller house next door had caught fire. The yard cottage had also been engulfed, but the flames were dying down. The door was ajar. A positive sign. "Mama...!" I called, getting as close as I could to peer inside. There was no way I could enter, but it didn't look like there was anyone in there. No screams or movement. Just licks of fire. I peeked around the house, thinking Mama and the children might be hiding elsewhere. I didn't see them anywhere. Blasts were going off in the distance. Other than a few stray soldiers, the fighting seemed to have moved to another part of town. The streets in the neighborhood were deserted—except for corpses. Bodies were strewn everywhere. The clean white snow was splotched with blood.

"Let's go this way." Riva said when I got back. She led us to the fence where she looked up and down the street, trying to decide where it would be safest to go.

"I think we should go to the Sharpovs. Or the Avshalumovs," I repeated.

"I see movement down that way. It's probably the Reds," Riva said. "Might be better if we try the Minkovs." Lyonya and Ludmilla Minkov lived across the street. Though we'd been neighbors for years, the doctor and his wife were more acquaintances than friends.

"Do you think we can trust them?"

"They're in the same position we are," Riva said as she moved in that direction.

"Not exactly," I pointed out. "The doctor hasn't been arrested, nor does it seem the Reds have moved into their house."

"Even better," said Riva.

"Maybe." I wasn't so sure. "Where do you think Mama is?" I asked.

"We'll worry about that later. Let's get to safety ourselves first."

As we traversed the road, I tried to shield the children from the sight of all the death and destruction. It was impossible. Suddenly, Misha gasped. I followed his gaze to a body in our yard and recognized Igor, lying on his side, a grimace on his now very blue lips, blue as his eyes used to be. I felt a pang of grim delight; then, caught myself. I prodded the boy past the figure. Meanwhile, from afar, shouts could be heard and the occasional click/whistle of a rifle. The sounds appeared to be coming from the direction of the jail. Nobody said anything but it was obvious we were all hoping for the same thing: that Ilya, Esther and the other prisoners had somehow managed to escape as we had.

We cautiously crossed the road and banged on our neighbors' door. Ludmilla Minkov was an ample woman whose largesse seemed to slow her down. She had a flat round face with a large mole above her lip. It was difficult to avoid staring at it. Ludmilla looked surprised, then disappointed, to see us. Still, she expressed relief that we were alright and reluctantly invited us in. As she poured tea, Ludmilla explained that her husband had been called away. "The partisans came knocking at the door several hours ago. They said they needed a doctor... for Triapitsin," she explained. "He's been shot."

"Oh, if only that skunk would die!" The words slipped out before I could stop myself.

"Shah..." Milla said, shooting a fierce glance at me. "If he dies, they will blame it on Lyonya."

Gathered around the samovar, we were lost in thought as our extremities began to thaw. The steaming liquid and currant cookies she offered were soothing. Almost like the old days.

Riva leaned forward and embraced Ludmilla. "Don't worry. Perhaps Lyonya will make good and it will help us all." I closed my eyes and prayed Riva was right. As we talked, we could hear horses outside. Milla rushed to the window.

"Lyonya's back!" she shouted. Her voice wavered and the nervous woman seemed jumpier than ever. "Thank God.... He's back....He's alive." She kept wiping her hands on her apron and peering carefully out the window, afraid to be seen, like a girl awaiting a suitor. Quickly, she scooted us into her pantry, hoping to keep us out of sight. We could barely move in there, but I could see a little through the slightly open door.

The doctor, a compact man, brisk with determination, swept in. "We will wait for you here," said one of the partisans guarding him from the doorway. Lyonya didn't seem bothered by their presence but Milla's relief reverted to fright.

"What's going on?"

"I need more supplies," he explained. He ran his hands through his mane of wavy white hair. "They've set up a hospital in the Town Hall and they want me to supervise."

"And Triapitsin...?" she asked.

"He was shot. In the leg. I've just been treating him. At gunpoint, I might add. But he's fine. Just laid up a bit. Still very much in command, I'm afraid."

"Let's go!" The partisans were getting impatient.

"I've got to get to the hospital," he continued, ignoring them. "There are so many casualties." Lyonya went to a cabinet against the far wall and rifled through an assortment of vials, placing most of them in his creased leather bag.

"Any news of the prisoners...?" Ludmilla inquired.

"It doesn't look good," he whispered, then kissed her. "Stay calm. And inside. I'll come back as soon as I can."

As the men left, we emerged, wondering what was going on at the prison and in the rest of town. I began to think about Mama again. "Do you think she survived? Where might she have escaped to?"

Riva took me by the shoulders and stared into my eyes. "We must concentrate on our own survival. That, in itself, is not going to be an easy task."

Lyonya Minkov returned mid-afternoon. He seemed surprised to see us. "You're okay?" he said. Weary from exhaustion, the doctor's steps were labored and he avoided our gazes. He shook his head as he fell into a seat at the table. No one could hold back. We descended on him with questions. Ludmilla busied herself at the samovar, preparing a hot cup of tea for him.

"Nothing good," he said. Shielding his face in his hands, he looked like he was trying to suppress his emotions. The enormity of the day was settling upon us all. "It's unspeakable..." he uttered. "Beyond description. No one's left." I'd been holding my breath, willing everything to be alright. I stared at him and at Riva. No one knew what to say.

The children were chattering in the next room with Yumiko-san and Nessia who were playing with them in an effort to distract them. Their insouciant voices reminded me of a life we might never again know. The glass covered clock on the mantel ticked on, its longer hand stiffly counting off each minute as it passed. At the quarter hour, the brass workings began to move and a cheerful melody broke the melancholy. But as the music ended, the silence seemed even heavier than before. Nessia appeared in the doorway. After one glance, she must have surmised the verdict. Seeking comfort, she wedged into our midst.

We were unable to take in all the information right away. As a doctor, Lyonya must have realized the magnitude of the grief we were experiencing. As a human, he must have sensed how hungry we were to hear the story—no matter how ghastly it might be. He looked from face to face as if gauging our capacity for horror, then simply spat out the grisly facts: "The cells in the prison were opened up and emptied. Everyone inside was killed."

"But—How—?"

"It seems the prisoners were marched down to the river where half of them were shot."

I felt as if I'd just been shot. Could Ilya really be dead? As the news sunk in, I thought I was suffocating.

"To save ammunition, the others were pushed into holes in the ice where they were bayoneted before they could climb out."

"What about the Japanese?" I asked.

"They, too, were overpowered and slain. If only they had thought to attack the prison first," the doctor continued, "they might have been able to free the prisoners. The extra manpower could have reinforced them." Lyonya shook his head in dismay.

"They couldn't have gotten everybody..." I was trying to make sense of this information.

"Perhaps five...seven...a dozen people survived," Lyonya conceded. "But the chances are not good."

"You never know..." I refused to give up. Ilya had to be one of them.

"*Lubachka*," he said gently, "a few people did survive. If you could call it that." I looked at him questioningly. "This morning, at the hospital, I had just finished removing a bullet from a partisan's arm when I heard voices. 'Here's another White scum who wasn't killed off!' someone said. 'Get him now!' another shouted, but the two soldiers carrying the body, shooed the third one off and laid the victim on the table before me. It was Andrei Sharpov."

"Andrei?" Iulia hadn't won Ilya's heart as I had, but her husband was still alive.

"The poor lad was unconscious. And practically frozen. He was covered with bayonet wounds—twenty-six lesions— all over his body." I winced. "Eventually, he came to and described to me what had taken place." We listened in rapt disbelief as Lyonya continued his sordid tale. Tears poured down our faces, but Lyonya didn't stop. "I fixed him up, as well as I could, wrapping him in layers and hoping that we wouldn't have to amputate his frostbitten limbs. I managed to sneak him out of the hospital as I left and I just dropped him off at his home."

"What about Mama? Any word of her whereabouts?"

"Thankfully not. I'm sure she's found somewhere to hide. Speaking of hiding, I think it would be safer for your family if you were to find a better refuge." Riva and I looked at him. "I just don't think it's safe for you to remain here," he continued. Behind him, Milla was nodding.

"What?" I said. "Why not? We can pay you. We have a little food."

"Luba, it is not that. The partisans that brought me here earlier may have seen you. The ones living in your house have returned. At the Lury house just now, tending to Triapitsin's leg, I overheard talk of the enemies they're looking for. Your names are at the top of the list they've drawn up. There's a reward for bringing you in. We just want you to be safe."

"But where can we go? We can't return to our house."

"No. You must remain out of sight," Lyonya cautioned. "But the partisans will come looking for you. Soon."

"There's nowhere that's safe," I cried.

"Perhaps you could stay with some of your relatives?" Milla interjected. But who knew what relatives remained alive?

We spent the rest of the day in the Minkov cellar. Our hosts had given us a kerosene lamp and a few coverlets. Riva was slumped in a heap, propped between the wall and a crate. Her head was in her hands, her eyes completely covered. What must have been going through her mind, having just heard that two of her children were gone, I wondered, as Viktor crawled over me and I looked at my older children sitting nearby with Nessia and Yumiko-san. What would I do if my babies had been brutally murdered by the bloodthirsty men who'd been living in our home? The very men whom we'd been waiting on daily. Thinking about Ilya and Esther, I remained numb. Unbelieving. In my depths, I was convinced they'd escaped by some miracle. But Riva's inner strength had completely dissolved. The woman who had weathered poverty and storms, who defied anyone who got in her way, was withering before my eyes.

I signaled Katya to go over to her granny. But the girl's presence did little to lift the old woman's spirits. Nessia looked despondent, having lost her brother and sister. And now seeing her mother in this state. What were we going to do? I realized again that it was up to me to take charge. First, we had to find a safer place to stay. Afterwards, I could try to find out more about the fates of Mama, Ilya and Esther. I wondered if any of them had come looking for us. We were directly across the street from our own home, yet unable to return and knowing our time was running out.

"I can't believe they want to send us away!" I exclaimed, channeling my fright into fury.

"Well, it isn't fair to put the Minkovs at such risk. After all, they have been generous enough to take us in—" Nessia defended them grudgingly, also with an eye on her mother, hoping she would add her two *kopeks* to the conversation. But Riva remained slumped in the corner.

"They're our neighbors...!" I said.

"Their lives are as much at stake as our own. If we were to be found in their house—" Nessia continued.

"Everybody's lives are at stake! If we don't stick together....That's what brought this whole situation on. Everybody afraid to stand up for one another, to defy the intruders!" My own defiance shocked me.

It caused Riva to look up for a moment. "Lubachka, calm yourself," she scolded.

"Mama, don't talk to me like that!" I snapped. "I am well aware of the situation. Our situation...theirs....everyone's! And we have to do something...."

"Shh," Nessia put her arm around me. "Mama didn't mean anything. We're all a little—"

"Never mind! I've as much to lose as anyone." I wrested myself from her grasp, then paused to catch my breath. I realized the children were watching. But perhaps this would wake Riva up.

"What about Judi Avshalumov?" I said, knowing that she and Riva were good friends. "She would take us in for sure."

"Perhaps," Riva consented weakly. "Ask Lyonya what he thinks."

"I fear she may have been arrested," Lyonya said when we told him our plan. "If not, her name is definitely on the list."

"Judi?" I was astounded.

"Her house has been taken over by partisans," Lyonya confirmed.

"The Shimkins," I said. "Eda would—"

"There's only Papa left now. And little Natasha."

"You mean...?"

Minkov nodded. "That's what I heard."

"No. This can't be." I was thinking of my friends Sammy and Eda. Nessia tried to comfort me again.

"Perhaps we could go to the Mersons?" Riva perked up slightly. The Mersons were business associates of Matvei and Ilya.

"Isidor's name is on the list along with yours," Minkov said. "He has somehow avoided arrest so far, but the whole family are fishery owners, *burzhui*...."

"What about Syoma and Tuula?" I suggested. "They're not wealthy enough to be..."

"That's an idea," Lyonya agreed after a moment.

"Syoma is your uncle..." Milla looked at me as she completed her husband's statement.

"Of course," I added drily. "And the partisans would never think of searching our relations, would they?" My sarcasm surprised everyone, including me.

"Perhaps their neighbors...?" Milla offered sheepishly.

But I realized that maybe Mama, Sophie and Tolya had sought refuge there.

I made the decision.

17

*W*e were to depart after nightfall and head for the Maremant house. Even though Tuula and Mama had an abrasive relationship, Mama was Syoma's sister. Certainly under these conditions, all grudges would have to be ignored. And where else could Mama be?

Before we left, Milla served us a hot meal. The children ate with gusto, but we adults had little taste for anything. Seeing that Riva and I were not participating, Lyonya pulled us aside. He glanced toward Yumiko-san. "Lubachka," he whispered, "you know that all Japanese are now even worse enemies than the Whites. Those still alive have been sentenced to death on sight. Anyone caught harboring one will be treated to a similar fate."

His words astonished me. He was probably right, but what were we to do? We couldn't leave Yumiko-san with the Minkovs and we weren't about to abandon her. I looked from him to Riva and back. Riva maintained her detached silence.

"I'm merely passing along what I've heard. These are not easy times...." His voice drifted off.

Then, he handed me a small pouch containing several vials. "Cyanide," he explained. "Just in case." For a moment, I didn't understand his intention; then I realized he meant it for us to commit suicide, if the time came that we wanted to avoid a worse fate.

I thanked the doctor for the information and the poison, which I stowed in the pocket of my coat, and our little caravan ventured out into the dark night. We walked so that Yumiko-san was concealed in our midst.

As we trudged through the snowy streets toward the less wealthy part of town, I no longer recognized our beautiful city. The thoroughfares had been somewhat cleared, but dead bodies were strewn on drifts and in gardens everywhere. Thankfully, it was dark, which made it more difficult to discern the details, but it was hard not to notice the ghoulish shapes. The houses we passed were shuttered. The icy air mingled with the smell of fires escaping from chimneys and masked the stench of death. It was invigorating, but my fingers were stiff and my cheeks tingled. The children complained of having to walk so far, and Riva was now an additional encumbrance. I hushed the little ones and prodded them along. Aware of their *babushka*'s condition, they didn't balk and fell into line like little soldiers.

"Riva! Luba!" Syoma's face registered relief as he opened the door and found us clumped on his doorstep. "I was afraid you were partisans here to arrest me," he laughed nervously. He ushered us in and fastened the bolt.

"Is Mama—?" I didn't need to finish my sentence because Mama was not in the tiny house which consisted of one central room that served as kitchen, dining and living room. Even the bed that Syoma and Tuula shared was shielded from the main room by the flimsiest curtain. The ceiling was low and darkly timbered. The floor was dirt, frosted with a layer of sawdust. It reminded me of Iosef and Oksana Dimchin's cottage in Mago. Why did my brother, Matvei, not help Syoma and Tuula out more, I wondered.

"Have you heard anything?" I asked. Syoma shook his head and frowned.

"Nothing. I've gone out to look for her. But....There is no sign," his voice faded. Yumiko-san, with Viktor in her arms, tried to be unobtrusive. Nessia settled Riva onto one of the four spindle chairs and Katya ushered her siblings toward the fire to warm themselves.

"Are you hungry?" Tuula turned to the pot on the stove just behind her. There was barely room to move. "We have a little kasha and..." She scraped together what she could find and prepared a meal. Nessia and I offered to help.

"We have some food," I offered.

"Keep it for now," Tuula said. "There's stew left over." She watered it down so there was enough for all. "We're almost out of water," she told Syoma as she dug deep into a barrel in the corner. "We need to fill it with more snow." He immediately got up from his seat.

"Misha, want to help me?" The boy nodded eagerly, happy for activity of any kind. "Let's get it from out back," Syoma said. "There's nobody there to see us."

"One thing about winter," Nessia commented, trying to be sociable, "there's never any shortage of snow for water." Tuula nodded.

Despite the lack of room, it was assumed that we would stay with the Maremants. With all the danger in the streets, everybody remained indoors. There was nowhere to move about and not much to eat. We started consuming some of the supplies we'd brought, but doled them out thriftily. Riva remained in her state of semi-consciousness. Nessia, Yumiko-san, Tuula and I busied ourselves taking care of the children, washing nappies and preparing meals, but Syoma seemed unmoored. He paced back and forth, continually pulling back the white cotton curtain and peering out the small window. I imagined he was unused to having so many people in his house—women and children in particular. The fact that the Maremants didn't have any of their own had always been a sore spot for Tuula and I imagined our presence grated on her.

A kind and patient man, Syoma moved slowly. He had met Tuula when she'd come to Nikolaevsk from her native Finland one summer to visit her brother who worked with Syoma in Matvei's lumber yard. Syoma seemed completely enamored of his wife, despite her reserved exterior. Certainly, he buffed her rough edges.

"I'm going to go in search of provisions," he said after a couple of days of confinement. "We're going to need more."

"I'll go with you," I announced.

"No, Lubachka. You stay here. I'll let you know what I find," he told me.

"I can't. I want to look for Mama. And Ilya. I won't accept

that everybody's gone. It's not possible. I need to see for myself."

He looked to Riva to help him out, but she said nothing. Tuula shrugged as if to say, "If that's what she wants..." I suspected she was happy to have a little more breathing room for a few hours.

No sooner had we come out of hiding, than grim reality rudely intruded. Without the cloak of night, the harshness of our new world could no longer be shrouded. Lying hand to foot or in heaps, face up, face down, oozing blood that stained the vast tableau of snow, bodies were scattered everywhere, along the streets and in yards, like discarded plates after a banquet. Wooden carts, driven by Chinese workers, rattled through the arteries of Nikolaevsk, clearing them away.

Syoma and I trailed the carts, curious as to their destination. Down the hill from the warehouses that lined the wharves, the vast frozen Amur resembled a field dotted with recently harvested haystacks. In the past, the mounds had represented Chinese gunboats frozen into the ice. There were too many now to be only boats. It took a moment to realize that many of the mounds were made up of bodies, not boats. The sanitation crews were discarding their loads, then returning to the city for more. I tried to take it all in. I glanced at the looming wooden structures on the riverbank where the stores from Ilya's and Matvei's businesses had once been held awaiting export, certain that the buildings must have been looted of any remaining goods weeks before.

"Perhaps we should go," Syoma suggested, pulling me back.

"No. I need to know," I insisted. We followed the path

down to the river. In front of us lay destruction. To the left stood the gunboats, like pawns on a chess board. On the right, nearer the prison, the surface was full of holes. I'd seen people using these to fish in the winter, but the circles I now saw had been crudely hacked into the ice and were clogged with corpses. I put my hand over my mouth but ventured closer. Syoma tugged at my arm. As I drew nearer, mountains of cadavers became more defined. Other people, appearing seemingly from nowhere, like swarms of mites, were also scouring the piles for their beloved ones.

The first mound contained mostly Japanese. Not only soldiers in uniform, but civilian men and women.

"Oh my God!"

"What?" Syoma turned and saw what had stopped me in my tracks. "Piotr Nikolaevich," I cried, recognizing the proprietor of Shimada's.

Syoma shook his head sadly. "Such a kind man, he was. And one of the few Japanese who tried to convince Major Ishikawa to stand up to the Reds."

The next stack was comprised of torsos that had been hacked to pieces. I recoiled as I spotted a headless corpse draped over the top.

The third mound was enormous. Perhaps three hundred remains. A guttural moan escaped from my depths as I recognized Old Man Kvasov, the town's beloved shoemaker, a look of fright frozen on his face. Some of the victims' hands had been tied behind their backs; their fronts were covered with stab wounds. I cried out as my gaze wandered over a young woman, naked, her stomach ripped open. Syoma pointed out the notary, Kozlov. His forehead had been pierced by a gunshot wound. A lucky one. Another victim's eyes had been poked out. I turned away and retched until my empty stomach brought all the bile up.

"Luba...come," Syoma gripped my arm. "This isn't right... it's—" I broke down in his embrace and let him lead me away. I didn't need any more proof. "You've got to get back home and stay put," he said and I quietly consented.

We turned into Syoma's street and several armed partisans blocked our path. "Halt," they said. "Where are you going?"

Syoma and I stammered, trying to figure out how to answer. The men were looking us over closely. I recognized one of them as Nelibuov's subordinate. He pointed at me and said, "You! Aren't you the widow of Ilya Kaptzan?" The widow? I knew Ilya was most likely gone, but I still couldn't accept the reality of it. Hearing the word caused my stomach to cramp.

"No!" I gasped, unable to accept my husband's fate. But my words were misconstrued by the men. Even Syoma thought I was denying my identity and decided to corroborate.

"She's my wife," he told the Reds.

"And I'm Triapitsin," he chortled. "Both of you, come. You're under arrest."

"For what—?" Syoma balked.

"You'll soon find out."

It had begun to snow. Wedged in between Syoma and Nelibuov's aide, I squeezed against my uncle, recoiling from any contact with the Red. A combination of garlic and whiskey washed over me as the man exhaled in my direction. His closeness brought to mind Igor's assault on me that day outside the prison. At the time, I hadn't thought things could get much worse. And then I'd seen Ilya. And then... Looking back over the past few months, I couldn't escape the sense that a frayed thread had broken loose, causing the sweater of my life to unravel leaving me completely exposed.

As our sled coursed through town, we passed the homes of people I'd grown up with and I wondered what had become of each of them. There was little sign of activity. No candles or lamps glowing in the windows. No shouts of children in the yards, or barking dogs or chattering goats. No scents of fresh bread or soups filling the air. We pulled up in front of my childhood home. The fire in the yardman's cottage seemed to have burnt itself out before reaching the main house which appeared unscarred. I hadn't been inside since before the Reds had entered town.

We were directed into the living room. I hardly recognized it. Yet it was as familiar as the alphabet to me. The straight-backed sofa upholstered in imported silk fabric from Japan no longer retained the delicacy of its embroidery. It was stained and a ragged tear exposed the cotton stuffing underneath. To make room for the stiff wooden benches we were told to sit upon, the comfortable armchairs had been pushed aside. Our beautiful carpet was splotched with mud. and the room smelled like a pigsty. The oil portraits of Mama and Papa that used to be proudly displayed over the mantel had been removed. In their place hung the new Bolshevik flag. The regal two headed eagle had been replaced by a plain yellow hammer and sickle over a bright red background. A woman I didn't recognize was bawling. I tried to keep my mind off everything that was happening, afraid that if I thought too much, I would get hysterical, too. Syoma must have sensed my agitation because he reached his arm around my shoulder and gave me a squeeze for support. I looked at him, thankful not to be alone, but guilty that he was there

because of me. Disconcerted voices sounded in the hall. The
soldiers were clearly annoyed at the racket. I heard a smack,
followed by silence. Other people were brought in and told
to wait with us. Many of them looked familiar; some I even
recognized. We nodded with our eyes but said nothing. Reds
moved about everywhere, completely at home in my parents'
house.

Finally, Syoma and I were summoned. We followed the
partisan who'd arrested us into the dining room. He whispered
something to Triapitsin and Lebedeva, but I was distracted by
a stooped couple who'd just been led from the room toward
the kitchen. "Spare us, please." I could hear them pleading. I
knew their voices. The Avshalumovs. I heard the door to the
yard bang shut and a moment later two shots punctuated the
air. I stood immobilized.

Behind our long table sat a row of eight men and two
women. Zhelezin, the baboon who had taken Ilya away, was
among them. I could see his moist pink lips parting the black
forest of his beard as he broke into a leer at the sight of me.
Dmitri Nelibuov was there, too. I hadn't seen him since the
night of the attack. I caught his gaze but his eyes flicked away.
In the center, next to Triapitsin, sat Lebedeva in Esther's usual
spot. She was wearing one of Esther's dresses and my sister-
in-law's pearls hung from her neck.

"You lied to our soldiers about your identity," Lebedeva
accused me, as Nelibuov's deputy left. "You claimed to be the
wife of this man and not your husband. What do you have to
say for yourself?"

I wanted to lash out at her, but I tempered myself and
spoke more humbly. "You don't understand. The man called
me a widow. He asked me if that is who I was. When I said

'No' it was out of disbelief that my husband is gone. The soldier was mistaken."

"And why did you not make yourself clear? Admit your mistake?" Zhelezin asked.

"I tried. They didn't let us."

"Isn't it true that this man pretended to be your husband?"

"He was just trying to protect me."

"Protecting Whites is a crime. Of the highest rank." Triapitsin declared.

"Luba Moiseyevna," Lebedeva's voice was shrill. All attention was turned on me. I tried to focus on what she was saying but I was distracted by the clatter of a cart stacked with corpses passing in front of the window. Suddenly, I heard Zhelezin telling me that the safe in Ilya's office had been broken into and emptied. He was accusing me of having removed all the family's belongings and demanded to know where the money and jewels were.

"How could it have been me?" I sputtered bravely, trying to figure out a way to convince these men to set me free. "We weren't allowed in there and we left in such a hurry, fearful for our lives. We never stopped to even think about—"

"Don't lie to us," Lebedeva threatened. She lifted one of Mama's delicate China tea cups to her lips and sipped from it, then replaced it on its saucer with such force I thought it would crack. The man seated to the left of Zhelezin, whom I'd never seen before, shifted uncomfortably, as if he believed me and was aware of the sham the Reds were concocting.

"I swear to you, on the life of my mother and my children, I didn't break into..."

"That's not worth much," Zhelezin laughed.

"Perhaps not to you," I retorted, emboldened by anger. "But—

"Bourgeois lies," another of our persecutors wheezed, scratching behind his ear. His fingernails were split and encrusted with dirt.

I stared directly at Nelibuov, trying to hold his gaze. I noted that Triapitsin wasn't joining in. In fact, he was looking at me with a strange intensity. I was grappling with how to respond.

"Wait," I stammered. "Didn't you say the safe was broken into?" There was a brief moment of silence. "Well," I continued daringly, "if we'd wanted to empty our safe, don't you think we'd have just used our key?"

"Perhaps you lost it," snickered Zhelezin. Several others nodded and grunted in agreement.

Nelibuov continued to sit in silence.

"Do you think I have the ability to break open an iron safe? How would I do it? And wouldn't it cause a great deal of commotion?" I tried to engage the sympathetic man next to Zhelezin. "Do you think the soldiers would sit by and—"

This seemed to make sense to him and one or two others on the panel. I grew bolder. "Wouldn't it seem more likely that your own soldiers broke in and stole the jewelry themselves?" I looked directly at Nelibuov who twitched as if he were crawling with lice.

Furious that I was being allowed to speak at all, Zhelezin tried to shut me up. "No matter who did it," he replied, "...it was your jewelry and you must pay for it."

"Enough. Silence." It was Triapitsin.

"Please," I mumbled, exhausted from my outburst, "We are good people." I peered directly into his piercing eyes, marveling again that someone so handsome could be so heartless. "My family built this town...my husband, Ilya Semyonovich...my brother..."

"Never mind."

"You're all filthy skunks who took advantage of—" Lebedeva was now at the helm. She puffed out her chest revealing an emerald pin underneath the pearls. It was the one my father had given my mother on the occasion of Nikolai's bar mitzvah. It was one of her favorites.

"Ninotchka, enough." Was Triapitsin really standing up to her?

I closed my eyes, awaiting the worst, realizing there was no reward for goodness, no compassion in this arena of ferocious, blood-thirsty wolves. But I had to go on. "Please, your Honors..." I addressed the entire panel, trying to be deferential. I made eye contact with each individual as I scanned their stony gazes. "Have mercy on us. I have four small children, an elderly mother, a sick sister. You've already taken my husband, a good and honest man. He put himself on the line and even saved the lives of some of *your* men." Again, I glanced at Nelibuov.

"That's enough." Lebedeva commanded. Triapitsin leaned over and whispered into her ear.

I saw Nelibuov's eyes darting around, clearly uncomfortable. Finally, he spoke. "If we kill her now," he addressed the table tentatively, "we are never going to see those jewels. What if we give her twenty-four hours to bring them back to us?" He looked at his fellow judges. "Where can she run? If she doesn't produce the jewels, then we can kill her," he murmured.

There was a tense silence. I held my breath.

The man next to Zhelezin nodded. "This is true," he said.

"She is the widow of Ilya Kaptzan," Nelibuov continued.

Zhelezin looked as if he wanted to lunge at both these men. "Of course she's his widow. That's why she must be expunged."

The word again stung me to the core. The reality was beginning to sink in. That Ilya had been killed.

"Her husband saved my life. He stood up for me against the whole city. Let us at least give her a chance to repay us." Nelibuov was growing more confident.

Triapitsin stared at him, then consulted with Lebedeva. Finally, he spoke. "Very well," he addressed me. "If the commissar will vouch for your honesty, we will give you twenty-four hours to find and bring back the jewels which were in your safe. If you can do that, you will be set free. If not, not only you but your entire family..." He looked pointedly at Syoma, "will pay for your crime. Along with you, Nelibuov." He motioned for some soldiers to show us out.

Once released, Syoma and I clung to one another as we hurried back to his house. No sled transporting us now. But we were glad to be on our own. The snow was coming down heavily and not only was it difficult to walk through the drifts, but it was also a challenge to find our way. I let Syoma lead me.

"What are we going to do," I bawled. I half hoped we would get lost in the profusion of flakes. "Where can we go?" The wet snow mingled with my salty tears. I imagined sinking into the snow and disappearing forever.

"We can give them what's left of our jewelry," Nessia

suggested when we got back to the Maremant house and told everyone our predicament. "Or just some of it..."

"But there's no guarantee they won't kill us anyway," I said. "And if we're to hang on until the Spring, we will need every piece." I looked around the room, evaluating possible options. Finally, I said, "I think it's best if we leave."

"What's going to happen to *us*?" Tuula turned to her husband. "They'll surely come looking for you here and if you're not—"

"Shah..." Syoma quieted his wife.

I looked away. "It's my fault," I cried.

"No," Syoma reassured me. "But you must go somewhere safer. We will take care of ourselves."

We all looked at one another, knowing nowhere was safe.

"What about Raissa?" Syoma suggested to Riva. Riva's daughter and her husband lived outside of Kerbi, forty *versts* away where they owned and ran a gold mine. "Or Ilya's brother, Pavel?" Pavel spent the winters with his mistress, a peasant woman who lived outside of Mago. But how could we get there? And who knew what we would find?

Then a thought occurred to me. "Cook-san. We can go to him," I whispered to Riva.

For once, the older woman perked up.

"We'll be much safer buried in Chinatown, away from here," I went on. "And maybe he'll know how to find Ivan." I knew Ivan would help us if he could.

Riva nodded, starting to come back to her old self. "Yes," she said. "And there's no time to waste."

We decided to leave the following morning, before dawn. As we prepared, I looked at my children in their shearling coats. "We're never going to pass for peasants dressed like this," I said. It was a wonder we'd made it to the Maremants. But it had been dark. I didn't want to take any more chances.

"Do you have any spare rags, Tuula?" Syoma asked. Tuula pulled out a basket with soiled shreds of cloth. We began to tie them around the children's heads.

"It's too cold to leave our coats behind," I continued, trying to figure out how we could camouflage the outerwear so it would look more bedraggled. The adults' coats were of dark wool.

"We can soil them with some dirt so they look less ostentatious," Syoma suggested. "Misha, let's go into the yard and..."

Great idea, I nodded. Veronika went with them. "We should probably remove our fur collars, too," I said.

Tuula produced a pair of heavy scissors and we set to work. Moments later, Syoma and the children returned with a bucket of snow and dirt. "Help me spread this mud, will you?" he winked at his helpers and they dug into the slushy mess with a purpose.

"As for the children's coats...maybe it will be better if we turn them inside out," I said.

"Yes," said Riva. "Good idea." I couldn't believe that she was re-engaging. And no longer challenging every word I uttered. We inverted the shearling coats so that the wooly linings were on the outside, but in doing so, we came upon several brooches that had been concealed there. "We better remove these," she chuckled, "...and hide them somewhere better." She started to unclasp the jewelry from the fur and pin them on the reverse side. Nessia, Yumiko-san and I helped her. Handling each item, the occasion on which it had been bestowed on me—Christmas, birthday or anniversary— flashed through my mind. Silently rebuking myself for my sentimentality, I took several of the articles and placed them in Syoma's palm along with the fur collars. "Please use these," I whispered as I hugged him tightly.

18

We looked like a couple of shepherdesses with a flock of dirty lambs as we herded the children along. The streets were mostly deserted at this pre-dawn hour, but we walked quickly, keeping our heads down. We broke into groups, but stayed within sight of one another, ducking into alleys, when necessary. Riva and Katya led the way followed by Nessia with Misha and Veronika. Yumiko-san had Viktor on her back and I came last. It was starting to get light so we kept to the back streets as we headed toward Chinatown. The depth of the drifts hindered our progress. The overcast day boded more snow and the wind slapped our cheeks.

At every turn we confronted death. Bodies were heaped at the seams where buildings met pavement and, though obscured by snow, their outlines were detectable. Occasionally, we would hear moans from underneath the thick wet blanket

as we passed. I attuned my ears in case I might recognize
the voice of somebody close to me: Ilya, Esther, Mama. It
wasn't likely and we didn't have time to stop. I tried to ignore
them and walk faster. The children didn't ask questions. After
a while, we switched places. I took Viktor from Yumiko-san
and Veronika straggled back to hold my hand.

Suddenly, the door of a rickety building swung open. A
group of partisans reeled into the street and I got a glimpse
inside. In the dimly lit space, I could make out women,
heavily rouged and wearing flimsy robes. A whiff of strong
perfume sauntered our way. The men pouring out reeked of
whiskey and we tried to take advantage of their condition
by dispersing quickly. In our haste to disappear, Veronika
tripped. Yumiko-san ran to help her. As she turned back to
me with the girl in her arms, one of the Reds caught sight
of her.

"What's this?" He grabbed her by the collar and looked
into her face. "A Japanese traitor? Still alive?" He pulled out
his revolver and twirled it menacingly on his finger.

I handed Viktor to Nessia and rushed forward. Riva tried
to signal me to stay back, but I ignored her. Seeing me, the soldier turned on me, "It's against the law to harbor any Japanese.
Are you not aware of this?" he asked. Riva gathered the other
children and slipped quietly away as I confronted the soldier.

"She's Chinese," I lied.

"Is that right?"

"Yes. And she is part of our family," I told him. "She
hasn't harmed anyone. I swear it on my life." Veronika looked
from me to her *amah* to the soldiers.

"Well then, you can die along with her, if you wish."

Before I could do or say anything, the Red pulled

Yumiko-san away and shot her, point blank, in the temple. Veronika screamed. I stood, speechless. The partisans assailed the inert body, her blood seeping into the snow as they scavenged for anything valuable on her. I grabbed Veronika and ran around the corner. The girl was hysterical. I clasped her tightly and we flattened ourselves in an archway, waiting for the soldiers to disband. Would they come looking for us next? "Please, please. Don't let them hear you," I whispered as Veronika continued to sob. I didn't know how to quiet her. Some more Reds came down the road. Curious, they joined the culprits who were crowing over their prize. Veronika and I managed to slink quietly away.

By the time I felt it was safe to come back in the open, I'd lost sight of Riva and the others. It was no longer dark and too dangerous to call out their names. So, I re-oriented myself and continued searching for Cook-san's home on my own.

"What about Granny?" Veronika asked.

"Your *babushka* will find us at Cook-san's," I promised, hoping we wouldn't be disappointed. My mother-in-law was more familiar with Chinatown than I was. I'd only driven by the edges of the district in our coach or sleigh.

The streets were narrow and the ramshackle, wooden buildings were stacked one on top of another like presents on Christmas morning. There were signs in windows and on gate-posts, all written vertically in large, black Chinese characters. I had no idea what they said nor where Veronika and I were headed. But being in that interior district, I felt safe enough to ask for directions.

"I'm hungry," Veronika said. We'd had nothing to eat since we'd left Tuula and Syoma's several hours earlier. I reached into my pocket and came up with an apple. "Here,"

I said. "Have this. Granny and Nessia have the satchels with the rest of the food."

A woman came out of her house with a pail of refuse. "Wu Sun Yee," I said to her. The smell was so powerful, I gagged. She looked at me blankly, set the pail by her fence, then went back inside. Did she not understand what I was saying? Or was she too frightened to be seen conversing with a stranger? Finally, a stooped, old man pushing a wheelbarrow filled with branches and twigs came to our aid. "Wu Sun Yee," I repeated with desperation. He shakily nodded his head and indicated for us to follow him. He pointed at a house at the end of the lane. I thanked him and we parted ways.

As I was about to rap on the door, Veronika and I heard voices. I pulled my daughter into my coat and we crouched behind some discarded wooden crates in the street. Had we been tracked? Was this the end? The lilt of Katya's voice drifted over the others and a mewl escaped my throat as Veronika and I tiptoed out of our hiding place. "Thank God!" I sighed.

"Mama! Mama!" My children's voices were a soothing fugue.

I knocked on the door softly. Consolation spread through me when Cook-san himself answered. Seeing our family, he ran out to greet us. He smiled and bowed, so pleased that we had landed on his doorstep, then ushered us all inside.

One look around and I knew we'd made a mistake. The flimsy cabin which he shared with his wife and children was dark and crowded. There was a small window that let in a little light and an unlit kerosene lamp sat in the center of the rough hewn pine table around which Cook-san's family was arranged. It emitted scant light. The table took up most of the room. Seated on benches on both sides, his children were

eating their midday meal out of wooden bowls with chopsticks. They were dressed in rags and I wondered how they
didn't freeze or get sick. There was barely enough room for
them in the house, let alone for us newcomers.

I recognized Cook-san's wife and daughter who came
once a week to do our laundry. Or used to. I nodded at the
rest of the family whom I'd never met, including a toothless,
wizened woman who must have been Cook-san's mother or
mother-in-law. His wife prompted her children to get up and
give us their seats. She ladled some water from a bucket in the
corner into an iron kettle sitting on a small hibachi. While it
warmed, she shyly offered whatever was left of their meager
dinner, embarrassed that it was mostly rice. I told Cook-san
we'd already eaten and that he should tell his family to finish
their meal. But he could see the hunger in the children's stares
and insisted we join them. He found several more bowls and
scooped a small amount of rice into each, stretching the meal
as best he could. He lay a stray vegetable, which he fished
from a pot on the stove, atop the rice. My children voraciously
accepted the bowls and used their fingers to shovel the food
into their mouths. I watched, with a mixture of pity and relief,
as the little ones gobbled down the modest offering. The kettle
began to steam and Cook-san's wife doused some dry green
tea leaves and branches in the ceramic pot. I wondered if we
should offer the food we had with us, but I didn't want to
lessen Cook-san's generosity. Finding some simple cups on a
shelf, she poured us each a serving.

After we'd warmed up, Cook-san spoke. "*Gospozha*
Kaptzan," he bowed. "You must stay here."

"No, Cook-san," I said. "There's no room."

"There room," he insisted. He took me back outside and

pointed to a dilapidated structure in his yard. It wasn't as large as the gardening shed we had on our property and it was crumbling under the weight of snow on its roof. "My family, we stay there."

"No, no, Cook-san, you cannot do that," I told him. "This is your house." I couldn't figure out where anyone slept in there. Did they put mats down on the table and benches?

"My house you house," he insisted.

"But where will you sleep? How will you stay warm out there?"

"Never mind. We Chinese. We manage. But you must to stay here." He would not take no for an answer. His wife gathered the children, lit a second lantern and set out.

"No, Cook-san," I called. "You must stay here with your family. We will stay in yard house."

"No, *Gospozha*..."

"Yes. It will be better for everyone. More safe," I explained. "If soldiers come to look for us, they will find you and we will have a little warning. You understand?"

He thought it over and nodded tentatively. "Ah-so. Yes. May-be..." He called his wife and children back into the house. But he gathered a few of their futons and blankets in his arms and then led us outside. He bid us enter the low wooden shack. I felt like a giant. Cook-san cleared a corner of his tools—a shovel, hoe and some pails—and threw some old cloths down along with the futons and blankets to make a semblance of proper bedding. There was hardly any room, but we were growing accustomed to tiny spaces.

Cook-san apologized profusely for the lack of comfort and suggested bringing more blankets from the house.

"No. You need for yourself," I told him though it was

freezing in the wooden building and the wind whistled through the cracks.

He placed two pails by the door, not needing to explain their use. "Leave outside when full," he told us. "Now I bring hot tea," he suggested.

We nestled on the makeshift bunk and clustered together under the blankets, squeezing against one another for warmth. Viktor began to cry. The older children couldn't stop talking about their beloved *amah*. Would they ever see Yumiko-san again? This made me think of Mama. Don't, I told myself. When Cook-san returned, I showed him the food we'd managed to salvage. "We will share this with you and your family," I said.

"No, no. You must keep this. I find food for now. Winter last long time." I understood that he was referring to what surely lay ahead.

The rest of the day passed slowly, but after our long trek and the nightmare of Yumiko-san's murder, everyone was spent. I pulled my children close and put my baby to my breast. With all my anxiety, my milk was drying up. Viktor fussed in frustration, but perhaps the mere closeness of my body comforted him because he managed to fall asleep. Soon, the others did, too. Except for the wind and the sound of my children breathing, the barn was quiet. I closed my eyes and tried to imagine how I would keep us all safe.

The squawking of a rooster in the yard woke me. The others continued to sleep and, through a tiny round window above us, I could see that it was snowing again. The wind beat against the flimsy walls causing me to shiver. I could also hear pigeons cooing, though I couldn't detect where they might be.

Cook-san entered with a steaming pot of congee. He was covered with a dusting of snow and the vapor caused the contents to resemble a witch's brew. The little man ladled the soupy cereal into several small bowls as the others began to awaken. The mixture would warm us and fill our bellies.

I stared at Cook-san and then at our surroundings. It was a far cry from our family kitchen and dining room, but just having this dear man nearby alleviated some of my tension. It was better than living at home under the same roof as the partisans, never knowing when we might be assaulted or what might befall us.

Cook-san had worked for Ilya's and then our family for years. His smiling face with the silver tooth in front and the gap on the side never failed to make me feel cared for. And dear Yumiko-san. She had been part of our family, beloved by us all. I couldn't erase the image of her ashen face and limp body lying on the ground being pawed at by those drunken Reds.

19

*W*e'd been in Chinatown for over two weeks, remaining out of sight in Cook-san's shed. It was early April, but no one was thinking of the upcoming Easter or Passover celebrations. The Bolsheviks had renounced religion, wanting no part of God. Just as well because how would they ever explain themselves to a Higher Being? I thought about our family's annual celebration and couldn't believe that just one year before, we'd all been gathered at Matvei's laughing and eating. All the men swearing we were not in any danger. Having to deal with Riva had been one of my biggest irritations. And here I was wishing she'd be more like her contrary old self.

The recent events had clearly taken their toll. Though she was sixty, Riva had never been frail or retiring like most women her age. Now she'd begun to stoop under the weight of her sadness. I'd catch her staring blankly into space, no doubt trying to make sense of our situation. For the first time, my heart went out to her. I wanted to reassure her. Did it have to take Ilya's death to bring us together?

After another snowfall, we were visited by an unexpected warm spell which was a tremendous relief. The skies cleared and no more crystals fell. The wind ebbed and during the short hours of sun, when nobody was around, I let the children sneak outside to absorb a little of the warmth behind Cook-san's shack. Riva didn't stop me. Her abrasiveness was diminishing as well. The children peered longingly through the splintered fence, eyeing local youngsters playing in the street. From the brief snapshots of life which we glimpsed, it was as if we had moved to another land. The language was different. The people looked different.

Cook-san was generous with the little food he had, offering the best available to us and subsisting on plain rice himself. We meted out what we'd managed to take from the cellar. I insisted we all partake of it. "Cook-san, please..." I said. "I will not take the food from the mouths of your family."

"Is okee. We used to eat little food. You, not so much."

"You are very generous. But we all must share," I insisted.

"Your family save my life," he told us. "Give me good job. Help my children. I do anything for you."

And he did. Everyday, he would search for news and try to scrounge up more food. We'd asked him to look for Ivan in town, but his queries had turned up nothing. I hoped Ivan hadn't been held responsible for our disappearance because he was associated with us. The Reds would stop at nothing. I doled out pieces of our remaining jewelry for Cook-san to barter with, each parting a piece of my old life chipped away. At the same time, I was so grateful that it was saving our lives. I only hoped the items wouldn't be recognized. If anybody wondered where Cook-san had gotten them, he might be followed home and then we'd be found out. Even worse, Cook-san might be branded a thief and executed. But he was shrewd. He wouldn't let anything fall into the wrong hands.

Being cooped in such cramped environs was difficult in and of itself. I blamed the children's constant fidgeting on their youth. To pass the time and keep our minds off our fears as we sat hunched in Cook-san's backyard, Riva, Nessia and I helped Cook-san and his wife with any mending they needed. We sewed the children dolls out of some rags. And we told stories—fairy tales as well as our family history. Listening or relating personal anecdotes about those members of our clan whom we had no idea we'd ever see again was difficult for me. But the children couldn't get enough of them. Over and over, they would ask for details about their father, grandmother, Auntie Esther and Uncle Kolya. They also devised possible scenarios of how and where we might meet them again.

When we discovered that Misha and Veronika had lice, we helped Cook-san's wife wash our clothes and bedding in vats in the yard. Cook-san brought us oils mixed with petrol to apply to our heads, to kill the infestation and prevent it from spreading. It smelled horrible and the tiny pests continued to haunt us. While we were fretting over that, toward the end of our third week, Cook-san came running into the shed, his face pinched with worry. He had just passed a group of partisans making their way through Chinatown, pounding on doors and demanding entry. "I no think here safe for you now."

My heart fell. Would we never be secure? Would we bring danger to everyone who sheltered us? Hesitantly, Cook-san told us he had an idea. A few streets away, in the basement of an old storefront, was an opium den. It would be safer for our family there. Cook-san knew the owner.

"An opium den?" I gasped.

"What choice do we have?" Nessia said nervously. Riva merely shrugged. I looked at my children and decided that if this man would agree to take us in, we probably should go.

"I be very quick," Cook-san told us. "I hope nobody come before I return."

"I can be the lookout," Misha said. "I'll hide just outside and—"

"No!" I shouted.

"Maybe good idea. Just in case," Cook-san suggested. "Misha hide behind big barrel of water outside and listen in case somebody come this way."

"Yes! Please. Let me help," the boy pleaded. I didn't know how to respond. How could I put my son in danger's way? I looked at Riva, but her mind was elsewhere.

At last, I relented. "But you must be very quiet and still. And don't let anyone see you."

"I won't. I promise!" His serious face broke into a happy grin.

"If somebody come," Cook-san whispered before he left, "climb over fence in back and wait for me on other side." Eager for the adventure, Misha followed Cook-san outdoors. Veronika was disappointed she wasn't allowed to go, too. And I could tell Katya resented the attention her brother was receiving. The rest of us held our breath and prayed that the Bolsheviks wouldn't arrive while we were still there. At least we had an escape plan.

During the afternoon, while we awaited Cook-san's return,

Nessia began to moan and writhe, seized by one of her fits. Up until then, I had marveled that she'd been alright. She started to gag and gasp and groan and the children stared at me, wide-eyed with fright. "Mama!" I shouted. "It's Nessia. Help!" I shook Riva until she took notice. She glanced over at her flailing daughter.

Suddenly she woke from her haze. "Quick!" she instructed. "Hand me that blanket. A rag. Something!" While I shuffled through our bedding for something to give her, Riva squatted over her daughter's torso and held Nessia's arms down over her head. "Take her arms," Riva snapped at me as she grabbed the cloth I produced from my grasp and stuffed it into her daughter's gaping mouth. "Bite, Nessyinka," she said. "Bite down on this. Hard." Nessia's eyes were rolling back in her head and she looked as if she were possessed. Viktor started to cry. Katya and Veronika tried to soothe him. Misha ran in.

"What's going on?" he asked. The stupefied look on his face expressed his fear.

Slowly, the episode abated and Nessia began to relax and return to normal. Misha went back to his post, looking relieved to absent himself from the situation. Viktor quieted down as Nessia sat up and Riva removed the cloth gag. "Everything's alright, children," Riva cooed. "You see?" She nodded at Nessia whose wan complexion was paler than usual. Riva hugged her daughter and as Nessia smiled apologetically, a nervous laugh escaped me.

Later that night, when the streets were empty, Cook-san led us through a web of alleys to a shanty at the end of a murky lane. Chinese characters painted on the dusty windows were chipping. A bell tinkled as the door creaked open. Mr. Wong, the proprietor, appeared from behind a beaded curtain in the back, carrying a candle. The beads clicked softly as they swung back and forth. A small man with a rotund belly, Wong was dressed in a shabby embroidered jacket over wide cotton pants. A shiny black skull cap covered his bald head. A long skinny braid hung down his back like a rat's tail. He waddled forth and bowed politely in greeting. The men exchanged a torrent of Chinese words, punctuated with glances and nods. Mr. Wong and Cook-san ushered us toward a rickety spiral stairway at the back. "Mustn't make noise," Cook-san warned.

A smoky perfume pervaded the air. The thick, sickly sweet odor was mixed with the stench of body odor and the bad breath of the occupants, reminiscent of an outhouse. But who were we to complain? At least it was warmer than Cook-san's shed. The lighting was dim and it was hard to see into the numerous areas that we passed. They were sectioned off by screens, some paper, others wooden with inlays. As our eyes adjusted, more details emerged. Though the screens may once have been ornate and lovely, they were now shabby and dilapidated, the rice paper torn and wooden sections hanging limply like broken sparrows' wings. Where once the decoration had been of ivory and jade, the precious stones had long fallen out or been removed, no doubt stolen to pay for more drugs.

Inside the various compartments were wooden platforms. Patrons lay on them while they inhaled their narcotic elixirs. The surfaces looked hard and were covered with sheets or shawls, filthy from use by numerous patrons who did everything from drool to vomit on them. We passed several old men in various states of intoxication as Wong led us through the warren. The clientele in this establishment were all Chinese and the faces I was able to discern in the darkness looked dazed. Some of the men wore dark spectacles.

"Why do they wear those little round glasses?" Veronika asked. Riva explained to the curious children that it kept the light from hurting their sensitive eyes.

"They remind me of Baba Anya," Misha said. I didn't know whether to laugh or cry at the thought. Though Cook-san had made it his mission to squirrel for information, we'd still had no word about Mama's whereabouts. At least there hadn't been any more bad news.

One man we passed was writhing on his platform and moaning, from pleasure it seemed. I hurried the children forward. Another lay, passed out, and resembled the corpses that littered the streets, his arms hanging limply over the sides of his "bed." A third man, in a stained satin jacket, was sitting up and smiling a funny smile. He looked like a sinister sorcerer. Fortunately, none of the men seemed to register our presence.

I was a bit unsteady on my feet, feeling as if I might faint. Was I really bringing my children into such a sordid environment? Misha and Veronika stared open-mouthed at all we passed. I glanced at Nessia. If she were to have another seizure, she would certainly give us away. Worried as I was about Mama, I was thankful she wasn't with us. I couldn't picture her in a place like this, nor Tolya who was growing more nervous and worrisome by the day. Where and how were they? I tensed at the thought of their fates. Viktor was my other major concern, for his cries could attract unwanted attention. And if I were unable to feed him, he'd yell even louder. I bounced him in my arms to appease him.

Finally, Wong showed us to a corner cubicle at the end of the hall. He arranged several screens to conceal our presence and also to provide us with a degree of privacy. After he and Cook-san left, we settled in for the night. Someone needed to remain alert at all times and I elected to stay awake because my thoughts were churning and I doubted I'd be able to sleep. Riva put up a bit of resistance, but before long, she and the children had fallen into a stupor. In fact, I had to nudge Riva to quiet her snores. How I envied her ability to abandon herself to such deep slumber. My mother-in-law seemed to have gained a little color. Oddly, I was beginning to miss the feisty and robust woman who used to repel me. I could no longer look to my former nemesis for strength and consolation. She'd shown a glimmer of her old self during Nessia's recent fit, but then retracted under her cloak of melancholia. I worried that she was becoming as much a burden as Nessia and the little ones.

While guarding my entourage, I took stock of our circumstances. I was still in shock over Ilya's demise. He was dead. I had been told of it. But the reality of that loss was still floating on the surface of my consciousness much as oil floats on water. I couldn't absorb its finality. I'd fought away the pictures that haunted my mind, images of him in prison, being interrogated, beaten. Had he been allowed to keep my coat? To eat the food I'd left with him? How badly had he suffered? But nothing could compare to the realization that he was actually gone. That I was unable to touch him one last time. To kiss him good-bye. I couldn't bear the pain.

Esther. My dear friend and confidant. I couldn't imagine anyone ever filling the gaping hole she was leaving in my life. I prayed she and Ilya had been together and consoled myself that at least now their misery was over.

Yumiko-san, so good and blameless, had been like a fairy

godmother. She'd stood by me, always helping, never judging, asking only for love from the children, which she received in abundance. There was no doubt she was a second mother to them. To have her life end so brutally—it was too much to fathom.

And what about Mama? Would I ever see her again? I swore to myself I would never complain about her constant nagging if only she would survive this winter. And this time I meant to stick to my promise.

During the days and hours we hid in the den, I struggled with the knowledge that the fate of our family was up to me. I thought of both Ilya and Esther's strength. I would aspire to emulate them. Yet my own despondency was so great that sometimes I just wanted to pick up one of those pipes myself and enter a world of oblivion. If it hadn't been for the children, I probably would have.

The youngsters beckoned for attention, food, answers. The older ones seemed to innately understand the need to be quiet. Viktor was still too young to comprehend the danger. He required constant mollification. Whenever he started to whimper, I'd unbutton my blouse. Together, he and I would lapse into a relaxed lethargy and, for a brief span, I was able to shut out the world. But Viktor was less and less pacified by my breast, which no longer produced much sustenance. He was growing quickly and wanted to be in constant motion. He didn't understand the need to be quiet or still.

Ilya had always been the central focus of my attention. I'd been happy to relegate the children's care to Yumiko-san and Riva. Now that Yumiko-san was gone and the children were all I had left, my primary reminder of all I'd shared with Ilya, my attitude toward them altered dramatically. I became aware not only of their love for me, but of their need. I was astonished by their mature behaviour and their lack of anger at our plight. But what did their lives hold for them? If we were to survive this ordeal, how would the experience affect their psyches? Would they grow up to lead normal lives? Would they grow up at all?

These thoughts meandered into questions about what all of our futures would be like if we lived through this. Where would we move to? And how? We had almost no jewelry left. No money. I had no talents or abilities with which to earn a living. Could I be a teacher? A seamstress? I was a capable woman. There must be some trade I could learn. All I knew was that watching my children and needing to keep them safe imbued me with a strength I never knew I had.

Time passed in an amorphous fog. There was no day or night, nothing to do, nowhere to go and barely anything to eat. Every few days, Cook-san would appear, toting bread and sometimes rice with vegetables or a couple of hard-boiled eggs or yams. The lice still lingered and we continued to itch and scratch. Cook-san brought us a few ill-fitting garments to change into so that he could take away our dirty clothes and launder them. We were unable to bathe, but it did give us a lift. The clean items smelled of fresh air, a reminder of the outside world. I wondered where he'd rummaged about to find the spare articles. He always had been amazingly resourceful.

We remained in our refuge for several weeks. We were told it was late April already but with no windows it was hard to tell. Our life passed in a haze of opium. We were lulled into numbness by the drugs, the darkness and the singsong lilt of Chinese around us. The patrons were also in a daze and, luckily, nobody heeded our existence. I was horrified to have my little ones in such an atmosphere, inhaling drug-infused air and privy to the sounds of sexual exploits that were occurring just out of view. And the filth and squalor...! Between the sights and smells, it was hard not to want to vomit. Katya had caught a cold that was turning into a hacking cough. Each time she broke out in a fit, I froze, wondering if she would give us away. She would try to suppress it, often turning bright red in the process. I prayed the rest of the children and Riva wouldn't catch it.

I refused to let the children out of my sight. Noises emanated from behind other partitions and the youngsters were curious to look around. I explained that spies were lurking everywhere and one never knew who or where they might be.

I'd grown accustomed to the spooky silences, the muttering patrons and the occasional angry chattering of Chinese that broke out when someone was disturbed or asked to pay for his pleasure. It had become as natural as the aroma and the filth. Up to that point, I'd felt relatively safe being surrounded by only Chinese. Then, one day I heard male voices speaking Russian down the hall. I stiffened, suspecting the men were Reds looking for us. One glance at my shocked face and the children knew not to say a word.

When Cook-san arrived later to check on us and bring food and water, I told him what we'd heard. He returned after consulting with Mr. Wong. The men were indeed partisan soldiers, he confirmed; but they were only there for their own pleasure and for the relief that opium would offer their damaged psyches. And Mr. Wong was trying to keep them as far from our cubicle as possible. I was slightly relieved that they weren't on our tail, but petrified that they might stumble on us by chance. Or that Mr. Wong might turn us in for a bribe. Our store of valuables was ever diminishing and I didn't know how much more I could spare to keep him quiet. In the days that followed, each time we heard our native tongue spoken through the screens, we'd stare at one another and hold our breath. It did seem that the men were only seeking asylum in the oblivion the drugs provided. I heard them crying out in anguish over the atrocities that they'd been committing daily.

"God forgive me! I beg you!" one cried. "I swear I was only following orders."

"Give me that pipe," said another, "so I can blot out the memories of my actions!"

Nothing like the drama of a tormented Russian soul. Escalated by the potency of local vodka and drugs. I recalled similar liquor-induced dramas, even in happier times. When I'd been little, I'd laugh as my inebriated father had recited Pushkin, shedding tears that left tracks on his cheeks as they settled in the hedge of his mustache and beard.

Now that they'd discovered Mr. Wong's den, the Reds continued to patronize the establishment. From their conversations, we learned that Triapitsin, Lebedeva and their partisan army had been wreaking havoc throughout Nikolaevsk. Not only had they killed all the wealthy citizens they could find, but the Bolsheviks were now starting to arrest some of their own people since there weren't any *burzhui* left. For the most minor indiscretions, Russians were brought in and executed on mere whims. Anybody who'd had a run in with someone could denounce him with the likelihood of an arrest. The Reds were starting to wonder how long it would be before their leaders turned on them as well. Listening to some of their laments and fears made me realize how tortured their minds must be. I was beginning to almost feel sorry for them...until I overheard a frightening fragment of conversation.

"They still haven't found those damn Kaptzans. The wife and her mother seem to have disappeared."

"I heard Zhelezin and Triapitsin are in an uproar."

"It seems they've just vanished..."

"They never thought the woman would get away from their clutches..."

"They've upped the reward..."

"And that poor man who vouched for them..."

"Nelibuov?"

"...Executed in their place..."

Was I hearing correctly? Nelibuov was hardly *that poor man*. Yes, he'd tried to help me...though, I was quite certain he'd known all along that I'd never be set free in the end. And what about all those other people the Bolsheviks had murdered?

The wretched man had deserved to die just like the rest of them—perhaps even more so. Like Ilya and Esther and who knew how many other friends and relatives who'd been captured. But his wife...and children... My mind thrashed about like hay at harvest time. So many mean-spirited musings entangled with merciful instincts. I didn't want to reflect on them because of the dreaded images that constantly beleaguered my mind. But I had so much time to be still and think....And to worry.

Fortunately, Cook-san had brought some chalk and a slate for the children to play games on. He'd also managed to procure some old sweaters and needles. We unraveled the sweaters for wool and took turns teaching the children to knit and crochet with it. They were able to make a scarf for warmth and some small dolls, as well. I thanked God and Cook-san for providing us with the diversion. The busier our hands were, the less time we had to think and worry. And it helped us remain quiet.

Again, guilt about Ilya plagued me like the sour smells that pervaded the air. I felt so alone. How could I ever enjoy the thrill of life again without him at my side? How I regretted all the times I'd harped on him, annoyed at his hesitancy to leave Nikolaevsk; and, even more so, my lack of courage to insist. I felt numb. Perhaps it was the drug saturated air having its effect.

Suddenly, Misha poked me.

"Damn it," I heard one of the Reds exclaim. "I dropped my money clip." Sure enough, at that moment something shiny came rolling under the partition that blocked off our space. "Where did it go?" the voice said.

"Under that screen there maybe?" one of his friends suggested as the item twirled to a stop near Viktor who was sitting on the floor quietly playing with a rag doll I'd sewn for him while at Cook-san's. The shiny object captured all of our attention. I dared not move. But what if Viktor did?

Suddenly, a large hand reached in the tiny space under the screen that separated us from the room filled with partisans. Everyone stared at the hairy fingers feeling around for what had dropped. What if the screen was upended? Or the man realized there was a room behind it? We sat still as tombstones. Misha quietly got on his knees and surreptitiously reached for the money clip. Rather than picking it up, he carefully slid the silver piece into the path of the hand as it swept back one more time.

"Aha! Got it!" the voice was joyous. Just as we were about to breathe relief, a head poked around the screen. It was the man from the Tribunal, the one seated next to Zhelezin. He had seemed sympathetic at the time, but was he still? Knowing what a prize we were, I couldn't expect that he would pass up an opportunity to turn us in.

"What's back there?" one of his comrades asked. It sounded like he was coming over to see.

"Just some mops and brooms. Nothing interesting." The man turned his back on us and steered his mate away.

20

*I*t was dark and chilly but I could smell that winter had begun its retreat as I inhaled the sweetness outside. Cook-san was leading us through Chinatown to a new hiding place. Despite my fear and weariness, I was awed that the earth's rebirth could manifest itself in the midst of such miserable circumstances. I'd never quite understood how, out of the depths of snow and ice, green leaves would suddenly appear and shoots of grass miraculously spring from the hard, brown ground. After the harrowing winter through which we'd been struggling to survive, it seemed as if there was no God left to call forth such magic.

And yet, He'd been watching over us. I had no idea where we were headed or what we'd confront next, but the freshness of the night air made me realize that at least we were alive. So far, we'd been able to evade the unthinkable fate that lurked in every shadow like the steel chomp of a bear trap. And for what we'd been able to avoid, I was supremely thankful.

Over a month and a half had passed since the fateful night when the Japanese had opened fire on the partisans. Two months since Ilya's arrest. While we'd been bouncing from one haven to the next, we'd only been peripherally aware of what was going on in the outside world. We were focused on our own safety and wondering about those with whom we'd lost contact: Mama, the Maremants, the Minkovs. Cook-san was our sleuth, but so far he hadn't offered any concrete details.

Although it was almost definite that they were gone, in the absence of any confirmation, I still found myself clinging to grains of hope. Not having seen any actual evidence of Ilya, Esther and Nikolai's demise, it was hard to fold their fates into a neat pile and close the cabinet on them. Even though it was completely unlikely, I didn't want to abandon hope of anyone's survival. But the more we witnessed and heard, the starker the realization became of how unlikely it was that we'd ever meet again. I wondered what my brother, Matvei, in Japan knew of our situation. I was certain he'd pull any strings he could to come to our rescue. Then I realized how much I sounded like Mama with her endless faith in our Matvei.

Behind the stately home of a Chinese official, Cook-san led us toward a large warehouse. Extracting a large brass key from the pocket of his quilted jacket, he opened the creaky, padlocked door and showed us in. I wondered what we would find there.

Scattered on a smattering of straw toward the back, I could

discern the dark forms of sleeping bodies. "Mama?" I called, hoping she might be among them.

"Luba?" It wasn't Mama but Eda whose familiar voice I recognized.

"Eda?" I stared at my childhood friend as she approached in the dark, hunched over and painfully thin. It made me wonder what I must look like to her. "Oh, thank God, you're not...I thought—" I took her into my arms. Aroused from sleep, other figures began to reveal themselves. There was Iulia Sharpova, her two teenage sons, Papa Shimkin and Eda's little girl.

Iulia wept as she recounted the arrest of her husband, Andrei, his promising return and then his succumbing to his injuries. So he had died after all. Eda told of Sammy's demise, which was much like Ilya's. She described how the Reds had arrested him but had spared his father because two of them had worked in his tannery. Ultimately, those Reds had even given the survivors refuge in the back office for several weeks.

There was neither food nor water in the warehouse, only whatever our Chinese helpers managed to smuggle in to us. It was usually not more than one large can of water a day with more dry bread, rice or kasha. Some days they didn't come at all because they were afraid of attracting attention. Reds were lurking everywhere, searching every closet and corner. We subsisted on our wills. But for the little ones, it wasn't so easy. We saved most of the food for them.

Outside, pigs squealed in the yard. Iulia's sons were plotting how they might sneak out and kill one. Until they realized we had no way of cooking it. Some of us resorted to chewing on stalks of hay just to have something to gnaw on that had a reminiscence of flavor. Veronika had caught Katya's cold and was feverish. If we'd been at home, Riva would have made her warm milk with butter and honey and rubbed her chest with pine oil. But here there was nothing. I was worried about the others getting sick. Riva and Papa Shimkin, in particular. I attempted to feed Viktor my milk or at least offer him some consolation. Because I was barely eating, he howled as his tugs produced nothing. Listening to him was worse than being hungry. No one complained. Doing so wouldn't make things better and there was no one who could help us. Viktor was now fourteen months old. He'd started to walk but he looked so pale and undernourished. His soft blue-gray eyes almost blended in with his skin. We'd all lost weight and none of us resembled our hearty former selves.

The interior of the warehouse was dim and shadowy. We could hear rats scurrying in the rafters and bats beating their wings as they flew above us—incentive enough to remain close. There had been talk of eating them as well. If only we had a small burner or hibachi.

At least we weren't worried about being overheard here. We were able to talk as much as we'd been forced to remain quiet previously. To fill the time, we exchanged stories and compared details. We tallied the countless deaths of friends, relatives and neighbors and heard more horror stories about the torture everyone had been enduring. We also heard snippets about our captors and how they'd been enjoying their spoils. No one had seen Mama.

"It won't be long now until the Amur begins to thaw," Papa Shimkin said, trying to brighten our spirits. "Help is sure to arrive from somewhere."

"Yes," Riva agreed. "The outside world may not be in contact with us anymore, but they must have an idea of what's going on here."

How were we going to rebuild our lives, I wondered. Our town.

"Have you heard about Traipitsin's plan?" Eda asked. "There are rumors that he is planning to leave the city and that he's drawn up a list of those allowed out. Everyone else will have to remain. He's posted guards everywhere so no one can sneak away."

This was news. Though not surprising. "Surely none of our names would be on it," I said.

"He wants to kill every last one of us," said Iulia. Looking at her now, I tried to recall the statuesque beauty I'd always envied.

"Well, he's not going to succeed," said her eldest son. Most of us echoed his resolve, however faintly.

The warehouse was much colder than the opium den. But at least the air was fresher. And the weather was definitely getting warmer. It was now the second week of May. One day, Cook-san arrived, a huge smile filling his face. "Ice start to break up!" he announced, confirming that Spring really was coming and had begun to melt the frozen Amur. We knew from experience that the thaw wouldn't occur overnight. But also that it wouldn't take much longer. By the time the Amur began to splinter off in jagged ice boulders in Nikolaevsk, it meant that further upriver, toward Khabarovsk and Vladivostock in the south, the water must be running freely. That little ray of hope kept us going for several days. As did the extra loaf and eggs he'd brought that day.

We needed both because all of a sudden Cook-san and

the other servants stopped coming. Three days passed with no food, water or contact. Thank goodness we'd vowed not to consume everything at once. But what could have happened? Had they been caught? Killed? Every time footsteps sounded in the yard or horses whinnied outside, we froze.

A loud, ominous pounding of hooves coming down the street startled us. Horses halted outside and we could hear voices yelling—in Russian—followed by an incessant banging on the gate. Someone from the house had come into the yard to see what was going on.

"Open this gate immediately so we can enter!"

"No one home," came the answer. "What you want?"

"We want to get in so we can search your house and your warehouse." It quickly became evident that this was where our luck would run out. We heard the creak of the gate and more conversation.

"So sorry. Cannot open storehouse. No have key."

"Search him," a Red commanded.

"Try the door. Maybe he's lying." The huge door rattled in response to tugging from the other side. But it didn't open. "Let's break it down then."

"No, no. Cannot do that," he was told. "Owner of house very important man. Secretary to Chinese Consul. He need you bring papers." There was a tense pause. "You go get papers, I go find master and get key for you. Okee?"

Again silence, followed by the horses cantering away. The moment the Reds left, we heard the sound of glass breaking. Through a side window the servant crawled in. "Quick!" he said. "Come." He motioned that we should follow him. He unlatched a side door and we snuck across the yard to the pigsty. Just as the door to the sty shut behind us, the Reds returned. Their captain was shouting for the Chinese servant while his men began to strike at the warehouse door.

Inside the sty, there was a loft above the area where the swine were housed. Only one scrawny specimen had outlived his companions. Two barrels stood in a corner and the Chinese servant directed us to roll them over. We stacked one on top of the other, then quickly clamored up into the loft. It wasn't easy, especially for Riva and Papa Shimkin, but adrenaline fueled our scramble and the two old people were practically tossed overhead into the loft. We were aware that as soon as the soldiers found the warehouse empty, this would be the next place they looked. But where else could we run? A dozen people scattering in the street would surely rouse attention.

Weary and frightened, we settled deep into the hayloft and covered ourselves with the dried grass while, below, the Chinaman rolled the barrels away. He then deftly slid out, unnoticed. Holding my breath, I silently prayed that we hadn't reached the end of our fortune. Outside, the horses neighed. Suddenly, Viktor began to cry. Like the blade of a guillotine dropping, the sharp and instant gaze of everyone turned on me. I shoved my bawling son under my coat, praying that he'd latch on. He refused. He fought with me, showing more spirit than usual.

At that very moment, the downstairs door was broken down and soldiers surged in. A dog barked wildly. I prayed he'd continue. I instinctively pulled my coat tighter, pressing down to mute Viktor's yelps as the men searched below.

"I heard a baby," one said.

"Where?"

"I think it came from up there."

I pressed my entire bulk onto the bundle inside my coat, begging Viktor to forgive me. The men were discussing the likelihood that anyone could be hiding up in the loft.

"How would they have gotten up there? And so quickly."

"Perhaps it was the pig." The dog started to bark again outside.

"Or the dog."

"There couldn't possibly be a whole family hidden in that tiny space."

"They're not going to welcome us back empty-handed."

"No," his comrade agreed. "But if we take this porker with us, we won't be empty-handed, eh?"

"That's right! Good thinking!" For a moment the pig's shrill squeal sliced the air as it was chased around the sty. Then a shot rang out and the pig's whines subsided. Finally, the Reds departed, taking their prize with them. The last we heard, they were discussing what a delectable feast the unlucky swine would make for them that evening. By the time they were out of earshot, Viktor's sobs had stopped as well.

I quickly unwrapped my coat only to find my youngest lying there, blue and stiff. Riva grabbed the child and began pressing on his chest and breathing air into his lungs, trying desperately to revive him. A vestige of the woman I remembered resurfaced as I burst into a cavalcade of sobs, unable to believe what I'd done. After a horrible few moments, Viktor let out a meek cough followed by a cry. I swept him into my arms and rocked him back and forth before again offering him my breast. This time he was happy to suckle, even if no nourishment responded to his fierce tugs.

21

We remained in the pigsty for seven more days. Food was scarcer and nerves raw. Our heads were alive with lice and the children scratched interminably. Sometimes I thought it might have been more merciful if we'd just been shot, ending the dreadful nightmare. We'd experienced so many close calls. What if the next time...? I'd envisioned our capture and death in so many scenarios and dreams and the prospect of it was so awful that I was more afraid than ever to fall asleep at night. But remaining awake was worse. My fingers often slipped into the pouch containing the cyanide vials that Doctor Minkov had given me the night we left his house. Would I have the courage, I wondered as I gazed at my children.

The wooden walls of the loft were mottled with cracks and crevices. Through them, we could see the world outside. The black and white and gray of winter was turning into a pastel of greens, pinks and yellows. Even the wind that blew through them was fragrant. I tried to situate myself. It was obvious we were on a hill because below us, in the distance, was the city. The rustle of horses passing or a hungry dog yelping in a yard occasionally floated up from the street. But there was scant evidence of people anymore. Was everybody dead? Or hiding like us? We discussed leaving the safety of our haven to find food. But where would we go?

Then, one morning, we awoke to the smell of smoke. Looking through the fissures, Misha reported that he could see great billows of black air and flames in the distance. "It looks like the entire city's on fire." The wind was blowing in our direction and dark clouds were sweeping swiftly toward us. It wouldn't be long until the flames reached us as well. For the first time in a while, footsteps could be heard outside. "Soldiers," Misha whispered. "They're carrying cans and pouring something onto the ground."

"Kerosene," Riva said, recognizing the smell drifting upward. "That Bolshevik skunk is trying to fumigate us out of hiding." Since the incident with Viktor, Riva seemed to be regaining her previous spirit. "We've got to get out of here."

Nobody was around to help us from the loft. If only Cook-san would return. Iulia's sons jumped to the ground, located the barrels we'd used to get up to the second story and rolled them out. Once they were stacked, the rest of us climbed down. Any moment, the Reds might torch the fuel, sending us all up in flame. We tried to open the door. It had been padlocked from the outside for our own protection. We picked up one of the barrels and pounded it against the wall, running forward and backward trying to balance the unwieldy, awkward weight until we managed to break a jagged hole in it. Then we swarmed through.

We ran down the street to get as far away as possible in case of an explosion. From the top of the hill, there was a clear view of the harbor, full of broken ice chunks, floating upstream. The Chinese gunboats and barges, which had been docked there all winter, frozen in place, were now floating amid blocks of ice. I wondered about the piles of cadavers. We broke into two groups and hurried down the hill toward the port. Behind us, the buildings began to ignite, one after the other, like dominos.

The streets were muddy and deserted. Near the bottom, I spied an old peasant woman on a wagon, being pulled by a horse. I gathered my brood and confronted her. On the seat next to her was a large metal container with a ladle protruding from it. It had to contain some food or liquid. Most likely, milk. "Please, good woman," I uttered breathlessly. "Could you spare something to eat or drink for my children? They're starving."

She looked at us hesitantly. It occurred to me she was on her way to town to sell it. She could probably get a good price with all the shortages.

"Please," the children chimed in. "We're so thirsty. We haven't had anything at all for days now."

She looked pityingly at the waifs. Her flat round face broke into a compassionate smile. "Help yourselves." She lowered the dipper in and offered it to them. They gathered around her like grubs, their dirty desperate faces gaping up at her. She couldn't scoop the milk out fast enough and the children began to laugh deliriously as it splashed over their faces and into their mouths.

"Where are you headed?" the woman asked.

"To the port."

"Don't go there," she warned. "That's where all the Reds are."

"But where else can we—?"

"Try to get to the edge of the city, beyond the harbor. There are many common people there and it will be easier for you to hide among them."

"Oh, dearest lady," I said. "How can we thank you?"

"Just hurry and be on your way." We looked at one another and there was a moment of recognition. Was it kindness, or pity, at shared suffering? Not knowing what to say, we headed in separate directions. Suddenly, I stopped in my tracks. I looked back. The wagon was receding from view, but the woman was looking at us, too. I was seized by a revelation. Could the woman driving the cart be Olga Nelibuova? The wife of Dmitri Nelibuov? Whether or not it was, my thoughts flew to the woman who had come to our house to enlist Ilya's help in her husband's defense. How much we'd both been through since that long ago day! I had felt so sorry for her, having no money and so many children to raise. Now, we were both widows and my situation was hardly better than hers. Did she know that I had been the cause of her husband's death?

We made our way through the back streets of Nikolaevsk, hoping to avoid being seen or followed. The city was no longer recognizable. The center of the town was also in flames. Fire could be smelled everywhere and the sky was black with smoke. On the outskirts, where we now were, houses were mere skeletons of burnt shards or had been broken into and abandoned. Corpses lay everywhere. The frozen snows had preserved many of them, but now that the sun was getting stronger, the bodies that hadn't been removed were beginning to thaw and rot. There was no one to clean up the mess and the stench was piercing.

The city resembled a ghost town. But despite the desolation, trees had started to bud and crocuses pushed up from the ground. We barely encountered another soul in our travels. In a way, this was a relief. Occasionally, we heard footsteps or horses' hooves and dashed quickly behind a fence or a deserted structure until it seemed safe to continue. We were never sure whether the approaching sounds were Reds or others, like ourselves, who were trying to escape. It wasn't worth the risk to find out. We skirted the harbor. The pier was so overcrowded with refugees, it looked as if it were sinking under their weight. On the beach upstream, campfires burned. Around them, clusters of the displaced warmed themselves. Once again, my heart leapt at the thought that perhaps we'd be reunited with Mama. We found a secluded corner near some bushes and I left the children with Riva and Nessia, knowing I'd cause less attention if I went searching on my own.

"*Gospozha* Kaptzan..." I immediately recognized Ivan's deep voice. I was about to run to him when I realized he wasn't alone. Though I'd been longing to find him, now that I had, I was filled with trepidation. I'd known Ivan my entire life and I was certain he'd never harm any one of my family. But times were different and people had changed. Could I trust him? He said something to his comrade, then walked over.

"Are you alright?" he asked, looking me over and registering obvious shock at my appearance. "They're still looking for you," he whispered. "They've questioned me and even offered me money if I could find you and bring you in. Don't worry," he responded as I reflexively pulled back. "I would never do anything so despicable."

I let out a relieved sigh, feeling badly that I'd doubted him. I couldn't help thinking that he might hold our family to blame for this entire wretched situation, for his not having been able to rise above being a coachman while we led such lavish lives. "Where is the rest of your—"

"Ilya—*Gospodeen* Kaptzan," I corrected myself, "...is gone."

"In the prison...?" Ivan asked. "During the Japanese attack?"

I nodded, tears suddenly stinging my eyes.

"Never mind. And your mother...and *Gospozha* Riva...?" he ventured gently. "The children...?"

"Thank God the children are alright. And Baba Riva. But I haven't seen my mother or Sophie and Tolya in weeks. I don't know what's become of them. I've been looking here... but not a sign."

"I will help you find them. But first, we must get you to safety. It's not wise to remain here. The partisans are everywhere, hunting for any Whites that remain. Like dogs sniffing out ducks....Even Russians like myself are trying to get out."

"Where can we go? What can we do? I know there's a list and—" I sounded like Veronika the way I was babbling on.

"Perhaps I can get a permit."

"For us?" My eyes widened with hope.

"For myself. I am just a simple comrade. You could pose as my family. Not everyone knows me. I'll approach someone who won't recognize me." His willingness to put himself at risk made me want to reach out and hug him. "I will find a boat. I can row you to Mago. I think things in that village are quiet these days..."

"Come," I clutched his arm. "Let me show you where we're camped." I led him back to where I'd left Riva and the children. But they weren't there. "Oh my God! They're gone! Ivan! What could have happened?" I was on the verge of hysteria when Misha came running toward me from behind some shrubs a few yards away.

"Mama!"

"Where were you? Where's Granny?"

"Ivan!" Misha exclaimed as he recognized my escort. The boy ran uninhibitedly up to the man and hugged him.

"Misha!" the tall figure boomed in his familiar bass.

"We're over there...behind the hill," Misha pointed. "Baba Riva thought we should move because she heard some soldiers talking and..."

"Lead the way," Ivan said, lifing the boy to his shoulders. "You've grown!" he laughed.

Everybody jumped up with relief at the sight of our beloved coachman. Even Riva beamed. "Do you think it will work?" she asked after Ivan outlined his plan.

"We can only try. It could—if no one looks at us too closely. We must not make them suspect anything, okay?" Ivan winked at the children, turning our escape plan into an adventure. Ivan instructed us to remain hidden while he went to obtain the permit. In his absence, we peered through the bushes and absorbed the scene before us. Because the gates of the city were heavily guarded, mobs of people were exiting by sea. But every so often, a boat filled with passengers set out from the pier only to go up in flames once it was too far out for its occupants to swim back. Or, even more horrible, shots would ring out from some of the boats, followed by screams of pain and terror. Clearly, those people had been duped into thinking they were sailing to safety only to be executed by their saviors.

Hours passed without any sign of Ivan. Had he been sincere? Had he been turned in by a suspecting friend? Or, worse, would he return with soldiers to arrest us? Riva and I wondered whether we should hide somewhere else or remain where we were. The sun was sinking behind the hills on the opposite shore and it was getting cool. We'd gotten so used to our cramped corner in the pigsty that wind was a new sensation.

Finally, Ivan returned, triumphant. "I was able to get an exit permit. And a boat." He led us further upstream where a rickety rowboat was tied to a tree. As we crawled in, Riva and I exchanged a glance. Ivan had driven us to weddings and funerals. He'd run after Misha when the boy had taken his pony out for rides, he'd told the children stories while he cleaned the harnesses and allowed them to feed the horses and help him clean out the stalls. I couldn't imagine that this man would ever deceive us. And yet, an inkling of doubt still lurked. So much had happened in the past few months. Nothing was as we thought it was. So many people had been betrayed. The rowboat didn't look as if it had been tampered with and would either sink or explode once we set out. And Ivan wasn't carrying a bayonet, though a smaller pistol could have been concealed on his body. We had to trust him.

We pushed off from shore and Ivan began rowing out to sea. "This way! I saw them go this way!" Several partisan soldiers materialized from the trees and pointed in our direction.

"It's them!" Ivan began to row furiously as the men aimed their guns at us and fired.

"Get down. Cover your heads," Ivan commanded. We stooped down as much as possible. Shots pinged all around. One hit the boat, taking part of the wood with it. Another grazed Ivan's arm. Viktor was crying. All around us the sea was in flames. Other boats had been hit and caught fire. Some of them had been doused with kerosene before setting out. I sniffed the air, but could detect nothing suspicious. Ivan continued rowing until we were finally out of the soldiers' reach. Riva wanted to take a look at his arm, but he insisted he was okay for the time being.

In the distance, barges and gunboats with lanterns shining on their decks bobbed on the choppy sea. People were shouting, offering asylum. Ivan was bleeding heavily and Mago was many *versts* away. We decided to row toward one of the boats instead. Waving at those on deck, we requested permission to board. It was a Chinese gunboat and the captain indicated that his vessel was full. "Please..." we implored. He was about to turn us away but we must have looked so forlorn that he finally relented.

On the boat were other families who had escaped. I scanned the faces, but there was no sign of Mama. There were other survivors on other boats. But we couldn't get to them. At least there was a little food and water. The sky glowed red in the darkness behind the harbor. The city was breathing erratically. Every so often, a burst of flame erupted as another structure capitulated to its fate. But Nikolaevsk didn't want to concede defeat.

Just when it seemed all was over, there was a flicker of luminescence, like an ember being coaxed to give up more heat. The silhouettes of brick chimneys left standing and the trees along the river in front of the flames once again reminded me of that German horror film I'd seen with Ilya, Esther and Kolya the previous Spring. My taste for such entertainment was forever lost. Lost...like all those I had loved. I forced myself to snap out of my despair. We were almost in the clear and wouldn't have to hold on much longer.

22

*A*s the Amur began to flow again, bloated corpses released from the grip of the now melting ice floated randomly in the water. The unfortunate victims who had been lured to their deaths and shot instead of saved were constant reminders of how fortunate we were.

I dreaded looking at the dead, scared to find myself staring into the face of someone dear. Imagine coming upon Ilya or Esther like that. I couldn't bear the thought. The bodies were mostly face down and unrecognizable. Seeing that Misha, too, was obsessed with the sight, I pulled him away from the edge of the boat and tried to divert him with optimistic conversation. The flames from our burning Nikolaevsk were slowly beginning to subside as we moved further away. Smoke lingered in the air and every gust of wind swept up clouds of ash, transforming them into spectres dancing on the grave of our city.

———

We had been on the Chinese barge for two days. Ivan remained with us and his arm had been cleaned and bandaged. I'd questioned everyone I encountered about Mama, but no one had seen or heard about her. I couldn't imagine how she'd have traipsed through the snow, burdened with fussy Tolya and overeager Sophie, not to mention her own poor eyesight and lack of an independent spirit. Then, late in the afternoon of the second day, as the sun was descending inland, Katya suddenly called out. "Look!" She was such a quiet girl that her voice astonished us all. "Everybody, look. Over there!" Something in the distance had caught her eye.

She jumped up and pointed toward the horizon. "Aren't those boats out there?" The commotion was so great and the passengers' movements so sudden that the boat nearly tipped as the entire load ran in the direction Katya was pointing. Far out at sea, an armada was steaming toward us.

Not until the sun rose from behind the ships the next morning, could we identify the bright white rectangle with its blood red target rippling gaily from each mast in the breeze, confirming that the vessels were Japanese. Giddy with expectation, we began waving and crying, screaming and praying. The boats chugged closer and I recognized my darling brother Matvei's gravelly voice bellowing from a megaphone before I made him out standing in the prow, gesturing urgently.

When the hull of his ship rubbed against our barge, I rushed forward to greet him. But my tongue was frozen. I had no words. We scrambled aboard. I could see his eyes scanning the crowd behind me, looking for Mama. "She's not here," I whispered. I buried myself in his strong arms and burst into uncontrollable tears.

I finally composed myself enough to speak a bit of our excruciating ordeal and to ask how much he had known of what was going on.

"We'd heard rumors and obviously knew something terrible was afoot when the telegraph went down. But because of the snow and what was going on in Khabarovsk and Vladivostok, we couldn't get through." I looked at him questioningly. "Those cities were also taken over," he explained.

I told Matvei about Ilya and Esther. Our brother Kolya.

"And no word at all about Mama?" he asked tentatively, as if he couldn't bear any more bad news.

"The last time I saw her was two days before the Japanese attack. I have no idea...Every night I pray for her...." Matvei and I were standing on the crowded deck. Our city was growing faint in the distance. The vessel, with us onboard, was sailing toward the island where the fisheries were located. Other ships remained to comb the bay, picking up those who had found refuge in other Chinese gunboats.

"Perhaps no news is good news," Matvei said.

I nodded, but I felt queasy with fear. Matvei put his arm around me and held me close, my one remaining family member. How reassuring it was to be back in his dominating aura. But it so reminded me of Ilya that his presence was bittersweet. I looked up and caught him staring at me and I became aware of how I must look, tattered, graying, worn. I could see him searching for the little sister he used to care for and spoil. I surmised that the sadness in his usually playful eyes was reflected in my own.

———

Practically overnight, as is always the case, the seasons had changed. All along the banks as we sailed upriver, Spring was trumpeting its arrival. The silver bark of birches glistened under a fluttering mobile of leaves. Delphinium, irises and lilies fought with wildflowers for space in meadows surrounded by larches, pines and walnut trees. Apple trees coiffed with pink and white blossoms looked like young girls in ruffled pinafores. The scent of scallions and wild garlic filled our noses.

The barracks that used to house the workers during the fishing season were being transformed into temporary shelters for us. We disembarked and began searching for those we recognized. Matvei had gone back to Nikolaevsk with the boat to search for more survivors. He would return in a few days, but watching him disappear after finally being brought together was like a wound re-opening once it had begun to heal. I watched jealously as people around me were reunited with relatives and friends who had made it through the ordeal.

For the first time in two months, we bathed and put on fresh garments brought from Japan. Because everyone had lost so much weight, the clothing hung on our bones, like washing set out on a line. Who cared? We were clean and dry. Someone rounded up the children who were taken behind one of the tents where a man with shears cropped their hair to get rid of the lice. The skinny little things looked funny, running around with their smooth heads and it was difficult to differentiate between boys and girls. Then the adults were beckoned. I felt naked and embarrassed without my long hair; but everybody was in the same predicament. The women wore rags or anything they could get their hands on as kerchiefs, to feel less exposed. So hopeful to be on our way to safety, nobody asked questions or put up resistance. We were grateful to be alive.

Buckets of fresh icy water from the river renewed us with its delicious simplicity. Enormous vats steamed over fires and soup and kasha were spooned out to us. We were warned to eat slowly and not too much as our stomachs were unused to food. I was trying to explain this to the children, who were gobbling their portions, when I heard, "Veronika! Misha! *Tyotia* Luba!" Little Sophie rushed toward us from the bushes. I grabbed her up in my arms, looking over her shoulder for Mama and Tolya.

"Where's your *babushka*?" I asked, holding my breath.

"Over there," she squiggled out of my embrace and took me by the hand. Together, we ran toward a clearing where my mother was resting on some rocks.

"Mama!" I screamed and rushed to fold her in my arms. I hardly recognized the skinny little woman whose black hair was now striped with white. The chubby cheeks I remembered were inverted. One of the lenses of her spectacles was missing and I could see that she'd also lost a few teeth. But she was alive. And her throaty laugh was only slightly subdued. We looked at one another, then hugged again as the others looked on and joined in the reunion.

We learned that, with the help of Iosef and Oksana Dimchin, Mama, Tolya and Sophie had escaped to Mago just after the Japanese attack. They'd spent the winter there, living in the Dimchin's cottage. I couldn't believe that she was okay and that Mama's suffering had been lessened by her luck.

More survivors straggled in all week. We wandered around, in a state of shock, still traumatized. While the Japanese authorities searched the nearby fort, woods and villages for Triapitsin, Lebedeva and their gang, officials and journalists asked questions and recorded the testimonies of those of us who remained. It was very difficult to talk about what we'd been through, reliving the horrifying details over and over. But after a while it became a relief to spit out our stories. I supposed it was a way of putting the gruesome events behind us. Every day, with a little nourishment and lots of sleep, our bodies were becoming fortified with a renewed will to live.

———

On June 18, 1920, almost four months after our ordeal began, Mama, Sophie, Tolya, Riva, Nessia, the children and I boarded the vessel Matvei had chartered and set sail for Japan. Iulia's remaining family and the Shimkins were coming, too. With our city a bed of ashes and only the remnants of some chimneys left standing, there was nowhere for anyone to return to in Nikolaevsk. Ivan saw us off. He would remain in Russia and return to his village. Who knew if or when we'd ever meet him again? And what about Cook-san? Since we'd escaped from the pigsty, we hadn't seen or heard from him. Would we ever know if he and his family had made it? These men had saved our lives. How could we say good-bye to them?

Tinged with sadness was our parting. And filled with so many questions. We were enveloped with relief that our nightmare was finally over. Yet it was countered by the overwhelming realization of what had been taken from us, what we had seen. Our home was gone forever. But the truly irreplaceable hole in all our lives was the loss of our beloved fathers, mothers, sisters, brothers, friends and neighbors who had suffered so heinously and died so needlessly. That sadness tempered our gratitude for having survived.

What lay ahead? Would we ever return? Where would we live? Would we remain in Japan and build new lives there? And what would I do?

As we sailed upriver, the bright June sun ablaze, I glanced back toward the fisheries we'd just left, remembering the day we'd visited with Ilya. Under the looming gaze of Fort Chinnarakh, the shimmering backs of the spawning salmon were making their way upstream again to lay their eggs. Only this year there was no one to harvest them. Could it have really been less than twelve months ago? So much had come to pass in our lives and yet the river still ran, the salmon swam and the blood that was spilled merely flowed out to sea.

Postscript

Triapitsin, Lebedeva and their remaining commissars were arrested when the boat on which they were trying to escape was seized outside of Kerbi later that June. They were brought to trial in Khabarovsk and were, by overwhelmingly majority, sentenced to death by hanging on July 9, 1920.

During the decades that followed, the city of Nikolaevsk was rebuilt as a secret military base. For seventy years, it was closed to civilians. Today, Nikolaevsk is a thriving modern city. A monument commemorating these events stands in a park. Yet, the details of that Red winter are unknown to most of the population of Russia and the world. It is just another sad footnote that passed unnoticed. Nikolaevsk-on-Amur is truly a lost city.

After surviving the winter of 1919-20, my grandmother, on whom Luba's character is based, moved to Japan with her family. They settled there with her brother for several years. He took care of them and everybody learned Japanese and began a new life. But three years later, at noon on the 1st of September, the Great Earthquake of 1923 struck, razing the city of Yokohama where they were residing, upending their lives and sending them once more on the run in search of a more stable home.

Finding refuge in China this time, Luba's children grew up in various cities—Tientsin, Harbin and Dairen—before settling in Shanghai which they called home until after the second world war. Without any legal documents, Misha (my father) traversed the world with a single yellow sheet of paper stamped with a variety of entrance visas as his passport. Because of huge quotas, the family was put on an extended waiting list to enter America. But Misha secured a job helping the U.S. with Japanese reparations after the war and he and his family were finally allowed to settle in the United States in 1946. There, they lived a comparatively peaceful and happy existence.

Acknowledgements

It really does "take a village." If I were to thank everybody who had a part in my Red Winter journey, this would no doubt be the longest section of my book. Truly, there are so many people to thank and to whom I owe so much for listening, encouraging, reading, re-reading and reading yet again. From my very earliest sounding boards: Anita Gold, Lydie Raschka, Ahna Bogyo, Ava Chin, Ann Mallen, Miriam Camitta, Liz Pinnear, Richard Leslie, Sandra Van Pelt Hogue, Tom Mitchell, Joslyn Cooke and Suzanne Lamb; to more recent ones: Jeannie LeResche, Donna Limoges, Vida Olinick, Alexis Gargagliano, Barbara Bluestone and Margarita Jozwiak...your comments, criticism and suggestions heartened me to keep going.

Ella Wiswell, Hee-Gwone Yoo and Patricia Polansky—who tirelessly answered questions, provided facts, maps, photographs and feedback—without you, I would never have known the true events behind the fantastic tales I'd heard from my father and grandmother. Tibor Zonai, Christina Anderson and Anina von Haeften, thank you for your discerning eyes and graphic expertise. Elenka Bobrova and Mara Gordon, your social media skills are helping me get the word out there. Kristin Rocco, thank you for putting me in touch with Tony Brasunas who gave me great feedback and advice and led me to Estelle Kim whose beautiful map graces this book. Judy Bullard and Therin Knite, you transformed my words and visions into a beautiful finished product. All of you, with patience, understanding and your individual talents.

Josie Joffe Franklin, Jimmy, Robin, David and Mikayla Kaptzan...your encouragement to get our family story out there and your constant appeals to hurry up continued to ring in my head as I honed the story to make it the best I could.

Joanne Bramsen, Diane Lech and Siobhan Burke, your unflagging support buoyed me, knowing I could always ask for yet another honest opinion. Katherine Lim, Katya Redpath and Daniela Petrova....my writing partners, ruthless editors, fearless cheerleaders and chief hand holders. How many times did I turn to you for editing assistance, guidance and a request to "please read one more version" or "look at one more book cover"?! You never let me down, keeping my spirits up and relieving my anxiety with laughter.

Patrice Fitzgerald, without your persistent urging, knowledge and help on all fronts, Red Winter would still be sitting in my drawer. You're a lifelong friend and guiding light!

Finally, David, Michael, Larissa and Mom....You have stood by and emboldened me throughout all the years it took to get this story completed. Thank you for always being there, cheering me on and loving me no matter what. You fill my life with so much love and joy that I can't help but be inspired. You are my everything!

Daddy and Granny Luba...I hope I did your story justice.

About the Author

Kyra is a lifelong New Yorker with deep Russian roots. While weaving her grandmother's history into this fictional narrative, she did extensive research into 1920s Siberia. Kyra holds degrees from NYU's Tisch School of the Arts and Graduate Musical Theatre Writing Program. Her recent musical, *To Dance*, tells the story of Russian Jewish ballet dancer Valery Panov whose struggle to emigrate in the 1970s made international headlines. *Red Winter* is Kyra's debut novel.

For further information, please go to:
www.kyrarobinov.com

Printed in Great Britain
by Amazon